Praise for Meredith Schorr

BLOGGER GIRL (Blogger Girl Series #1)

"What a fun book. The characters were incredibly well-written. I felt like I understood everyone's personalities and quirks, almost as if I knew them personally myself. Meredith Schorr is a talented author and I'm glad she has other books out for me to read!"
— Becky Monson, Bestselling Author of the Spinster Series

"Sassy, sexy, endlessly entertaining, and full of laughs (as well as some heart-wrenching moments), *Blogger Girl* is one of those books that keeps you up at night because you can't wait to see what happens next."
— Tracie Banister, Author of *Mixing It Up*

"America finally has its own version of Britain's Bridget Jones!"
— *Books in the Burbs*

NOVELISTA GIRL (Blogger Girl Series #2)

"A strong and confident heroine, a sexy boyfriend you can crush on, supportive friends, and plenty of conflict leading to comical results, culminating in a very satisfying ending...Once you start this book, you won't be able to put it down."
— Erin Brady, Bestselling Author of *The Shopping Swap*

"A perfect mix of romance, conflict, and humor, *Novelista Girl* solidifies Schorr's place among best-sellers Sor͏ ͏ ͏ ͏ ͏nd Emily Giffin."
— Carolyn Ridder Aspenson, Bestselling Author ͏ ͏ ͏ ͏ ͏ve

"Absolutely brilliant chick lit, I couldn't put it d͏ ͏ ͏ly, highly recommend."

The
Boyfriend
Swap

The Boyfriend Swap

Meredith Schorr

HENERY PRESS

THE BOYFRIEND SWAP
Part of the Henery Press Chick Lit Collection
First Edition | November 2017

Henery Press, LLC
www.henerypress.com

Trade Paperback ISBN-13: 978-1-63511-271-9
Digital epub ISBN-13: 978-1-63511-272-6
Kindle ISBN-13: 978-1-63511-273-3
Hardcover ISBN-13: 978-1-63511-274-0

Printed in the United States of America

To the Beach Babes

ACKNOWLEDGMENTS

Thank you so much to everyone at Henery Press for believing in this book and for helping to make it so much better than it would have been without your assistance—Art Molinares, Kendel Lynn, Erin George, Rachel Jackson, and Maria Edwards. Thank you to my fellow Henery Press authors for always being so generous with your knowledge and support.

Even before I handed the book off to my amazing editors (Erin and Rachel above), my brutal but awesome beta readers, Samantha Stroh Bailey and Natalie Aaron, ripped it apart until it was tighter, funnier, more logical, and simply put, stronger than it was before. I couldn't be more grateful to you both.

I offer my sincerest gratitude to Shanna Eisenberg, Andrea Bube, and Marc and Gina Vicari for offering their expertise in the areas of teaching, educational administration and budgeting, and musical education.

I am always thankful for my family for their unconditional love and support now and well before this writing gig was even a blip on my radar.

The journey of being an author can be quite lonely, which is why I feel so blessed to have so many author friends like Hilary Grossman, Stacey Wiedower, and Lily Barrish with whom to exchange ideas, experiences, and frustrations on a regular basis. On the flip side, I'm also lucky to have friends who aren't writers. You might not quite understand that side of me, but you love me anyway, and you keep me sane (and often tipsy). I love you all.

Special shout-outs to Ronni, Jenny, Shanna, Megan, and my wild and crazy vacation posse (Hilda, Abbe, Jenn, Jen, and Marisa).

Eternal gratitude to my guardian angel, Alan. Damn, I miss you!

Thank you to my street team and all the wonderful bloggers who support my writing—Lindsay Lorimore, Rebecca Moore, Aimee Brown, Melissa Amster, Ashley Williams, Kelly Perotti, Bethany Clarke, Amanda Lerryn, Isabella Anderson, Gina Reba, Kaley Stewart and so many more.

Finally, to the Beach Babes to whom this book is dedicated—Samantha Stroh Bailey, Josie Brown, Eileen Goudge, Francine LaSala, Jen Tucker, and Julie Valerie—you all mean so much to me. I cherish every one of you and, except for the week we are together in California, I'm always counting down the days until we'll be together again.

Chapter 1

Robyn

If asked to choose between a world without music and one without my mother, the choice would be a no-brainer—I'd give up music. I might feel dead inside, without a song to sing or a beat to dance to, but at least my mom would be there to comfort me. The decision was easy, but sometimes, like now, when she put on her matchmaking cap, I was tempted to change my answer.

"He just moved here from Boise to work in the Treasury Service team at JP Morgan," she said, referring to the guy she'd befriended while standing in line at the DMV for two hours. "He said you reminded him of a blue-eyed Selena Gomez."

I allowed a small smile at the comparison, but promptly clamped my mouth shut. "I'm flattered, but why did you show him my picture?" I already knew the answer. My mom was always trying to fix me up with eligible men, especially those employed by companies like JP Morgan, where employees were forced to dress business casual and infrequently required to use their imaginations.

"I thought you'd make a great couple. Someone like him— attractive, successful, nice, funny—won't be single for long."

I banged my head against my desk in frustration. "I'm already taken. Have you forgotten?" I asked in a hushed voice before glancing at my boyfriend, Perry. He was lying on his back on my bed with his t-shirt riding up to showcase his six-pack abs. I turned down the volume on my phone so he wouldn't hear.

"Ah yes, Perry. His teeth-whitening commercial aired while your dad and I were watching the *Legends of Freestyle* documentary last night. Too bad he can't cultivate an entire career around his talent for flicking his tongue across his upper teeth."

I chose to ignore the portion of my mother's statement aimed at my boyfriend. "You watched *Legends of Freestyle* again? Aren't you sick of it by now?" My parents were high school sweethearts who performed together and even released a Freestyle album in the early 1980s. They never hit the bigtime, possibly because there wasn't a smidgen of Latino in them, unless you counted my maternal grandparents, Sephardic Jews from Argentina. But they shared the stage at many New York City venues with some of the best, including Lisa Lisa and Cult Jam, until they gave it up to raise me and my younger brother, Jordon.

"How many times have you seen *High School Musical*?"

"Point taken."

"Does Perry get a lifetime supply of teeth whitener now? One less expense could come in handy until he catches his big break," she said, her voice dripping in sarcasm. Perry, my boyfriend of almost a year, was a struggling actor/musician—*struggling* being the operative word.

"Speaking of Perry, I'm preparing my grocery list for the holidays. Is he coming for Chrismukkah?"

I gulped down the unease of bringing Perry home with me for the holidays. His last callback fell through, which meant he probably wouldn't have anything promising to tell my folks when they asked about his acting career—which they would. They would then outwardly encourage him to keep on keeping on, while using the famous Lane mental telepathy to invade my brain space and urge me to choose a more "stable" boyfriend. As former musicians themselves, my parents would never discourage a performer from shooting for the stars, but they didn't want a performer dating their daughter.

Perry sat up. "Don't forget to tell your mom I want to demonstrate the vocal exercises my voice coach taught me." Perry didn't have the money to fly to his parents in Portland for Christmas and, oblivious to my folks' discouragement of our relationship, was looking forward to an intimate family celebration.

I smiled fondly in his direction. It wouldn't even matter if he could hear my mom's side of the conversation. He wasn't lacking in self-confidence, and any disapproval by others, including my parents, tended to go unnoticed by him. Unfortunately, what attracted me to Perry—his focus on the here and now rather than the long term and his ability to make light of almost every situation—was what repelled my folks. They worried he wasn't husband material. It was their job as my parents, but at only twenty-six, I wasn't thinking about marriage yet anyway. Perry made me happy day to day, and that was good enough for me.

"Is he still gluten-free?" my mom asked.

I sighed into the phone. I could picture my mom holding her breath and crossing her fingers, hoping I'd say she didn't need to stock the house with gluten-free products because I'd broken up with Perry and was now dating someone new, like an attorney in a prominent law firm. Before I could tell her there was no cure for celiac disease, I heard a knock on the door followed by my roommate, Anne Marie, peeking her blonde head in my door.

"Almost ready?" Anne Marie and I had played together in a recreational kickball league a couple years earlier and quickly discovered we were both about to lose our current roommate to a serious boyfriend. Neither of us made enough money to live alone in pricey New York City so we decided to move in together. Our complex was advertised as a "luxury" apartment, but it catered mostly to twenty-somethings like us, who were happy to share very little square footage with a roommate to live in a doorman building with a pool on the roof.

"I've gotta run. We're hosting a wine party tonight. I'll call you over the weekend, okay? Tell Dad I love him. And you too." I hung up the phone and let out a deep breath. Then I walked over to the bed and pulled Perry up by his hands. "Time to go."

"I seriously can't stay?" Perry asked, pushing out his full lower lip.

I shook my head and gave him a sad smile. "Sorry. Girls only." Perry's large eyes were blue like the deepest part of the ocean, and his longish blond hair managed to look masculine even when pulled into a man bun. With biceps that toiled to break free from his well-fitted t-shirts, I was sure if the girls saw him, they'd wish I'd made an exception to the "no boys allowed" rule.

Giving himself a once-over, Perry said, "Suit yourself, but I think a room full of your girlfriends would be more exciting if I tagged along. It would be like an episode of *The Bachelor*."

I placed my hands on my hips. "Are you in the market for a bachelorette?"

"An episode *after* the final rose which, of course, I gave to you."

"Good save," I said with a laugh.

Perry took my hand and kissed my pointer finger. Running his thumb along the chipped sea-green nail polish, he said, "Maybe you guys can give each other manicures too."

"It would be a waste of time and nail polish and you know it." I pushed him out of my room and toward the front door of my apartment. "Will you be home later?"

"Eventually, yes." He leaned down and kissed my forehead. "Have fun at ladies' night. If it breaks out into a pillow fight, record it on your phone."

"Don't be a douche," I said before closing the door behind me. Then I smiled at Anne Marie, who was returning the vacuum cleaner to the hall closet. "What can I do to help?"

Sidney

I logged off my computer, slipped into my Burberry trench coat, and turned off the light. It was almost eight o'clock—past the acceptable time to leave work on a Friday night, even for a lawyer— but I'd never take off for the weekend without responding to all my client's emails. The advent of the smart phone meant I could communicate remotely from anywhere with cellular service or wi-fi, but once I left the office on a Friday night, I liked to unplug at least until the morning. My assistant, Anne Marie, had invited me to a wine party she was throwing with her roommate, and I wanted to get there before all the bottles were empty.

When I opened my office door, I came face to face with my father. My hopes of making a quick escape dashed like a reindeer through the snow on Christmas Eve.

"Sidney, I'm glad I caught you." His eyes, the same jade color as mine, twinkled. If I didn't know him so well, I'd think he was going to share a humorous anecdote or even invite me out to dinner to celebrate another successful week at the law firm where he was one of the name partners and I was a third-year associate. But I knew better—he wanted to talk shop.

"You're leaving?" He gestured to my coat and pointed toward my dark office.

"I'm guessing the answer is 'no' if you have anything to say about it," I mumbled. The man was my boss, but he was also my dad, which made maintaining professionalism at the conclusion of a long work week more challenging.

He waved me away. "I was going to ask you about a case, but we can do it tomorrow." It didn't matter that the next day was Saturday—lawyers didn't do weekends. "Is it a date? Your mother will ask me."

"No comment." I *was* seeing someone, but since my father was privy to all my professional activities, keeping my personal ones from him and my mom helped maintain a sense of independence (and my sanity). I was twenty-eight years old and some aspects of my life, specifically ones pertaining to love and sex, screamed for privacy.

He scratched at his hair—salt and pepper and impressively thick for a man in his late fifties. "Fine. Keep your secrets, but she's planning the Christmas party and will ask who you're bringing." He paused. "Preferably someone in a leadership position in the field of power and construction. The industry is booming, and the firm can use an in to a new client."

I rolled my eyes. "I'll see what I can do, Dad." I stepped into the hallway, closing the door behind me for emphasis. "I'm late for a party, and you should head out soon too before Mom loses it." She was accustomed to my father's late hours, but her patience ran thinner on Friday nights and weekends.

My dad glanced left and right as if finally noticing the lights were off in nearly every room on the floor. With a wave goodbye, he headed in the direction of his office, which was blessedly on the other side of the hallway from the elevator bank.

I grimaced as my stomach growled in hunger. Anne Marie had said there would be food at the party, but I was positive the pickings would be slim to none two hours into a gig attended by all women. I'd purchase some goodies on the way to both satisfy my appetite and apologize for showing up late.

When the doors of the elevator opened, I stepped out into the lobby and almost collided with Michael Goldberg, a senior associate at the firm with a distaste for country music, solid-color neckties, and me. As far as many of the junior partners and senior associates, including Michael, were concerned, the reason I received a summer associate gig followed by an invitation to be a first-year attorney at Bellows and Burke LLP was because my last name was Bellows and had nothing to do with the fact that I was editor of Colombia Law Review and graduated at the top of my class. Three years later and I still had to work twice as hard for half the credit.

"Leaving so early, Sidney?" He raised the bag from Main Noodle House in his hand, no doubt wanting me to know he was working through dinner.

I tried to bite back the desire to say something snotty or defend myself. Nothing I said would make a difference anyway, but I couldn't let Michael have the final word. "I need to make an appearance at a wine tasting. Sitting behind a desk for twelve hours a day is not the way to bring in new business. Sometimes you need to get out there and network." Planting on a smile, I said, "I already made myself late sending out last-minute emails to clients, so I must go. Enjoy your Chinese food." I hoofed it toward the exit without awaiting his response. He probably didn't buy my story, but I'd find a way to beat him at his own game—maybe impress one of his clients into requesting me as his direct contact. My billing rate was lower and my work product was the level of a fifth-year—more bang for the buck. In the meantime, my skin burned with annoyance, my belly cried for food, and my liver begged for wine.

When I got outside, I spotted an available cab headed in my direction. I also saw a trio of tourists waving their arms frantically to get its attention. With one gesture of my hand, it stopped at my feet. I climbed inside, pretending not to hear the girls shouting at me. Being a native New Yorker had its advantages.

Robyn

Two hours into the party, and enough red wine varietals from the southern hemisphere in my system to feel a buzz, I raised the volume on my iPod and moved my hips to Rhianna's "Where Have You Been." I pulled Anne Marie away from the plate of cubed cheese to dance with me as a clear loud voice called out, "Sorry I'm so late." I twirled around to see a pair of long slender legs in tight blue skinny jeans, a designer trench coat, and high heels. Her face was hidden by the layers of boxes she was holding.

Afraid they would topple over, I ran over to her. I stood on my toes to remove the top box and smiled up into a pair of forest-green eyes. "Let me help."

"I've got it," she said, walking over to the bridge table we'd set up for food. She placed the other two boxes on the nearest surface and turned to face us. "Sorry I'm late. I think it's a rule in the law firm bible that associates must always be late for Friday night festivities. Anyway, I brought mini cupcakes and pizza so I hope you'll forgive me." She smiled. "I'm Sidney. Friend of Anne Marie's. Well, technically her boss, but not for tonight."

I should have known. Anne Marie said her boss was larger than life, and I could tell already the leggy redhead before me was a force. After putting down the cupcakes I was holding, I returned her grin. "Robyn. The roommate."

Sidney scrutinized me. "You're very pretty. I bet you get called 'cute' a lot though. Am I right?"

Amused, I said, "Yes, actually." I was only five foot three and many people equated lack of height with cuteness. Some of my younger students called me Truly Me, after the American Girl doll with the long wavy brown hair and blue eyes.

Nodding knowingly, Sidney said, "I thought so." Before I could thank her and return the compliment, she peered over my shoulder. "Is Anne Marie here?"

"She's here some—"

"Sidney!" Anne Marie raced over to us and wrapped one solid arm around Sidney's waist and the other one around mine in a group hug.

I giggled to myself, thinking the three of us, a blonde, brunette, and redhead, probably looked like the modern-day Andrew Sisters. I kept it to myself since I doubted either of them had heard of the American close harmony singing group from the mid-twentieth century.

"Someone's had plenty of wine, eh?" Sidney locked eyes with me before we both turned to Anne Marie, whose fair skin was flushed to a deep shade of pink.

I shrugged. "I knew somehow the wine 'tasting' would turn into a wine 'drinking.'"

Separating from Anne Marie, Sidney grabbed a cupcake and an empty glass. "I wouldn't want it any other way. Now, excuse me while I taste some wine." She used air quotes around the word "taste" and winked at us before heading over to where the expert was standing a few feet away.

"Isn't she a pip?" Anne Marie asked.

I watched as Sidney instantly drew the attention of the expert away from the crowd and toward herself. "She sure is," I said with a chuckle. Anne Marie had mentioned Sidney was a driven and focused attorney, and I was surprised she'd accepted our invitation. Fortunately, it appeared she knew how to play hard too. Assuming she didn't ask Anne Marie to send an email or make copies, I was confident my roommate would enjoy her own party even with her boss in attendance. As Lady Gaga's "Born This Way" played on my "Best of 2011" playlist—I was in the mood for "classic" tunes that night—I bumped my hip against Anne Marie's. "I love this song. Let's boogey."

Sidney

I read the text from my boyfriend, Will, and frowned. He was having drinks with a friend from work. The wine expert and all the other guests had left, but I didn't feel like going home yet if it meant being alone in my apartment. Maybe Anne Marie and her roommate would want to go out for another drink. After scanning the living room area with no luck, I spotted them in the small eat-in kitchen. As Anne Marie bent down to put leftover food in the refrigerator, her sturdy freckled legs stuck out from the red athletic shorts she'd already changed into. And slim Robyn, in striking hot pink pants and a black and white polka dot top, was simultaneously rinsing dishes and dancing in front of the sink. She had moves.

I walked over to them. "Can I help you guys?"

Robyn turned around and smiled. Still bopping to the music, she removed the rubber yellow gloves from her hands and placed them on the dish rack before sitting down at the round hardwood table. Waving me away, she said, "I'm finished and, besides, you're our guest."

Joining Robyn at the table, Anne Marie said, "Want to help us empty another bottle of wine?"

"It would be my pleasure," I said before plopping myself on one of the high-backed kitchen chairs and accepting a generously poured glass of Malbec.

During the next couple of hours, the three of us went through almost two bottles of wine and laughed like sorority girls, making me homesick for Lisa, my best friend since childhood. We were inseparable until her family moved to the suburbs of Chicago in middle school, but we remained as close as sisters. I didn't have the best track record with other female friends and hoped tonight would go a long way toward developing a friendship with Anne Marie outside of work. I delighted in witnessing her relaxed and in her comfort zone. And her roommate was like an encyclopedia for all things music. Since sitting down, I'd already downloaded three new songs to my iPod.

We'd reached the boy-talk phase of the evening, and Robyn had just told me about her boyfriend, Perry.

"I can truthfully say you're the only person I know who met her boyfriend when he pulled her onto the stage in the middle of a live performance." I doubted a tactic of that nature would have worked on me. I didn't take kindly to being put on the spot.

"I think you misunderstood," Robyn said with a giggle. "Perry was fronting a cover band at a bar where I was celebrating a fellow teacher's birthday. When he learned I taught music, he pulled me on stage for a duet of Pink's 'Just Give Me a Reason.'"

"Your version makes much more sense," I said with a nod. "I think I've had too much of this." I lifted my glass before topping it off. "And what about you?" I jutted my chin toward Anne Marie. "Any cute boys in your life?"

Anne Marie confided about the crush she had on the bartender at a neighborhood dive bar. "I have no game, but my drinking tolerance is growing from all the time I spend in his pub." She hiccupped, immediately belying her earlier comment.

I considered myself somewhat of a connoisseur in the art of seduction. "Let me be your wingman sometime. He'll be in your bed before you can say 'tequila.'"

"Word," Anne Marie said before giving me a high-five.

"What about you, Sidney?" Robyn said. "Are you dating someone?"

I opened my mouth to tell them about Will as my phone pinged a text message. "Yes, and this must be him now." I hoped he'd be game to meet up later. Drinking with the girls was a good time, but sleeping with my boy was a *great* one. My lips curled into a grin as I reached for the device on the kitchen table. Only it wasn't Will. It was my mom. She wrote: "Your father said you were on a date tonight. Good luck! Any chance we'll meet him at Christmas?"

A surge of annoyance at my parental figures coursed through my veins, but it was nothing more alcohol couldn't fix. I placed the phone back on the table without responding and took a swig of wine. "Sorry for the delay. My boyfriend's name is Will and he's a tall glass of water."

"Bring him to the office one day. I work hard for you—the least you can do is provide me some candy to eye up," Anne Marie said. She glanced out the window and beamed. "It's snowing."

I followed her gaze to the light dusting of snow outside.

"It's almost Christmas," she yelped while waving her hands in glee.

Robyn and I let out a groan at the same time, and I shot her a curious glance. Between chair-dancing to every song that played on the iPod and her generally giddy demeanor since we'd met, I pegged her as someone who lived for the weeks between Thanksgiving and Christmas, kept her holiday playlist on constant rotation, and didn't even mind the crowds at Macy's.

"Personally, I wish we could skip straight to New Year's Eve," I said. Will's parents were going to be in London for the holidays. In a moment of particular fondness—after he'd given me a mind-blowing orgasm—I'd asked him to come to my family home in Scarsdale for Christmas. Once the feeling returned to my legs, I regretted my spontaneity. The four months we'd been together had been filled with lots of laughs, great sex, and zero pressure. There was no doubt my parents would love Will—he was handsome, polite, intelligent, and funny. And he was a lawyer, which would automatically gain him points with my dad and assure my mom he had the requisite social graces to work a room. But I feared their fondness for my boyfriend would have an adverse effect on my own attraction to him. I was enjoying myself too much to risk it. But the invitation was out there, and I couldn't bring myself to renege on it now.

"I love Christmas. McAdvenille is the home of the biggest holiday light display in the United States," Anne Marie declared proudly before taking a bite from the bottom of a red velvet mini cupcake.

I snorted. "Christmas in North Carolina sounds like a dream. Quite the opposite of Yuletide in the Bellows home. All Harvey does the entire weekend is boast to anyone pretending to listen about his latest wins in court or new cases he's taken on." For Robyn's benefit, I clarified. "Harvey is my dad. One of the two named partners in the firm. Anyway, we try to change the subject, to anything—the weather, the final season of *Orphan Black*, politics— but he seamlessly ties everything to the successes of the firm. I'm proud of if too, but give it a rest."

"Sounds exhausting," Robyn agreed.

"It is. I really don't want to subject my boyfriend to it. He's also a lawyer, which means my father will grab his ear the entire time to talk shop and no doubt make passive-aggressive digs about Will's firm not being as good." I grimaced. "He might even recruit Will to work at Bellows and Burke. I like to keep my professional and personal lives decidedly separate." My stomach clenched as I imagined Will taking a job at my firm. It was one thing for my dad to watch over my professional growth, but if my personal life was at his disposal, he and my mom might install surveillance videos around the office to keep tabs on the progress of my romantic relationship too.

"But you're definitely taking him?" Robyn asked, leaning forward in interest.

I sighed. "Going stag would be equally as painful. Without an escort, my mom would entrust me with entertaining every unattached male at the very well-attended dinner party—mostly overgrown bachelors with egos as inflated as their stomachs or widowers over the age of sixty-five." It was rare she thought any of them were appropriate life partners for me, but if I was unattached, she considered it my duty as their only child and junior hostess to make the single men at the Bellow shindigs feel at home.

Anne Marie chuckled. "You two have something in common."

"Your parents stifle you so much, you're thinking of asking them for an oxygen tank for Christmas too?" I asked Robyn.

She chuckled before slowly shaking her long raven waves. "No. But Anne Marie knows I'm on the fence about taking Perry home for the holidays. My parents make it no secret they think he's a flake. I don't want to spend the entire time defending my relationship choices or playing referee to my mom and Perry. But the only other option is to leave him home alone." She pushed out her naturally glossy lips. "I can't do that to him on Christmas."

I closed my eyes and smiled dreamily. "I *wish* Will were a flake. My parents would take no interest and I might actually enjoy Christmas in peace." Opening my eyes, I said, "As it stands, the minute I introduce them to him, any semblance of personal space I've managed to maintain thus far will burn to ashes. A struggling actor would serve me much better this Christmas."

"And my parents would love for me to bring home a lawyer or anyone whose job comes with health insurance," Robyn said with a sigh.

Anne Marie adjusted the black elastic headband keeping her long bangs off her forehead. "If only you guys were dating each other's boyfriends, it would be a holly jolly Christmas for all. Maybe you should swap boyfriends for the week."

Her comment elicited a hearty laugh from all of us and we clinked glasses to the notion before opening the final bottle of wine. The subject of conversation turned to our plans for the rest of the weekend. I listened as Anne Marie complained about the early start of her Saturday morning boot-camp class. While Robyn spoke of an electronic music festival she was attending with Perry, I had a vision of a family dinner with Will. During the appetizer and dinner courses, my dad and Will would enjoy courtroom humor, and after dessert my mom would display my baby pictures across the kitchen table and gush to Will about my chubby thighs and ginger baby hair. At the conclusion of the evening, a professional photographer would take a family portrait of the four of us—my dad, Will, and me wearing matching "Trust Me. I'm a Lawyer" t-shirts and my mom donning one that said, "They're my lawyers" with arrows pointing in all directions.

Then I pictured the same night with an out-of-work actor as my date. My dad would bring his laptop to the table and work through dinner until my mom told him to put it away. He'd do as told only for her to ignore him in favor of her latest *Celebrate* magazine. Neither would balk when I excused myself and my "boyfriend" early from the table. Then he'd go to the guest room to do his acting exercises or whatever activities guys like him did and I'd go to my childhood bedroom and sext with Will. A sudden lightness took over me at the possibility.

"What about you, Sidney? Doing anything fun this weekend?"

I shook myself out of my fantasy and faced Anne Marie. It was balls-to-the-wall crazy, but it could work. I swallowed hard before locking eyes with Robyn across the table. "I think we should swap boyfriends for the holidays."

Robyn

I cackled. "You can't be serious."

Sidney took a sip of wine. "I know it sounds deranged, and when Anne Marie first said it, I laughed it off too. But the more I imagine the possibilities, the more I'm convinced your roommate here was touched with genius." She pointed her elbow at Anne Marie.

"Thank you. Thank you very much," Anne Marie said in an Elvis Presley impression.

I visualized walking into my parents' colonial-style house and introducing some random dude as my boyfriend while Sidney claimed Perry as hers hundreds of miles away. "Genius? I'd call it absurd." I laughed again.

"Give the idea a minute to percolate," Sidney said calmly. Her mouth remained in a straight line, indicating she wasn't joking.

My stomach quivered with unease, but I took calming breaths to settle down. According to Anne Marie, Sidney was very opinionated and sometimes wouldn't shut up until she got her way. I'd just let her keep at it until her throat hurt or she passed out from too much wine.

Sidney continued, "If left to our own devices, the holidays are going to blow chunks, but if we pool together, we'll all be better off. And it's only for a few days. It's the perfect solution to our mutual problem."

I stood from the table and removed a bottle of water from the refrigerator. I poured a glass and placed it in front of her. Hopefully she'd take the hint. The wine was clearly going to her head.

"What do you say?" she asked the minute I sat back down.

The girl had to be on more than fermented grape juice. Hallucinogenics maybe? Whatever influence she was under, she clearly believed her ludicrous plan had merit, and I was going to have to put my foot down. "I say that I'm a grown woman and shouldn't need to lie to my parents about who I'm dating."

Sidney nodded. "I agree. You shouldn't."

A breeze of relief zipped through my core. "Glad we're on the same page."

"You *shouldn't* have to lie, but in our case, we sort of do. If we want to make it to the New Year without requiring a straitjacket, that is." She smiled, a slick grin I was certain both assured her clients and put the fear of the devil in her adversaries in equal measure.

At the realization she was serious, my eyes bugged out. I took a huge gulp of wine, nearly choking on the contents. This was wrong on so many levels. For one, Perry was my boyfriend. I couldn't just lend him to someone else temporarily. It would be like prostitution. Only without the sex, of course. I also didn't feel right lying to my parents. They'd never believe me anyway. "My folks won't buy it. The closest I ever got to bringing home a lawyer or even going on a date with one was the time I had coffee with one of my student's dads to discuss how to register the copyright for the original songs I wrote for the school concert."

"What reason could you possibly have to lie? They'll be surprised, for sure, but they'll also be thrilled. Don't you think?" Sidney asked.

I covered my mouth with my hand and blew out a stream of air. Perry's ego wasn't fragile, but he wasn't made of stone either. He'd be hurt. Dropping my hand, I said, "Wouldn't you feel guilty handing off your boyfriend to another girl?"

Sidney appeared to silently contemplate for a moment and I held my breath. Maybe I'd gotten to her. "I hear what you're saying, but it's for Will's own good," she said.

I narrowed my eyes. "How so?"

"Let me count the ways. For one thing, Will doesn't like discussing law unless he's on the clock—an impossibility in my dad's company."

This surprised me, as I assumed most lawyers liked to brag about how important they were and how much money they made, while simultaneously complaining about how hard they worked.

"And more importantly, Will is really into me, and my family is like an anti-attraction injection. If they take to him, which they will, I'm afraid I'm going to lose interest. I know it sounds immature, but it is what it is. Will lights my fire, but my parents might as well be New York's Bravest—on duty to put it out. If our relationship stands a chance, I need to leave my parents out of the equation." She shrugged. "I haven't had a chance to think it through, but I'll probably emphasize the work part when I approach him with the idea. He doesn't need to know I'm uncertain whether our chemistry could withstand my family's influence."

I laughed despite myself, even though Sidney was acting like swapping boyfriends was a foregone conclusion. "What do you think of all this?" I said to Anne Marie.

Anne Marie opened her blue eyes wide and laughed. "I was joking." She took a sip of wine and jutted her head toward Sidney. "But if anyone can devise a foolproof plan, it's this one. I've seen her pull a diamond out of a trash heap many times. Metaphorically speaking, of course." Her face radiated admiration as she smiled at Sidney.

Sidney flipped her shoulder-length straight hair. "Why, thank you," she said before scraping the icing off a mini cupcake and licking it off her finger. She gazed at me squarely. "But I must have misunderstood you. I thought you sincerely dreaded bringing Perry for Christmas to the point that the lining of your stomach felt like it was being peeled away one layer at a time. That's the sensation I experience when I imagine Will around my parents. Even though I adore Will, I'm fully prepared to entertain your Perry as my fake boyfriend for a few days. But if you were exaggerating the extent of your distress, by all means, I'll drop the subject." She tapped her unchipped fire-red painted nails on the wood surface of our kitchen table.

I blinked at her in awe. She was good. No wonder she was a lawyer. The truth was I hadn't overemphasized my holiday-related anxiety one bit and she knew it. It was like she'd hovered over my bed as I tossed and turned the last few nights, trying to predict what my parents would say to Perry so I could prepare mechanisms in advance to get through. All I had come up with was excusing myself to the bathroom every time the subject of his career came up, but I feared my parents would think I had a weak bladder or irritable bowel syndrome. "Why would Will or Perry ever agree to this?" Sidney's poor boyfriend would be forced to sing Christmas carols (and the occasional Hanukkah jingle) at our piano after dessert—a Lane family tradition. My parents didn't take "no" for an answer and refused to let any guest sit it out. It was all in good fun, they'd say. I once even tried to defend my preference for song-and-dance men to my mom as more compatible with our family dynamics by saying a suit-and-tie guy would be so stricken with performance anxiety, he'd never want to come over for dinner. She assured me there were plenty of men who worked as accountants and computer software programmers who could hold a tune, but I wasn't so sure.

Sidney ran her tongue along her bottom lip and winked at me. "I'll make it worth Will's while. I'm sure you can do the same for Perry, no?"

I felt myself blush. Perry and I had plenty of sex, but whenever I engaged in conversation with others on the subject I closed up, reverting to my bashful younger self. I glanced down at my cracked nails and pictured Perry at my parents' house over Christmas. He'd joyously croon holiday songs, completely clueless to my angst and to my parents rolling their eyes behind his back. Maybe he'd be better off at Sidney's—even if he didn't know it. But I still had questions. "Okay, let's say Perry and Will agree to this farce. And I'm not betting on it. But for fun and games, we'll pretend they do. I introduce Will to my folks as my boyfriend and they buy it. What do I tell them after Christmas, when they ask how he is?"

"You tell them it didn't work out," Sidney said simply before downing the rest of her wine and emptying what was left in the bottle into her glass.

I frowned. "Just like that? 'It didn't work out.'" My mom was accustomed to more detailed explanations for my breakups even though she was usually thrilled regardless of the cause.

Sidney nodded. "I'll say the same to my parents if they ask, but I'm betting they'll forget Perry's name the second we leave."

Lost for a retort, I rested my head on the kitchen table and imagined introducing my parents to my boyfriend, the attorney. There would be no need for my mom to give me sidelong glances while Perry droned on about the impromptu song and dance numbers to which he treated his tables at Carmines, the Italian restaurant where he worked as a waiter to pay his rent. And no one would have to suffer through my father's tales of the "good" old days—when he and my mom had lived cramped in a two-hundred-square-foot apartment in Sunnyside, Queens and subsisted almost entirely on twenty-five cent boxes of Kraft Macaroni and Cheese and Ramen noodle soup because they couldn't afford to eat anything else on the meager pay they received from their occasional gigs.

When I raised my head, Sidney and Anne Marie were watching me. Anne Marie nervously chewed on her lip while Sidney's expression reflected assumed victory. Her idea was insane, but she had a solution for every potential issue I'd raised, and I was certain her answer well would not dry up any time soon. I took a deep breath and let it out. "Fine. Count me in. Assuming Will and Perry agree to it."

"Leave that to me," Sidney said, before proposing the four of us get together to discuss it in a few days.

I was only half listening by then. I was too busy praying all the alcohol we'd consumed had gone to Sidney's head and she'd wake up acknowledging how barmy her plan was. Maybe she wouldn't even remember the conversation. She'd definitely drank the most of the three of us. It also occurred to me that even if *one* of the guys said yes, there was no way they *both* would, and I smiled to myself as the tension left my body. Within seconds, my muscles knotted once again—if they didn't agree to the swap, I'd be taking Perry home with me. No matter which way the pendulum swung, it was going to be an anxiety-ridden Christmas. It was only a matter of which version was the lesser evil.

Chapter 2

Sidney

I perked up at the mention of coffee. My father suggested we refuel after we'd been behind closed doors in his office for the last two hours going over deal points for a talent agreement in dispute. The agency we represented was sold on the actor but wished his hard-edged attorney would get hit by a moving bus. "Coffee sounds great," I agreed, tossing my empty Starbucks Grande Blonde into the trashcan next to my father's desk.

Michael Goldberg glanced at me long enough to say, "Terrific. How about you grab one for all of us, JB." One of the partners had taken up the obnoxious habit of referring to me as JB—Junior Bellows—and unfortunately, it had stuck. I took it up a notch by assigning my dad the nickname SB—Senior Bellows—but the only other person who had the balls to use the initials within earshot of my father was his partner, Stan Burke.

I blinked at my father, who I could tell was working hard to avoid eye contact with me. My father considered his law firm his oldest child and made it clear as glass I was not getting a free ride, but he had no interest in office politics. We both agreed I should fight my own battles, but I was getting tired of the war. "Seriously, Mike? Don't you think there are better ways my time could be spent than fetching coffee? I'm a third-year associate, not an intern."

My dad rubbed his plump cheeks and subtly rolled his green eyes at me. "Shani can do it." He called his assistant and asked her to make a Starbucks run. "If there's a long line, cut it. You're working on a talent contract involving one of *People* magazine's sexiest men. Nothing they're doing is as important, I'm sure, or else they wouldn't have time to wait in line at Starbucks."

I snorted before giving Michael a sideways glance. He was adjusting his paisley-printed tie and shaking his head of receding dirty blond hair in amusement. One thing even *we* could agree on was the enormous size of my father's ego and inflated sense of importance of his work in the grand scheme of things.

"Thanks," my dad said before hanging up the phone and leaning back in his chair with his arms clasped behind his head. "Where were we?"

Two hours later, I was still in my father's office and high on caffeine. Michael had been excused, but my dad wanted to call my mother and asked me to stay. She phoned twice during our meeting and told Shani she wanted to speak to both of us.

My dad put the call on speaker and pursed his lips at me over the table. "Be nice to her," he said, wagging a finger at me.

I bounced my leg underneath me. "I'm always nice to her."

"She wants to talk about Christmas."

"Shoot me now," I muttered under my breath. It was stuffy in his office so I removed the navy tailored jacket I was wearing over my white dress shirt. Grabbing a pencil from his desk, I gathered my hair into a bun on the top of my head. I didn't feel the need to be as formal when it was just the two us, especially for holiday talk with my mom.

"I'll pretend I didn't hear that," my dad said as the phone rang once, then twice. "Your mother is a perfectionist when it comes to party planning, and I, for one, appreciate her hard work. I have two potential clients coming this year. I've been courting them for three years already. I'm hoping a bottle of Glenfiddich 1937 will seal the deal once and for all." He ran a finger along his thin auburn eyebrows, the same color as mine.

"I could buy myself a crazy shoe collection with the money you spent on that Scotch." It was five o'clock somewhere and, in need of a drink of my own, I smacked my lips, already tasting the grapefruit undertones from the bottle of Chilean Sauvignon Blanc chilling in my refrigerator. I didn't drink whisky recreationally. I reserved it for business dinners, as a way to minimize the divide between me and my predominantly male clients. It did little to sway their focus away from my tits and ass, but it made me look fierce.

"If you have a personal relationship with Jimmy Choo and can bring him to B&B, the money is yours. Otherwise—"

"I'm here," my mom's voice called out, sounding out of breath. "My phone was all the way at the bottom of my handbag."

My dad raised a finger to his head and made a circular motion. "Honey, I've got Sid with me."

"Great. I have you together," my mother said excitedly. "You there too, Sidney?"

My dad rolled his eyes at me and mouthed, "Isn't that what I just said?"

I chuckled and shifted my chair closer to my father's desk so she could hear me better. "I'm here, Mom."

"The count for Christmas is now thirty-nine people. I want to finalize the seating chart. We'll probably get some last-minute guests and a few will cancel—"

My dad interrupted, "Who's going to drop out? Unless someone has an aneurism or a last-minute stroke, assume everyone who said yes will be there. It's the party of the year."

I silently disputed his statement based on my attendance at the party for most of my twenty-eight years, during which I counted the minutes until it was over almost as soon as it began.

With an impatient edge to her trademark "Kathleen Turner" throaty voice, my mom said, "Fine. So we'll assume minimum forty people. I need to know if you're bringing a date, Sidney."

Wincing, I clicked the notes application on my phone to my running to-do list. "Plan double date with Robyn to discuss the boyfriend swap" was second on the agenda after "schedule appointment for underarm laser" and before "read through last three issues of *People* and *OK!* magazines in preparation for conference call with CAA." I'd been severely intoxicated when I transformed Anne Marie's throwaway comment about swapping boyfriends into a full-fledged plan, but five days later and sober, I still thought it was brilliant.

Before I could answer, my mom said, "Because if you're attending alone, I think we should seat you next to Aaron Davenport. He finally broke things off with his latest young trophy girlfriend. You can keep him entertained for a couple hours."

I didn't need her to clarify what she meant by "entertain." My mother was not the madam of a brothel. She was merely a real-life society Westchester housewife whose most important role the last quarter of every year was to plan, as my father called it, "the party of the year."

My dad yawned before saying, "Aaron hasn't cut Ashley loose yet. He just manages his dates with her more carefully. Someone mentioned the politician Bill Boner over Thanksgiving dinner at the country club and apparently Ashley asked if he was 'that guy from the porn movie, *Ram Me in St. Louis.*'"

I snorted. "Priceless."

"At least Sidney manages to be charming even when she's inappropriate," my mom said.

"It's my gift," I said.

"So?" my mom prodded.

"Sorry, but you'll need to find someone else to stroke Aaron's ego for the evening. I'm bringing someone." One way or another, I was bringing a plus one. Only time would tell if it would be Will or Perry.

My dad leaned forward in interest. "Potential client perhaps? Or someone with connections to the next big thing?" he asked, his face shining with hope.

"I don't think he'll be of interest to B&B, Dad."

His face dropped as if the only reason I could possibly have to date someone was to add to B&B's bottom line.

"Can you spare a tiny morsel of your life with your dear old mom? Is this 'someone' anyone special? A boyfriend? A friend? A plaything?"

Usually, I didn't break a sweat over my mom's desperate inquiries into my love life. She was used to them going unanswered ever since I broke up with my last serious boyfriend, Jake. We met in college, but our coupling didn't make it past my first year of law school. That was entirely due to my determination to graduate at the top of my class, leaving me little time to spend with him, even on the weekends he came to visit me. Ivy League educated with more than a splash of Midwestern charm, Jake was the son my folks never had, and they took our split badly. It was years before we could get through a family gathering without his name coming up in conversation. Ever since, I worked hard at keeping my love life close to the chest. But even though I kept the information to myself, I always knew the answers. This time was different. I shifted uncomfortably in my seat and looked down at my J. Crew suede kitten heels.

If I brought Will as my plus one, the answer was "some of the above." Will fell somewhere between "plaything" and "boyfriend." We were exclusive, which suggested "boyfriend," but at only four months, we were still in the honeymoon phase. Our relationship was mostly sexual in nature so far. Not that either of us were complaining. If Perry accompanied me, on the other hand, the answer was "nothing special." His only role was to be of as little interest to my parents as possible so we could all eat our baked ham, roasted artichokes, and apple pie in peace.

"Well, can you at least give me a name? I have an appointment with the calligrapher tomorrow," my mom said when I failed to provide the desired response.

I took a deep breath and let it out. "Perry." I should have asked Robyn for a picture so I'd know what I was getting into. I was usually more on the ball. If he was unattractive, at least I wouldn't have to actually sleep with him.

"Perry what?" my mom asked.

I gulped the rest of my coffee and winced from the stale cold flavor. After tossing the empty paper cup in my dad's trash can, I stretched my neck from side to side to work out the stress-induced kinks while simultaneously wracking my memory for Perry's last name. Did Robyn even mention it? If I'd asked, I could have stalked him on social media—party fail. Having stalled long enough, I said, "Perry..." just as a reminder showed up on my phone for my 8 o'clock dinner plans with Will at The Smith restaurant. It would have to do. "Smith. Perry Smith."

Robyn

My cheeks ached from smiling and my hands were red and sore from clapping so hard. Nothing gave me as much satisfaction as standing in the wings as my little protégés brought their parents, grandparents, and siblings to their feet with their well-practiced song and dance routines. Tonight was the school's winter concert, and the first graders' rendition of "All I Want for Christmas Is You" was flawless. When I first came up with the dance moves, I feared they might require a bit more coordination than many of the students possessed, but as if by magic, even my youngest pupils managed to memorize the lyrics and belt them out—albeit not 100 percent in tune—while simultaneously shaking their little hips to the music. I felt a burst of emotion as the performance came to an end and braced myself for impact as the little ones bowed to the audience before running off the stage and into my arms.

"You were all so great," I exclaimed, hugging one after the other as their faces beamed up at me with pride. I loved so many aspects of my job, but my absolute favorite was organizing and directing the spring and winter concerts and the fifth-grade graduation ceremony. Coming up with new routines was challenging, but seeing them play out in front of me after all the hard work left me with a sense of satisfaction I didn't know existed outside of performing until I first took on the task two years ago.

While the first-grade students followed their teachers back to the audience where they would sit as a class until the final performance of the evening, I lined up the second graders.

Standing in front of them, I asked, "You guys ready?"

Three rows of heads bobbed up and down in answer, along with a few fist pumps. Considering they'd forgotten all the words during the final rehearsal earlier that day, I didn't share their confidence, but I hoped for the best.

I faced the audience as my heart beat rapidly in vicarious stage fright. Speaking into the microphone, I said, "I'm excited to present to you the second grade's performance of 'Snowflake Lake.' This piece is extremely special because the students wrote the lyrics themselves with the help of their teachers, Ms. Eisenberg and Ms. Malfetta. Let's give them a round of applause." While the crowd clapped, I whispered, "Break a leg" and walked to the piano on the side of the stage. I clasped the fingers of my hands together and stretched them out in front of me. With one more nod of encouragement at the kids, whose heads were turned toward me for my cue, I played the introductory notes and waited for them to start singing. I tapped the piano keys with shaky fingers, and it wasn't until they belted out the chorus one last time without any bumbles that I let myself breathe.

"*Take me down to Snowflake Lake because winter's here and it's too cold to bike. Take me down to Snowflake Lake. Fall from the sky with no two alike.*"

The second the music stopped, the crowd broke into rambunctious applause. As a tear of joy peppered with relief dropped down my cheek, I jumped up from the piano bench and joined the standing ovation until the kids happily waved at their fans as they skipped off the stage.

During the brief intermission, I basked in the success of the concert so far. I didn't have much time before I'd need to mentally prepare myself for the third, fourth, and fifth grade performances still to come, but was enjoying a rare moment without the kids jumping on top of me when I heard my name being called. I turned around and smiled wide. "Lynn." I rushed into Lynn Berryman's waiting arms and squeezed tightly. I had replaced Lynn as the school's music teacher when she retired after forty years of service.

The school had taken a chance hiring me right out of graduate school, but the one year of training as her aide while getting my Masters in music education had proven invaluable. "I'm so glad you're here."

Lynn grabbed hold of both of my arms and shined her brown eyes on me. "Wouldn't miss it. You look beautiful. Your eyes pop in that dress."

I glanced down at my dark blue and turquoise silk dress and did a little twirl. "Thank you. You look wonderful too." And she did. At almost seventy, Lynn maintained the muscle tone of someone twenty years younger, not a strand of gray hair poked out of her brunette bob, and she hadn't lost an inch of height, towering over my five-foot-three frame by at least four inches. "Enjoying the show so far?"

She nodded. "It's wonderful. And the original song? Impressive. Your idea I'm guessing?"

"It was an experiment." I held my breath.

Lynn gave me a soft smile. "It paid off."

"Thank you." I exhaled as heat crept across my cheeks. Lynn was very protective of the traditions she'd introduced to the school's music program, and I hoped she wouldn't be offended by my introduction of new customs, like original music.

Lynn hugged me again, as if reading my mind. "I always knew I was leaving my babies in good hands," she whispered.

I grinned. "I learned from the best. Seeing you singing along from the front row at every concert is one of my favorite parts of the entire night."

"Thanks to you, I've got the best seat in the house after yours, which I need more than ever these days. Aging is not fun, but I guess it's better than the alternative, right?" She winked at me.

I nodded. "There will be a reserved seat in the front row with your name on it for as long as I'm the music teacher."

Surprised by the sadness that crossed Lynn's eyes at my words, I frowned. "Did I say something wrong?" After Lynn retired, I hesitated to talk about the job too much during our periodic meetings for lunch for fear she'd resent me for taking her place. But she'd expressed her love of retirement—spending time with her grandchildren, organizing shows at an assisted-living community, and simply catching up on her soap operas—on so many occasions since then, I stopped worrying.

Lynn covered her mouth with her hand for a moment but quickly dropped it. "Nothing's wrong," she said with a forced smile.

I tilted my head to the side and studied her. Something was up.

Glancing at her watch, she said, "You need to get going. I didn't mean to upset you. I'm fine."

"I'm worried now. Please tell me," I pleaded. What if she was sick? She was my mentor, but I loved her like a grandmother.

"I'm not ill," she said, once again reading my mind.

"Thank God. I can handle anything else."

She smiled softly. "Okay, here goes. A rumor is going around about the future of the music program at the school."

I pressed my lips together. "What sort of rumor?"

Lynn sighed. "You didn't hear it from me, but there's been pressure to up the foreign language curriculum at the elementary level and the budget is strained. My sources told me they're considering cutting down on electives like music to generate more funds." Patting me on the shoulder, she added, "It's only a rumor, so please don't let it upset you." She shook her head and mumbled, "Me and my stupid mouth."

Despite Lynn's plea to keep my worries at bay, I couldn't unhear her words. I feared the uncertainty would be permanently nestled in my gut until I got to the bottom of it. Staring down at my sparkly silver heels, I asked, "Who are your sources?" even though there was no way she'd tell me. I could probably figure it out on my own, but it didn't matter. My heart was shattered, not only for me— I could get a job at another school—but for the kids. How were children supposed to nurture their creative sides if schools focused entirely on academics?

"Miss Lane. It's time. It's time."

Motioning toward the third graders, who were dancing in place in line outside of the auditorium and ready to strut their stuff onstage, Lynn said, "Go to your kids, Robyn. The show is greater than great. And you, my dear, are spectacular. Whatever this rumor is, it's just that—a rumor—and it has nothing to do with tonight's performance. Who knows when, if ever, these changes would take effect? You might be retired by then." She smiled, and this time it reached her eyes. "The best thing you can do is lead those kids in the best concert this school has ever seen, and show them what they'd be missing without it."

I nodded as giddiness and nervous tingles for the upcoming number replaced my paranoia about the future of the music program. Lynn was right. It had nothing to do with tonight. Turning to the kids, I said, "Ready, everyone? Let's show them how it's done." To Lynn, I said, "Want to watch this performance from the stage with me?"

Lynn clapped her hands together like a child entering the gates at Disney World. "I thought you'd never ask."

"And last but not least, please put your hands together for our music teacher, Robyn Lane."

My breath caught in my throat and my legs wobbled as I walked to where Principal Hogan stood centerstage waiting for me. He had already thanked Lance, the band instructor, for heading up the instrumental portion of the performance. I waved at the audience, who were now on their feet and clapping, before taking the hand he offered and shaking it. Even though I knew what was coming from the prior year and the year before that, it didn't stop the butterflies that danced in my tummy as three of the first graders ran up on stage, each holding a giant sunflower.

"Thank you, Ms. Lane," they said one at time before handing me a flower and giving me a hug.

Sneaking up behind them, Aimee Clay, a fifth grader with red hair like Little Orphan Annie and a singing voice to match, said,

"We love you, Ms. Lane" before placing a large box wrapped in paper emblazoned with musical notes in my arms.

"What's this?" I whispered, raising and lowering the heavy box in genuine surprise.

Aimee's eyes twinkled as she feigned nonchalance. Shrugging, she said, "You'll have to open it."

My fingers ripped off the paper. "Did you guys know about this?" I asked the audience. Not surprisingly, the crowd responded with a collective "No."

I reached into the box, gasping when I saw what was inside: a wooden plaque engraved with the words, "Robyn Lane. World's Best Music Teacher" and signed by every student in the school. I held it up for all to see and blinked back my tears. Was this gift my swan song—a "thanks for everything, but we won't be needing your services anymore" present? My lips trembled and I locked eyes with Lynn, who had returned to her seat in the front row. She gave me a sad smile and mouthed "No" to my unspoken question.

Forcing myself to let go of the rumor—*it was just a rumor*—I embraced the moment. I smiled at Aimee and the little ones. "Thank you so much. *You* guys are the best." Into the microphone, I said, "Thank you all so much for coming and for helping to make this year's winter concert a massive success." I looked pointedly at Principal Hogan and then back at the crowd. "I look forward to directing many more amazing concerts in the years to come."

When Principal Hogan cleared his throat and said, "Thanks for coming everyone, and drive safely," before placing his hand on the small of my back and escorting me off the stage, I prayed it had nothing to do with the fate of the music program and everything to do with wanting the kids to get to sleep at a reasonable hour on a school night.

Afraid I would say something I shouldn't, I declined a teacher friend's invitation to go out for a drink and headed directly home. The brisk fresh air I breathed during the thirty-minute walk from the school in midtown to my apartment on the Upper West Side did wonders for my psyche, and by the time I waved at my doorman and stepped into my elevator, I was feeling better about things. Tonight was the first I'd heard about these so-called budget cuts. As a current teacher in the school and one who would be directly affected by any change, I would be the first to know, along with Lance. Lynn's sources were probably mistaken. I smiled as my phone pinged a text message. It was probably Perry on a break from work asking how the show went. Locking the front door behind me, I plopped myself on the gray fabric sofa and reached into my bag for my phone. The text wasn't from Perry but from an unknown number, and I opened it with curiosity.

Hi Robyn, it's Sidney. Anne Marie gave me your number. Are you free on Saturday night? I told Will we were having drinks with my new friend and her boyfriend. Waiting until we're all together to drop the TBS bomb. Let me know if it's good for you.

Letting the phone fall to my lap, I closed my eyes and leaned against the couch in confusion. TBS? I was only twenty-six, but felt too old for all the new lingo. Aside from the basics—LOL, FWB, TTYL—I didn't understand half of the coded vocabulary used by the kids at school. Wasn't TBS a television station? Oh. I opened my eyes. *Oh.*

TBS: The Boyfriend Swap.

Chapter 3

Sidney

"Who are we meeting again?" Will asked as we climbed the stairs up from the subway onto the street.

Will walked briskly, and despite engaging in at least an hour of cardiovascular exercise five times a week, I had trouble keeping up with him. I squeezed the hand I was holding to slow him down. "Whoa, buddy. I'm wearing heels."

"Sorry. I always forget you're older than me and might not be able to keep up," Will teased with a straight-teeth smile that, even though he'd implied I was a cougar, made me wish we had time for a quickie. He was only a year younger than me. He slowed his pace and blew on his hands. "It's cold."

Leaning into him, I said, "I'll warm you up later" before stopping in front of the restaurant. "We're here anyway." I opened the door and scanned the dimly lit room, looking for Robyn. "There they are," I said, pointing to where she sat at a table laughing with a guy, presumably Perry. Even though they were sitting, I could tell he was at least a foot taller than her and, to my relief, very attractive. Actually, he was gorgeous. Not that Will was a slouch in the looks department—he was totes sexy—but this guy looked like a movie star, with longish hair the color of caramel and giant blue eyes under full eyebrows. He had to be lacking in talent big-time to look as good as he did yet struggle to get work as much as Robyn had implied at her wine party the previous weekend.

"You never answered my question. Who's 'they'?" Will asked

from behind me.

Waving at Robyn, who had just looked our way and flashed me a timid smile, I said, "My new friend Robyn and her boyfriend." When the hostess approached, I pointed at Robyn's table, said, "We're with those guys over there," and kept walking.

"Hi. So sorry we're late." I gave Robyn, who had stood up to greet me, a kiss on the cheek.

Robyn straightened out her bright yellow pencil skirt and tucked a wavy strand of hair behind her ear. "No worries. I had a drink." Pointing at Perry, she said, "He had two." She introduced us.

"Good to meet you," I said, shrugging off my winter white wool coat and draping it against an empty chair. "This is Will." I turned around to the empty space I thought Will was filling behind me. "Where the hell..." He had stopped to chat with a couple at another table. "I swear, he's like the mayor of the Upper East Side. Knows people wherever we go." I watched him in amusement until he finally looked our way.

Approaching us with a smile, he said, "Sorry. Friend from law school." His grin broadened as soon as he set his dark hazel eyes on Robyn. "Snow White? Is that you?"

"Snow...what?" I repeated, looking at Robyn.

Robyn's cheeks flushed an almost fluorescent shade of pink. "Oh my gosh. *You're* Will?"

As Robyn's wineglass teetered on the edge of the table, Perry stabilized it before giving Will a curious once-over. He met my eyes and mouthed, "Snow White?"

I shrugged and nudged Will in the knee. "Sit down. And please explain how you two know each other." I hoped their prior acquaintance would help and not hinder our plan.

"We went to high school together," Robyn said, a distinct tremble in her voice, at the same time Will said, "We lived on the same street growing up."

"Snow White," Will said, shaking his head. "Wow. How've you been?"

Perry cleared his throat. "Someone please explain the origin of Snow White." He gazed over my head and lifted his empty glass. Within ten seconds, a waitress was at our table.

Conversation halted while we ordered a round of drinks and a truffle-oil popcorn appetizer for the table, but as soon as the waitress walked away, all eyes were on Robyn.

She smiled shyly, her face still flushed. "No one's called me that in ages. Somehow, I got the nickname in high school. Everyone assumed I was pure as snow." She fiddled with her cocktail napkin.

"Were you?" Perry asked in disbelief, making me question whether the missionary position was even in their repertoire.

I predicted Robyn's answer would be "yes."

Robyn took a sip of wine and mumbled, "No comment" into her glass. Then she looked up at us and giggled. "Totally." She reached for her glass again and knocked it over the table. "I'm sorry!" she yelped, jumping up from the table.

Will stood up and mopped up the spilled red liquid with his cocktail napkin. "No worries. Shit happens."

"Here," I said, handing her my napkin as Perry hailed down the waitress. She was conveniently headed our way with our drinks and the popcorn. Poor Robyn looked mortified, and I second-guessed her ability to pull off the swap. The meet and greet was the easy part, and she was already falling apart.

The waitress washed down the table, and after Robyn ordered a fresh glass of wine, we resumed the conversation.

I swept my long fringe-style bangs to the side. "So Robyn was awarded the Snow White nickname because she was innocent?" I found it odd, since there were plenty of girls in my high school who could have joined the virginity club. I was no longer eligible midway through my junior year after giving my v-card to the son of one of my father's biggest clients at the annual Bellows' Christmas party.

Will pursed his lips together. "Not exactly."

Robyn's electric blue eyes opened wide. "It wasn't?"

Will grinned. "It had nothing to do with your purity." He

glanced at me. "I wouldn't know." He stroked my hand gently under the table.

While Robyn shifted in her seat, I squeezed Will's knee to confirm I wasn't threatened. Robyn was pretty, but I wasn't the jealous type. She was also a bit of a spaz, albeit in an endearing sort of way.

Will spooned a portion of popcorn onto his plate and then focused his gaze on Robyn. "You were always so cheery, dancing in the hallways as if there was nowhere you'd rather be than in school. I could almost picture you cutting a rug in your room as birds sang, and deer, rabbits, and raccoons played at your side." He laughed. "Like Snow White. You even resemble her, with your black hair and blue eyes."

Perry's eyebrows drew together. "*You* could imagine? This nickname was your idea?"

Will shrugged and took a sip of beer. "It was a long time ago. I'm not entirely sure."

"Right," Perry said, sounding pathetically jealous over some stupid high school nickname.

I rolled my eyes and kicked Will under the table.

Robyn's eyes glowed as she gazed at Will. "That's funny, because you were so broody, I imagined you holed up in your room with the door closed silently pondering the meaning of life." She cleared her throat before darting her eyes between Will and me. "We didn't run in the same circles too much."

"Why not?" I asked, hoping her answer would segue to a good opening to discuss the swap.

"I was a grade ahead of her," Will said before smiling fondly at Robyn. "And she was a theater kid and I wasn't."

With a shrug, Robyn said, "Yes, Will was too cool to be in chorus or audition for a school production and I...wasn't."

"Some theater kids were very cool in high school," Perry said. "Like me, for instance. In any event, I can vouch that Robyn's purity is no longer an issue." He winked and kissed the top of Robyn's shrinking head as she slunk so far down her seat, she could be mistaken for a little girl. Perry and I laughed good-naturedly at her expense until Will reciprocated my earlier kick under the table.

Robyn

Remember to breathe, Robyn. In through the nose, out through the mouth. If I couldn't even share a drink with the guy without requiring medical attention, there was no way I could pull off pretending he was my boyfriend. It had never occurred to me that Sidney's "Will" might be Will Brady—my old neighbor and the object of my high school fantasies. Considering how many times I spoke his name and wrote it in my diary during my teenage years, something should have triggered in my brain weeks ago, but it hadn't. I'd previously doubted my ability to lie to my family, but adding Will Brady to the picture added another level of complication. There had to be a way out of this.

"Sidney mentioned you're a lawyer now?" I immediately berated myself for posing it as a question. If Sidney told me Will was a lawyer, there was no reason for me to ask, as if he'd correct me and say he was a doctor. *Moron.* I took a sip of wine, my trembling hand firmly gripping the glass. If I spilled it again, I'd die. At least we'd moved on from discussing the extent of my purity in high school. My near-constant daydreams about Will back then were most unwholesome, despite being a virgin until my freshman year in college.

Will nodded. "What about you?"

"I'm a music teacher at an elementary school." I gazed down at my drink. I needed to pace myself, but between the disturbing rumor at school, anxiety over asking Perry to pretend to be someone else's romantic partner, and now unearthing that my temporary boyfriend—should he agree to the task—would be Will Brady, foggy inebriation was looking good. As was Will.

When Will whispered something to Sidney, I snuck a furtive glance at him. His face had filled out a bit since high school, but he basically looked the same. His dark hair was shorter now and cut close to his head, but he had the same brownish green eyes that twinkled when he laughed and a smattering of freckles around his nose. My long hair felt hot against my neck as he caught me staring at him. I slid closer to Perry.

Will raised an eyebrow. "A music teacher fits you."

I squirmed in my seat. I bet he was remembering the plays I put on in my backyard in elementary school and junior high. I'd hold auditions for any interested kids in the neighborhood and we'd sell tickets to our parents. I always wished Will would join in, but he never did.

"You know what they say. Those who can, do. Those who can't..." Perry said, putting an arm around me and drawing me in close.

I rolled my eyes and punched him gently in the shoulder. I knew he was teasing, unlike Sidney, who gasped, and Will, who sneered in Perry's direction.

Perry raised his hands in the air. "Kidding." Into my ear, he whispered, "You know I'm only playing, right?"

I pecked him on the lips. "Yes."

Will cleared his throat. "Teaching is a great job. I'm sure the kids love you."

I swallowed hard, not wanting to think about my students and whether they'd be fluent in French next year but sorely lacking music in their lives.

"I can't even remember the last time I saw your family," Will continued.

"It's been a long time," I agreed. I flashed back to watching through my bedroom window as Will's parents helped pack up his navy Honda Civic before he left for his freshman year of college. The whole family moved away a few months later and I never saw him again. Until now. I wished I'd spent more time on my makeup or worn something else. I felt like a giant lemon in my bright skirt, especially next to Sidney. She was so sophisticated in her fitted black skirt and gray cashmere top. I darted a guilty glance at Perry.

I shouldn't care what Will thought. I wasn't in high school anymore.

Will took a sip of Guinness and wiped his upper lip. "How are your folks? What's Jordy up to these days?"

Even though my younger brother, Jordon, followed Will and his friends around like an unwanted shadow from grade school on, Will sounded genuinely interested. "They're go—"

Sidney glanced at her watch. "Speaking of our folks, we need to talk to you guys about something."

"Who's we?" Will and Perry asked at the same time.

"Buy me a Coke," Perry said, pointing at Will.

Will narrowed his eyes at Perry, saying nothing.

I chewed on my nail, torn between hoping Sidney knew what she was doing and a desire to sneak off to the bathroom, climb out the window, and make my escape from the insanity of what she was about to propose.

Once Sidney had our attention, she nodded. "Okay, here's the deal. Christmas is around the corner, and Robyn and I need you to do us a huge favor." She opened her green eyes wide and gave Will a pleading look while I slunk down into my seat and tried to slow the beating of my heart. I felt Perry glancing at me through my side vision but kept my head bent toward the scratched wooden table.

"What kind of favor?" Will asked.

I glanced up in time to see his brows furrowed in concern.

"Help make us not want to murder our parents," Sidney said matter-of-factly.

Laughing, Perry said, "Robyn doesn't even like to kill bugs. I can't imagine her parents' lives are in danger."

I twiddled a strand of hair around my finger and protested, "You paint me like I'm..." I paused to come up with a good comparison. "Snow White." I caught Will's eye across the table and my stomach churned nervously. "I can stomp ants to their deaths like a champ, and let's not forget the mouse in my apartment. I shed no tears over its passing. But, no, I don't literally want my parents dead. I am, however, afraid they'll drive me batty over Christmas and I'd prefer to avoid it." It occurred to me bringing

Will home would inspire a completely distinct yet equally substantial reaction from my parents, and I stopped speaking and turned the floor back to Sidney.

She leaned forward across the table. "Here's the thing. Robyn's folks are concerned she's on the way to destitution if she continues to date artsy types like Perry." She glanced at him. "No offense."

Perry waved his hand and said, "None taken" before turning to me. "They do?"

I nodded reluctantly. "They bug me constantly about it and have done so right in front of old boyfriend's faces, even yours. Just last month, they tried to bribe me with orchestra-seat tickets to *In Transit* on Broadway. I was dying to see the first fully acapella show and they knew it. When I refused to take my mom's colleague's son, a doctor, as my date, the tickets magically disappeared." I grimaced. "They have no shame, and I'm sick of it. It's nothing personal." I frowned and patted his leg reassuringly under the table, even though I probably needed the comfort more than him. He was like Teflon—nothing stuck. "They wish I'd date someone with a boring steady job for a change." I looked at Will and winced. "No offense." The irony of my past infatuation with Will given his current career choice dawned on me, and I giggled. Realizing no one else was in on my joke, I slapped a hand against my mouth.

Will regarded me with a crinkled brow. "None taken. I think. But what does this have to do with you, Sid?" He placed his hand over hers on the table.

Sidney gazed up at him from under her long eyelashes. "I have the opposite problem. If I bring home an attorney, or anyone whose business could potentially require a high-priced lawyer, my father will turn the entire holiday into an RFP." For mine and Perry's benefit, she clarified, "A request for proposal. Basically he'll pitch his services to you all weekend." She faced Will again. "If I bring you, my dad will brag nonstop about B&B and either rag on your firm and all the reasons he thinks it's inferior to ours, or he'll try to hire you. And when I say 'nonstop,' I mean *nonstop*." She shuddered. "I can't do it."

Will shrugged. "Then I'll stay in the city. I already told you I don't care what I do for Christmas."

"No," Sidney said so loudly, she drew the attention of the neighboring tables.

Chuckling, Will said, "What's the big deal, babe?"

Sidney sighed dramatically. "If I go alone, my mom will whore me out to all the single men at the party." Probably noting Will's horrified expression, she added, "*Her* intentions are PG. I'm not so sure about theirs. I have to take a date. I just don't want to take you." She patted down a hair on his head. "No offense."

I wondered if we were going to spend the entire evening apologizing for possibly offending one another and tried not to laugh again.

"And besides, if you stay home, where does that leave Robyn and Perry?" she asked.

Perry raised his hand and, after swallowing the popcorn in his mouth, said, "For the kids at home, what does any of this have to do with me?"

She pointed her fork at Perry. "Robyn and I think it would be best for all of us if she took Will home as her date and I took Perry. That way, Robyn is dating a businessman who has health insurance and a 401(k), and I bring someone of absolutely no interest to my father's business." She looked at Perry. "Still no offense."

"Can you please backtrack? You said it would be best for *all* of us. How is this idea good for me or Perry?" Will asked.

"I'll find a way to make it up to you, Brady," Sidney said, adopting a sensuous, throaty voice.

Will rolled his eyes but chuckled, while I shook off the unwanted visual of him having sex with Sidney.

"What about me?" Perry asked.

Sidney raised an eyebrow at Perry. "You want me to make it up to you too?"

Perry smirked. "Not exactly, sweetheart, but thanks for the offer. What I mean is there's nothing Robyn here can bribe me with that she doesn't already deliver willingly."

I shielded my face with a menu to hide my embarrassment. When I put it down, Will was watching me with an amused expression. I slapped Perry on the leg. "Be serious, Perry."

"I was looking forward to Chrismukkah at the Lane house. I thought you were going to accompany me on the piano. I sing, you play. Remember?" Perry asked.

Will pointed at me. "Robyn's a great singer too."

"Thank you," I croaked out before grimacing with embarrassment. If he only knew how often I thought of him when I belted out songs of unrequited love and yearning back in the day.

Sidney tapped a knife against her glass. "I still have the floor."

The three of us stopped talking and focused our attention on Sidney.

"I've been listening to what you're saying, and I might be able to sweeten the pot," Sidney said to Perry.

At once eager and wary to hear what idea she had percolating in her devious brain, I leaned forward.

Perry mirrored my body language. "Go on," he prodded.

Sidney grinned—the same evil smile she honored me with the night of the wine tasting party when she talked me into this crazy scheme in the first place. "Robyn comes from a household of singers. At *her* Christmas, you'll be one of many fighting for your turn with the mic."

Perry glanced at me questioningly.

I had a feeling where this was going and nodded. "This is true."

"At the Bellows' Christmas party, you can monopolize the ebonized Steinway and Sons grand piano for as long as you'd like. In fact, we can organize a show. And..." She graced us with her sly grin once more. "This will be a fantastic acting exercise for you. You'll have to convince upward of forty people we're boyfriend and girlfriend."

"I'm not sure." He gave me a wary glance, but there was a gleam in his eyes, and I could tell Sidney held his interest.

Piling on the incentives, Sidney said, "Have I mentioned the largest practice area in my firm is entertainment law? It's what both my dad and I specialize in. My father invites his most prestigious clients and business colleagues to Christmas. This means networking opportunities galore for you."

Perry pressed his lips together, appearing to ponder his next words. "Okay, I'll do it. I'll be Sidney's boyfriend for a few days—in name only, of course." He shined his baby blues on me. "I'll miss you, but if it's what you really want..."

I swallowed hard. It was what I wanted, wasn't it? Why else would I be on a double date with Sidney, a virtual stranger, and her boyfriend—*Will Brady*? I'd agreed to lie to my parents, something I never did, just to avoid their blatant disdain for my dating choices. So what if I had an unrequited crush on Will the entire duration of my childhood? I was an adult now, and I was dating Perry. I needed to protect him from my parents' judgement and maintain my sanity over the holiday weekend. This *was* what I wanted.

Then why did I feel like I was going to throw up?

"Of course it's what she wants," Sidney responded for me.

I nodded timidly. "Sure." Taking a deep breath in and letting it out, I clarified my answer with a more confident "Yes." I met Will's eyes across the table. "As long as Will's okay with it too."

"What do you say, Will?" Sidney asked, sounding certain the answer would be a resounding "Yes."

Chapter 4

Robyn

"Too bad Will had to be a killjoy," Perry said the next morning at my kitchen table as he crunched on a piece of bacon.

I was rehashing the events of the night before to Anne Marie over the scrambled eggs, bacon, and toast breakfast she'd generously prepared for us. She even used gluten-free bread for Perry. "Uh-huh," I said, swallowing a forkful of eggs even though the gnawing feeling in my stomach was competing with my usually voracious morning appetite.

Perry slumped down in his chair and shook his head. "Who knows who would show up at a party like that? Any of those tycoons could be a Broadway investor or a movie studio honcho." He dropped his fork onto his plate in frustration.

"Could be." Even though Sidney had clearly proposed the swap as a way to help the two of us, Perry was more focused on how Will's refusal to play along affected *him*. I lacked the energy to be annoyed.

Anne Marie scooted her chair closer to mine and whispered, "What are you going to do about Chrismukkah?" She motioned her head toward Perry, who was scooping the rest of his eggs onto a piece of toast, oblivious to how Will's negative response to the boyfriend swap idea affected me.

I stood up and walked to our coffee pot, my music note slippers scratching against the medium-brown wood floor of our kitchen. "I'll have to find some way to tune out my parents' nagging." Whether I ended up with Perry or not, my folks would eventually need to accept that my taste in men was not necessarily one a financial advisor would consider a conservative choice—it was more stock than bond.

"You think your mom will make those pumpkin pastries? What are they called again?" Perry asked.

I sat back down at the table. "They're called rodanchas, and no. We eat those on Rosh Hashanah. She'll probably make fried bread though. They're called sfinz. You'll like them."

Perry beamed, seemingly no longer upset about being stuck at the Lane holiday dinner, where his chances of being discovered as the next Matthew Morrison were nonexistent. Perry fanboyed over Morrison because he managed to succeed in both television and on Broadway. I wished my mom's cooking was enough to make me feel better about Will saying no. A part of me was relieved he wouldn't play along. There would be no need for me to lie to my parents, brother, and every other member of my extended family coming to dinner about who I was dating. And yes, bringing Perry along would be painful, but at least it was a familiar agony. But why wasn't Will *comfortable* with it? Was he distressed with the situation in general, or was it personal to me? I bet he remembered the time junior year when he walked in on me and my best friend James singing acapella upstairs at Cassie Milano's keg party while everyone else was using the bedrooms to get drunk or fool around. From the mystified expression on his face, you'd think he caught us practicing witchcraft, not belting out Carrie Underwood's "Before He Cheats."

Interrupting my thoughts, Anne Marie said, "What's Will like? The way Sidney talks about him, I bet he's hot. I can't believe you grew up with him. What a small world."

"Crazy, right?" I said into my coffee cup. I was desperate to confide my puppy love for Will to Anne Marie, but I couldn't do it in front of Perry. I also felt guilty given her relationship with Sidney.

Perry stood up and stretched his arms in the air. "I'm going to take a shower. Feel free to join me," he said with a wink before walking out of the kitchen.

Anne Marie stared after him. "His parents must have fed him a lot of milk as a child."

"They certainly fed his ego," I said with a laugh.

"You gonna join him?" she asked, waggling her eyebrows.

"No," I yelped, horrified. It was one thing to have sex with Perry behind closed doors in my bedroom, but I would never shower with him while Anne Marie was home.

Anne Marie giggled. "Not sure I'd have the same restraint."

"Obviously, I'm the more considerate roommate," I said, before sticking my tongue out at her. I stood up and patted my belly. "Thanks so much for breakfast. Just what I needed to fortify myself for some research. I'll do the dishes, kick Perry out, and spend the next few hours with my nose in the internet." I had told Anne Marie what Lynn had said about the music program, and even though I was afraid of what I might find, I wanted to see if other schools in the metropolitan area had suffered a similar fate. I'd considered commiserating with Lance, but thought better of it. If he hadn't heard the rumors, I didn't want to stress him out before I verified whether there was any truth to them.

Waving me away, Anne Marie said, "Leave the dishes. You can do mine tomorrow."

I smiled wide. "I take back what I said. You are the best roomie ever."

"Don't you forget it."

A few minutes later, I jolted from my desk chair as drops of water landed on my arm. "What the..." I looked up to find Perry, naked aside from an eggplant-colored terrycloth towel wrapped low around his hips, grinning at me. Wiping the wetness from my arm with my hand, I said, "You startled me."

"I know. You looked so serious hovering over your computer like that." He stood behind me and placed a hand on each of my shoulders. "What are you reading?"

I sighed. "Did you know eighty percent of schools nationwide have been affected by budget cuts since 2008, and fewer schools offer art programs than a decade ago?"

"Isn't that good news?" he asked, squeezing my shoulders.

I whipped around to face him. "In what way?"

"You teach music, not art," he said matter-of-factly.

My eyes bugged out. "Seriously? First of all, 'art' includes visual arts *and* performing arts, and second of all, I don't want Miss Cassidy to lose her job either. Besides, don't children deserve a well-rounded education? There's more to learning than reading and math." My heart slammed against my chest at both the unfairness of it all and Perry's nonchalance.

He knelt so we were eye to eye. "Whoa, sweetie. Relax. You're getting riled up over nothing." He paused and I watched as his eyes scrolled the piece. "The article mentions Chicago, D.C., Los Angeles, and Philadelphia, but there's no mention of New York."

I didn't respond. What if the Board of Education decided my school should be the guinea pig for these budget cuts in New York?

"What can I do to make you feel better?" he asked, snaking two fingers under the top of his towel suggestively.

"Nothing," I mumbled. I was more concerned than ever about the future of my school and in no mood for sexy time. Perry wasn't the type to dwell, and I mostly took my cues from him to maintain perspective. But sometimes, like now, I wished he'd take things more seriously.

"I have an idea. We're not leaving for your folks until Wednesday. We should go to BOB Bar on Tuesday night."

"Dancing to old-school hip hop would definitely help loosen me up, but aren't you working Tuesday night?"

Perry frowned. "Yeah, you're right." He glanced around my room with a pensive expression for a moment before tapping a finger to his head. "Got it. I have my casting director workshop tomorrow afternoon, but I'm free after. Let's go to the Birdland cast party."

One of Perry's regular hangouts for years, the Open Mic Night at Birdland brought together superstars in theater with up-and-comers, but after he snagged his first commercial—a teeth-whitening bit that aired mostly during late-night television and infomercials—he'd been less interested in the Broadway crowd and hungry for more screen work. Perry's manager, Wilson, encouraged him to keep a toe in all aspects of performing arts, claiming if Matthew Morrison could do it, so could he. I didn't often agree with Wilson, but I did in this instance. "Really?" I glanced up at Perry hopefully.

He nodded. "Anything to get you to smile."

I grinned at him. It was a bandage, not a solution, but it would lift my mood temporarily. "Mission accomplished." I tugged at the bottom of his towel until it fell to the ground. "What were you saying before about making me feel better?"

Sidney

I sat on my crème-colored English roll-arm sofa and rolled my eyes up to the high ceiling of my living room while my father droned on about work over the phone. "Can we talk about this tomorrow? I need to head out soon." After Will finished his shower, we were going for a late brunch at one of the many trendy tapas places in my Lower East Side neighborhood.

"I promised Scott we'd sit down with him at Christmas to discuss the rampant infringement of their assets in the Pacific Rim. Are you caught up?"

"Almost." I leaned over and straightened out the pile of industry-related magazines I kept on my leather-upholstered ottoman coffee table. "Do you think Christmas dinner is the best time to discuss business? Maybe we can, you know, eat, drink, and be merry for a while?"

My dad harrumphed. "The client comes first, Sidney. If this is your way of saying you're behind in your research, get to it."

"I'm not behind. I'm merely trying to enjoy what's left of my weekend and encourage some semblance of holiday cheer at the party." The shower turned off, which meant Will would be ready to go in less than twenty minutes. I preferred to use that time admiring Will's fresh-out-of-the-shower body over discussing clients with my dad. "I really need to get out of here. I'm meeting some friends for lunch." If my dad knew the "friend" I was joining was already in my apartment, he'd never let me off the phone. His time was more valuable than anyone else's.

"Your mother created a Word document with the guest list and included a column to indicate if they were family, clients, or potential clients." He paused. "It probably wasn't necessary to include family, but better to be overly inclusive than miss someone important, right? I'm emailing it to you now so you can familiarize yourself with anyone new. I just sent it. Did you get it?"

I buried my head between my legs. "I'm offline. I'm on my way out to eat, remember?"

"Can't you bring it to the restaurant? You can read it between courses."

With a dejected sigh, I rose from the couch and leaned my hips from side to side in a stretch. When my fitted white sweater rose over my belly, I pulled up my low-rise jeans. "Great idea, Dad. I'll do that. See you tomorrow."

I hung up before he could respond and walked to my bedroom with a renewed sense of dread for the upcoming holiday. The night before, Will had adamantly refused to take part in the boyfriend swap. He said he wasn't comfortable with it and that his boyfriend services weren't on the auction block. My reference to Perry as a "blond god" didn't help things. When I realized Will was jealous, I promised he had nothing to worry about. Perry was gorgeous, but from what I'd witnessed, he didn't have much else going for him. But Will wouldn't back down from his firm refusal, and I'd promised to drop the subject. It wasn't worth risking our burgeoning relationship to argue.

I'd tried to keep my vow, but I was afraid bringing Will with me to Christmas would have disastrous consequences. Will purposely chose an employer that embraced the work/life balance.

Subjecting Will to my father, whose motto was, "Work/life balance? What's that?" would be cruel. Even worse, my mother had been burying me with texts about Perry: How did we meet? Was it serious? Did he drink wine, beer, or hard alcohol? Did I want to invite his parents too? Was he a leftie or a righty? At some point, I'd come up with a way to explain Perry's sudden name change to Will, but I wished it wouldn't come to that. I shuddered at how much time I'd lost scrolling through her multiple messages and ignoring her questions. She was going to suffocate me to the point where I'd want to be holed away from everyone, including Will. For both of our sakes, I had to convince him to change his mind about the swap.

As I heard his footsteps approach my bedroom from the bathroom, I brought my phone to my mouth and said, "Yes, he's a lawyer." While silently counting to ten, I peered out my bedroom window and down eight flights at the pre-war buildings across the street. My newly constructed complex was one of the few high-rise apartments among century-old tenement buildings.

"A third year at Kensworth and Associates," I said. Breathe. One, two, three. Breathe. Four, five, six. "Good memory. They were opposing counsel on the Russell case." I let my head fall back and groaned. "Yes, he's intelligent, Dad. It's a good firm." I turned around and feigned a shocked expression when I saw Will leaning against my bedroom door. My father's inability to take a hint had made me too late to admire Will's freshly showered naked body. He was already fully clothed in blue jeans and an olive-colored sweater that brought out the green in his eyes. Placing my hand over the phone, I whispered, "Sorry."

Will raised and lowered his shoulders in a shrug before sitting on the edge of my bed and lacing up his Jack Purcell Signature sneakers.

"No, I'm not going to ask him to do research for one of our cases during Christmas. Have you heard of it? The one day a year almost everyone besides movie-theater and Chinese-restaurant employees gets the day off? He doesn't work for you." A tear lodged in my eye as I became more fully invested in my manipulation.

"Is Mom there?" I asked no one. "Well, Aaron Davenport will have to find his own date because I'm spoken for." I rolled my eyes at Will. "Okay, tell her I called. Yes. Bye."

I placed the phone on the windowsill and stared out the window. My hands were shaking and my stomach felt heavy. I wasn't sure if it was a result of guilt or desperation.

"You all right, Sid?"

I turned away from the window and joined Will on the bed. Wiping my eye, I said, "I've been better." I hated lying to him, but the more I allowed an idea to fester in my brain, the more determined I became to make it a reality—no matter what.

Will smiled sheepishly. "You weren't kidding about your dad, huh?"

I sighed and rested my head against his shoulder. With my eyes closed, I said, "I wish I was."

"I only heard your end of the conversation, but I can see how this might be equally painful for both of us." He stroked my hair. "Do you honestly think bringing Perry instead of me is a good idea?"

"I do. Crazy as it sounds," I said without opening my eyes. "I know you think I'm being a drama queen, but I only want to protect you. Your first introduction to my family should be during a shorter dose of time, not Christmas."

"It's only for one day, right?"

Finally opening my eyes, I turned to face him. He was so close to bending, I could feel it. "My family expects me from the twenty-third to the twenty-sixth. Since Robyn's from out of state, I assume she's planning a longer stay too."

Will stood up and whistled through his teeth. "I can't believe I'm saying this, but I'll reach out to some of my old friends from high school and if any of them are heading to Bala Cynwyd for the holidays, I'll go with Robyn. At least I'll have extra incentive."

I jumped off the bed and hurled myself into his arms. "Yay! Thank you, thank you, thank you," I said as I hugged him.

"We'll need ground rules," Will said, separating from me.

"I don't think we need to create a handbook. We're all grownups. Be as convincing as possible without actually getting naked and it should be fine, but we can talk about it later." I wanted to bask in my victory for a while before ironing out the details.

Will chuckled. "So anything goes as long as Robyn and I are clothed?"

"Don't sass me, Brady," I instructed, but a visual of Robyn and Will naked together appeared before me, and a ping of jealousy stabbed me in the gut. The emotion exited as swiftly as it arrived. Even if Will found Robyn attractive—he was a man after all—Robyn wasn't the type. Despite only meeting her on two occasions, and notwithstanding Perry's comments about her purity score, I'd bet my quarterly bonus Robyn would never screw someone else's boyfriend. I wouldn't either, and I was fairly certain Will would take the moral high ground as well. Just the same, I reiterated, "No rule book is necessary, but trust your gut. If it strikes you as inappropriate, it probably is."

"And the same applies to you and the 'blond god,' right?" Will asked with a serious tone.

"Of course." With any luck, I'd spend just enough time with Perry to introduce him as my boyfriend and then cut him loose to wear out the piano keys or serenade the kitchen staff.

Will cocked his head to the side. "How will you explain bringing home an actor after just telling your dad your boyfriend is a lawyer?"

My stomach clenched. If I told Will the truth—that my folks had no idea what my boyfriend did for a living—how could I explain the telephone conversation with my father he'd just overheard? My sprightly mind coming to the rescue, I said, "I purposely keep my family guessing when it comes to my relationships. They'll be surprised for a minute but will move on quickly." I breathed a sigh of relief and gave mental thanks to the god of quick thinking for being so generous with me.

My belly grumbled in hunger, but first things first. "Can you call your friends before lunch?" I wouldn't be able to enjoy my egg-white frittata until I was certain it was a done deal.

Robyn

"Ms. Lane?"

I stopped humming along to "Jingle Bell Rock" and followed the sound of the high-pitched but soft voice to where Aimee, one of my star fifth-grade students, was leaning against the classroom door. I glanced at my wall clock. "Hi there. I'm surprised you're still here." I'd stayed after school to remove the December decorations from my classroom wall. Then I remembered Aimee was part of the after-school program.

Aimee chewed on her lip. "I have to go to the doctor for my throat over winter break."

Her face was hidden by her curly red hair, but I could tell from the tremor in her voice she was on the verge of tears. I pulled out a chair and said, "Here, sit," before planting myself in a chair too. I pushed a strand of her hair away from her face. "What's the matter with your throat, sweetie?" Her voice did have a distinctively hoarse quality to it.

"It's sore," she responded before staring at her shoes.

"Do you have a cold?" My first telltale sign I was coming down with something was a sore throat.

"I don't think so," Aimee replied as a fat tear dropped down her cheek.

I scooted my chair closer to her and studied her face. "Why not?"

"Because it's hurt for a long time." Aimee averted eye contact, now focusing on my currently empty walls rather than her shoes.

"What's a long time?" To kids, three days was an eternity.

"Since the beginning of the school year. I didn't want to say anything because I was afraid I wouldn't be able to sing in the concert," she said quickly before inhaling a huge gulp of air.

Even as I burst with pride at how much value Aimee placed on the school performances, my heart wrenched that she felt she needed to keep her pain a secret. And if she was fearful of missing *one* concert, how would she react if the entire music program was abolished? *Don't go there.* I brushed the thought to the side. "Did you tell your parents?"

Aimee nodded, her teeth threatening to leave a permanent dent in her lips. "Yesterday."

"What did they say?"

"I have to go to the EMT."

Cocking my head to the side, I repeated, "EMT?"

"Uh-huh. The throat doctor."

"Oh." I smiled in amusement. "The ENT—ear, nose, and throat."

Aimee frowned. "That's what I said."

There was no point in correcting her, so I nodded. "I understand you're worried. Doctors are yucky, but they also have the power to make you feel better. I'm glad it's out in the open."

"What if he tells me I can never sing again?" she asked, her chin quivering.

I pushed my lips together. "I bet you overdid it with all the solos I gave you and your voice needs to rest a little. What better timing for a nap than winter vacation?"

Aimee looked at me with cautious hope. "You think?"

Nodding eagerly, I said, "Sure. So go easy on the Christmas carols, okay?"

Her face brightened. "Okay."

I beamed at her. "Because I need you good and rested for the spring concert."

"I'll be ready."

"Promise?" I extended my pinky toward her.

"Promise," she said, entwining her pinky with mine.

I let go and stood up. "It's settled then. Let's get you to the auditorium with the others. Do you want me to walk you back?"

"No thanks, I'm fine."

"Have a great Christmas, Aimee."

"You too, Miss Lane," she said with a wave before racing out of the room in much better spirits than she entered it.

Alone again, I glanced at my barren walls, contemplating whether to put the January decorations up now or leave them for after the break. I was also tempted to see if Principal Hogan was still around and corner him about those so-called rumors. But what if I didn't like what he told me? It might put a dark cloud on my entire vacation, and I'd have no one to blame but myself. I rolled my eyes to the ceiling as it dawned on me there was no way Principal Hogan was still in the building. With no students of their own, members of the administration were usually the first to pack up before a holiday. It was probably better that way. Still, not knowing was killing me.

The sound of my phone pinging the delivery of a text message startled me out of my internal debate and I rushed back to my desk anxious for a distraction. It was from Sidney. *"Will changed his mind. The boyfriend swap is on. I would have told you yesterday, but Will had to confirm a few things first."*

My heart pounded furiously as I read the rest of the message, which included a phone number for me to contact Will and set up a plan for departure. Sidney said he was expecting my call and I shouldn't wait too long since we were only two days away from show time. Then she asked me to forward along Perry's number.

She concluded the text with, *"Good luck, Robyn. And one last thing: no funny business. JK."*

Suddenly lightheaded, I threw myself in my chair as the room spun around me. I closed my eyes, wondering how Sidney had hoodwinked me into this plan, but I quickly accepted my own role in letting it get this far. I should have shot down the idea before it become fully formed, and certainly once I found out it would require me to pretend Will Brady was my boyfriend. But I didn't. With everyone else on board, it was too late to back down now. The curtain was about to go up on the biggest performance of my life.

With my eyes still shut, I reached around the desk for my

phone and gripped it firmly in my hands. Finally opening my eyes, I called Perry first. When voicemail picked up, I said there'd been a change of plans and he would be going to Sidney's party after all. I told him I didn't know the details and he should phone her directly. I left Sidney's number, said we'd talk at the cast party that night, and hung up.

Calling Perry was the easy part. I figured he'd be thrilled at the opportunity to be discovered as the next big thing. But what was I going to say to Will? I wondered what made him change his mind to be "comfortable" with the swap. Did Sidney succeed in persuading him with her sexual prowess? I swallowed down the queasy knot in my belly. I still couldn't believe Sidney's boyfriend and my ex-dreamboy were one and the same, but it wouldn't be so bad. All we had to do was pretend to be boyfriend and girlfriend for three days while we lived in the same house, ate at the same table, showered in the same bathroom, and slept under the same roof— correction, same *room*, since my folks were liberal enough to let me sleep in the same bed as my boyfriends. Easy like Sunday morning. I fell back against my chair. Compared to what was in store for me in the coming week, talking to Will on the phone was a stroll through a garden. Before I could chicken out, I keyed in his number and paced the room while waiting for him to answer.

"Hello?"

I gulped at the sound of his raspy voice. "Will? Hi, it's Robyn." I giggled nervously. "Your girlfriend."

Chapter 5

After meeting at the car rental place and driving through the Lincoln Tunnel, Will and I put aside small talk in favor of a more pertinent topic of conversation—how we were going to convince my family we were boyfriend and girlfriend. Will broached the subject first, asking about ground rules.

"Holding hands, some touching, and little pecks are fine. As long as we show some affection, my parents won't question the lack of making out," I said, almost choking on my words. I was having trouble focusing on the road with Will Brady as my passenger, and the current topic of conversation wasn't helping. I flashed back to the last time we'd ridden in a car together. School had closed early due to an ice storm. I was terrified to drive home and the buses had already left. Before I could protest, Jordy, who was a freshman, asked Will to give us a ride and, of course, he said yes. I remembered sitting in the backseat and trying not to get caught looking at Will's reflection in the rearview mirror.

"Do you and Perry full-on make out in front of your folks regularly?"

Even though I was looking at the road, I could still see Will's amused grin through my side vision. To talk myself out of blushing, I focused on the vanity plate of the car in front of me—GRNSON1. "Not at all. I meant if we make small shows of affection, no one will be skeptical."

Will tapped my thigh. "I'm teasing you. I don't think it will be too difficult. Unless your parents are suspicious by nature."

My leg tingled in the spot where Will's fingers had been. "They're not. But they'll be surprised." To my knowledge, Will had no idea of the extent of my crush back then. He probably assumed my parents would consider it a humorous coincidence that their daughter was dating an old neighbor—nothing more, nothing less. I should have warned them, but I was too afraid they'd see right through my lies.

"You haven't told them yet? Are they expecting Perry?"

I could see my knuckles turn white from gripping the steering wheel so tightly. I had managed to avoid extended conversation with my mother over the past couple of weeks. When the subject of Christmas came up, I fibbed some excuse to end the call before I could confirm or deny whether Perry would be joining me. This resulted in major half-Catholic/half-Jewish guilt, along with seriously unhealthy nail beds. As the traffic came to a halt, I mumbled, "Shit." Traffic so early in the drive was not a good sign.

"Snow White curses." Will laughed.

I turned my head toward him with a smile. "You better call the Brothers Grimm to confiscate my princess crown."

Will furrowed his brow. "I don't think Snow White wore a crown."

"Well-versed in fairytales, are you?" I teased.

"Just Snow White," he said with a wink, taking me back almost a decade to when we were in high school and a wink from Will Brady was better than an extended solo in the spring concert. My favorite one took place my junior year. I was in the hallway between classes telling my friend James about my new favorite movie, *Little Miss Sunshine*. I'd seen it with my family the previous weekend. To better express my enthusiasm, I acted out a portion of the scene where Abigail Breslin danced to "Superfreak" and was completely oblivious to the other kids who had halted their conversations to observe me, including Will. James's trembling lips finally clued me into the public display I was making, and I stopped mid-song and hid my face in my locker. I felt a tap on my back, and when I turned around, I came face to face with Will. He said, "Nice moves, Snow White," and winked at me before continuing down the hallway. Even though he was teasing me, I floated through the rest of the day.

I came out of my time warp and jutted my head toward the bumper-to-bumper traffic before us. "This might take a while." With no traffic, the drive from New York City to Philadelphia could take less than two hours, but so close to Christmas, I estimated closer to three.

"I'm not going anywhere." Dressed casually in blue jeans and a gingham button-down shirt, Will stretched out his long legs as far as the small space in the passenger seat of the economy car I'd rented allowed.

I snuck a quick peek at him again before turning back to the road. For someone previously uncomfortable with the plan, he was being a good sport. I yearned for an ounce of his coolheadedness. "Your parents don't like Perry, huh? Why do you think that is?"

"They have nothing against Perry personally, just his career." In all honesty, I wasn't confident either of them would approve of Perry even if he were an advertising executive, but I didn't like the hint of sarcasm I noted in the way Will directed the question.

"You guys serious?"

I shrugged in response to what could only be described as the most annoying question ever.

"You've been dating for how long now?"

"A little under a year." I tapped my fingers to the beat of the music. "I love Counting Crows," I said happily before raising the volume of "Mr. Jones" and singing softly. Good music always made sitting in unmoving traffic more bearable, and the Classic Rewind Sirius XM Radio Channel was one of my favorites.

"Me too," Will said, before enthusiastically belting out the lyrics along with me while slapping his hands on his thighs to the rhythm.

Within the first few notes, it became evident Will's status as

Mr. Cool wasn't the only reason he never sang in the chorus or auditioned for the school play—he had a horrible voice. If Adam Duritz's ears were blistering, it was probably because Will was demolishing his band's American Top 40 number one song from 1994.

Surprised Will was unself-conscious enough to sing out loud with a voice that could stop traffic—in a bad way—I was momentarily rendered mute. Continuing to tap his feet to the music with his eyes closed, he didn't even notice me staring at him. Which was a good thing, as I was visualizing him in the shower singing into his scrub brush like a microphone. Only bad singing wasn't supposed to be hot. Ashamed of my mind for going somewhere it wasn't invited, I Rick-rolled my mind until Will was dressed in gold sparkly parachute pants and a down vest and singing "Never Gonna Give You Up" by the painfully unsexy Rick Astley. I was unsuccessful in my mission since, naturally, Will made a much sexier Rick Astley than the man himself.

I released a grunt of frustration that Will didn't notice over his warbling. After the song ended, I lowered the volume. "What other music do you like?" I'd blessedly regained my composure by then.

Will opened his eyes and gave me a wry grin. "When I was 'pondering the meaning of life' in high school, The Killers, Fall Out Boy, and Red Hot Chili Peppers were usually in the background." He shrugged. "But I love almost all music. It makes everything better."

Unless you're the one singing. As the response perched itself on the tip of my tongue, my lips quivered and I mentally slapped myself. Who was this mean girl who'd invaded my body?

Will cocked his head to the side. "What are you thinking?"

"It's nothing." I slammed my fist into my mouth knuckles first.

Shaking his head in amusement, Will said, "You're such a bad liar, Snow."

I frowned. He was right, which didn't bode well for this trip.

"C'mon. Tell me."

"Not when you sing," I muttered.

"What?"

Good. He hadn't heard me. It was a sign I should shut it. "Nothing."

"No. I want to know what you said. Something about my singing?"

Groaning, I stole a glance at him before turning back to the road. It was a quick peek, but long enough to establish Will was fully invested in getting me to spill. "I don't want to hurt your feelings." I bit a fingernail.

"But?"

I turned toward him. "Do you think you're a good singer?" With any luck, he was well aware of his shortcoming and we'd share a laugh.

"Do *you* think I'm a good singer?" His hazel eyes opened wide in hope.

I licked my dry lips and shook my head gently.

"Oh." His shoulders dropped.

"But I'm sure you've got oodles of talent in other areas." I turned back to the road, afraid to look at him after going all Simon Cowell on his ass. What was wrong with me? So what if Will was under the false illusion he had a voice like Josh Groban? It wasn't my place to tell him otherwise. And I might be talented in the musical arts, but I could never color within the lines or hit the volleyball over the net. And after years of swimming lessons in summer camp, I still never mastered the butterfly stroke. It wasn't natural to be good at everything.

If Will's silence was any indication, he was taking my criticism very badly. I summoned the courage to look at him. My stomach dropped at the sight of him bent down with his face in his hands. Was he crying? I had no idea he was so sensitive. "I'm sorry, Will," I said, reaching over to tap the top of his head to soothe him. For years, I'd dreamed about being the person Will relied on to comfort him in his times of need, but I never imagined I'd be the cause of his distress. The boyfriend swap was off to an awful start thanks to me. Focusing again on the road, I begged, "Talk to me, Will."

Finally, he made a noise, but it didn't sound like crying. It sounded more like...wheezing? I darted my eyes toward him only to see his head bobbing up and down in the unmistakable throes of hysterical laughter. Embarrassed for falling for his aggrieved act, I demanded, "Stop it," and elbowed him in the rib for emphasis.

Releasing his hands to reveal his red-streaked face, he said, "I'm sure you have..." He took a gulp of air. "*Oodles* of talent."

"You suck," I muttered.

"I'm sorry," he said, wiping a tear of mirth from his eye. "I don't think anyone has ever been quite as apologetic over insulting me before."

Too mortified to respond, I focused on my foot on the gas pedal until I felt his hand on my shoulder. "What?"

"Please don't be mad. The expression on your face was so...earnest. You were so afraid to mock my singing voice as if you'd singlehandedly shattered my dream of going on the road with my one-man band." He eyes moved up and down my face and he smiled gently. "It was the cutest thing I've ever seen." With his lower lip pushed out, he asked, "Do you forgive me?"

I choked out, "I forgive you," fighting the squidgy feeling in my belly from him calling me cute. We locked eyes for a beat until I felt myself flush under his gaze. To drown out the awkward silence, I turned the volume back up.

"So what is it you see in Perry? Besides the obvious?"

I returned the volume to its earlier level. "What's the obvious?"

"Sid described him as a 'blond god,' which I assume means he's of above average appearance." He frowned.

It dawned on me that Will might be concerned with Perry being in such intimate quarters with his girlfriend. "Don't worry about Perry. Sidney will be safe with him. I promise." Perry was aware of the effect he had on women, but generally only took advantage when it meant getting immediate attention from female bartenders and waitresses. He barely even looked at other girls when we were together, despite them ogling him constantly.

"I trust Sid, but thanks for the reassurance."

"Then why all the questions about Perry?" I asked, before wincing at how defensive I sounded.

Will whipped his head back. "Just making conversation. If I'm going to pretend to be your boyfriend, I might as well know what attracts you to your real one."

I relaxed my shoulders and pulled up an image of Perry. "He's ambitious and really passionate about show business, but otherwise doesn't let things get to him. He's like a shield to negativity. It's refreshing to be around him." I smiled at the memory of him embracing me fiercely that morning before heading to his own apartment to finish packing. He warned me he might not call too often so he could stay in character as much as possible.

Will clucked his tongue. "You love the guy because he doesn't get stressed. Interesting perspective. This is probably none of my business, but I would imagine his nonchalance wouldn't be so refreshing in hard times when you need him to have your back."

Even though Will was right, it wasn't his concern, I pressed my lips together as I recalled the ease with which Perry shrugged off the rumors at school. "I never said I loved him."

Will squinted at me. "You've been together almost a year and you don't love him? How does he feel about you?"

Lost for a response, I cleared my throat to break the silence. I had no clue where Perry's head was long-term, and I was fine with it because I wasn't sure what I wanted either. I didn't need to know right this moment. I also didn't need to have this conversation with Will, of all people. "Sidney's something else. How did you two meet?"

"Our law firms co-chaired a moot court competition for law students." His eyes danced as he spoke of her.

Returning my attention to the road, I asked, "You guys serious?" It was obvious from the way Sidney spoke at the wine party that she dug Will, but she hadn't even introduced him to her parents yet, and most of her comments had been about their sex life.

"I have no idea."

I whipped my head in his direction. "Aha. You have no right to pick on me and Perry when you're in the same exact place with Sidney."

He chuckled. "I'm not picking on you at all. I was merely asking questions. But you can take back your 'aha' because it's not the same thing. I'm happy with Sid, but we've been dating less than half as long as you and Perry. If we're together in a year and you ask me if I love her, I hope I'll have an answer for you."

When he said "if we're together," I initially thought he meant the two of us and my heart raced, but then I realized he was talking about Sidney. I let out the breath I was holding. "Do you have an answer to everything?" I asked in mock annoyance.

"I'm a lawyer so...yes." He smiled dangerously.

Wanting out of the conversation, I raised the volume once again on the radio and sang "Free Fallin'" at the top of my lungs. Will watched me with an open mouth, seemingly stunned to silence, but I refused to stop. Noticing his mouth moving, I reluctantly lowered the radio. "What did you say?"

"If you can't beat 'em, join 'em," Will said before turning the volume back up. Shouting over Tom Petty's voice, he added, "And in my case, drive them to insert heavy duty ear plugs."

Still regretting my unsolicited feedback, I grimaced until Will's infectious laughter got the better of me and I joined in.

"And by the way, the answer to your question is no. I don't think I have a good voice. Hopefully your parents won't make me eat my dinner in the garage. I promise what I lack in singing skills, I more than make up for in showmanship."

I smiled to myself. My parents were in for a show, all right.

Sidney

"Does this car have satellite radio?" Perry asked.

"This vehicle has *everything*," I said, stroking the leather seat of my Glacier-white metallic Audi S7. Hard earned and well-deserved, the souped-up sedan was my twenty-eighth birthday present to myself. It didn't get much action in the city since I relied so much on public transportation or car services to get around locally, but the anniversary of my birth was the perfect excuse to replace the reliable but less luxurious Toyota Prius I purchased during law school.

"Can we listen to it? Or I have some seriously good road trip tunes on my iPod." Perry reached his muscled arms into the backseat and pulled his black duffle bag over to the front.

I frowned. "I really wanted to finish this audiobook. *Buried Bones*. Have you read it? It's seriously dark."

"I haven't read it, but listening to it from the middle would spoil it for me, wouldn't it?"

Staring him down, I said, "Be honest with me. You're not going to read it, are you?"

Perry smiled sheepishly. "No."

"Then there's nothing to spoil." I grinned. Logic won out every time.

Perry blinked his cobalt blue eyes at me. "Road trips are for singing, not reading."

I sighed and opened my mouth to tell him it was my car, which made me the entertainment DJ, but then I remembered Perry was doing me a favor and decided to play nice. I was dying to know how the book ended, but it could wait. "Music it is. What do you want to listen to?" I shook my shoulders. A little car dancing might do my stressed-out body good. As long as it wasn't hip-hop or country.

"I have some new Drake, but if you don't like hip-hop, how about Rascal Flatts?"

Even though it was winter, I liked keeping the sunroof open when I drove, but the wind coming through flopped my bangs into my eyes. Brushing them out of the way so I could see the road, I said, "You have anything less genre specific?"

Perry scrunched his forehead. "You mean like pop?"

"I guess."

His cheeks dimpled and he placed his iPod on the seat

between us. "It's all on here. Just skip anything you don't want to hear."

"Great. I'm not picky. You can man the music." The first song came on—a silly boy band whose name escaped me. "Not this one," I said.

"No problemo." Perry tapped his device and grinned as the notes of another song played out of the stereo speakers.

"I hate her," I said with a grimace.

Perry gaped at me. "How can you hate her? She's a musical icon."

I shrugged. "Not a fan."

Rolling his eyes, Perry muttered, "No accounting for taste."

"What did you say?"

"Nothing. How about this one?"

I pursed my lips. "Next."

Perry's eyes bugged out. "You're kidding me, right?"

Raising an eyebrow, I said, "Do I *look* like I'm kidding?"

He sighed. "Not unless you're pretending to be my eighth-grade history teacher, Mrs. McAndrews. She was mean, by the way, and never joked about anything."

We sat in silence for a few moments while Perry tinkered with his device. "This is like the least offensive song I can think of."

I listened as the first notes played. "Fine." It wasn't my favorite, but it would do.

"You sure?"

"Yes. I told you I'm not picky."

Perry laughed. "No. You're the most musically flexible woman I've ever met."

I frowned. "Are you toying with me?"

"I would never toy with Mrs. McAndrews."

The conversation halted for a while as Perry sang along to the music and I quickly decided I preferred his singing voice—a rusty whisper that reminded me of John Mayer—to listening to him speak. As traffic slowed down, I gazed out my window at the trees lining the sides of FDR Drive. Colorful fall foliage had given way to melting snow on bare branches.

"What kind of law do you practice?" he asked, breaking what I considered a contented silence.

"The kind I don't like to discuss after hours." Unlike my father, I avoided work-related dialogue unless I could bill my time.

Perry nodded. "Right. Is there anything you want to know about me, then?" He gave me a practiced smile as if I were one of the anchors on *Extra* asking who he was wearing on the red carpet.

Having discovered Perry's last name really was Smith—either I was totes lucky or a fledging psychic—I'd already looked up his IMDb page which, aside from a teeth-whitening commercial, an appearance on *Law and Order: SVU*, and a few Off Broadway productions, was sparse. "Not really." I paused. "Although we should probably discuss the game plan for this weekend." The ride from the city into Northern Westchester where my parents lived in Scarsdale was only about an hour and we'd already been driving for twenty minutes.

He shrugged. "If you want."

Amused by his nonchalance, I asked, "Don't you want to know who else will be there so you can prepare?"

Turning up the volume on his iPod, he said, "I prefer to be surprised."

If this was how he warmed up for auditions, it was no wonder his IMDb page was so unimpressive. "It would make me feel better if you didn't go in cold," I said over the music.

"I really need to practice my improvisational skills, if you don't mind."

A chill ran down my spine as I imagined Perry turning the entire weekend into an acting exercise. What if he adopted a British accent around my dad's English friends to practice for a role in the BBC's next *Masterpiece Classic*? I'd suggested Perry use the weekend as an opportunity to hone his talent to incite him to sign on. I meant it, but feared he'd lost sight of the big picture. "Like I said, you'll have full access to our piano and I'm sure the guests will love hearing you sing. You have a great voice," I said, figuring flattery was the way to this man's heart.

Perry smiled knowingly.

I knew it. "But let's focus on the real reason Will's with Robyn and you're with me this week."

Perry groaned. "I forgot about Will. He'd better keep his hands on the right side of Snow White's panties."

"Ew." I shook my head in disgust. "I'm sure our respective partners will behave. I keep Will *very* satisfied." I'd made sure our last time together was super memorable just in case.

Perry gave me a sidelong glance and smirked. "If you say so."

My mouth snapped open in response to the unexpected slight. My sex appeal had never been described as "understated." "Will was right about you." He didn't like the way Perry spoke to Robyn, and I had to agree his filter was nonexistent.

"Yeah? What did he say?" he asked with a wide grin.

Clearly, he assumed whatever Will said was positive. I got the feeling you could insult this guy six ways to Sunday and he'd say "thank you." Giving him a quick once-over as he absently pulled his fingers through his longish hair, I was taken aback by his blatant beauty. The gods of looks certainly didn't hold back the day Perry was born. Too bad they were so stingy with his humility. Ignoring his question, I said, "Anyway, back to the reason you're here."

Perry yawned and raised a hand to his mouth. "Man, I'm beat. You mind if I take a nap?"

"Actually, we need to go over a few things before we arrive at my parents' house. For instance, how we met, how long we've been dating. Once we get initial introductions over with, they'll leave us alone. And then we'll keep telling new people the same story. I have a few thoughts. Are you ready?"

Silence.

"Perry?"

The only response I received was the sound of Perry snoring away as if the passenger seat of my car was his own personal Posturepedic.

Chapter 6

Robyn

After almost three hours of driving, we finally arrived in Bala Cynwyd—the residential community in the Philadelphia suburbs where Will and I both grew up. As we drove along City Avenue, Will moved his head from left to right as if taking in all the sights for the first time. Amused, I asked, "Has it changed much since the last time you were here?"

Will grinned wide. "Not even a little bit. Although I don't think the LA Fitness was there nine years ago," he said, pointing to the gym in the Bala Cynwyd Shopping Center.

"You haven't been back at all since your family moved?"

Still gazing out the window, he said, "Nope. I never had a reason before."

"You're welcome then."

Will turned and smirked at me. "Yes. I feel like I've won tickets to the Super Bowl. How can I ever repay you?"

"I think you already have," I said sheepishly as jumping beans danced the jig in my belly. The last few hours of breezy conversation almost made me forget the real reason we'd taken this road trip together.

As a lump of guilt settled at the back of my throat for the lie I was about to tell my family, I thought about Perry. The last time he'd stayed over, my mom cut off his performance of "November Rain" because it was too long, but she let Jordy sing the equally verbose "Stairway to Heaven" in its entirety. Perry pouted for a few seconds before dancing to my mom's rendition of "Hit the Beat Now"—the incident already forgotten. My memory was longer. With a pang of gratitude, I glanced at Will. "Thanks, by the way."

Will cocked his head to the side. "For what?"

"For agreeing to this. Don't think for a second the absurdity is lost on me."

"You're welcome. No one, except maybe Santa Claus, should be as stressed out on Christmas as you and Sid were. As long as you realize it's a temporary fix to a problem that won't go away by itself." He chuckled. "Unless you plan to invite me to all of your holiday dinners from now on."

"What are you doing for Valentine's Day?" I joked before quickly turning my own gaze out the window to hide the blanket of red that crept across my cheeks. *Why couldn't I have gone with President's Day?* Thankfully, Will didn't comment.

"I'll have to meet the big bad Harvey Bellows eventually, but for now, if the only gift my girlfriend wants for Christmas is my blessing to let some other dude play her boyfriend for a few days, I'll play along." He sighed loudly and faced the window. "How did I get myself into this mess?"

I swallowed my weight in remorse and whispered, "I'm sorry, Will."

As if remembering he wasn't alone in the car, Will swung his head in my direction. "Don't worry about it. Like I said, I'm happy to do it." He smiled gently.

I grinned back even though I wasn't sure I believed him.

"You game to meet up with some of our old classmates while we're here?" he asked.

"Absolutely. James is around too." My spirits soared at the thought of seeing my best friend since the third grade. He lived in California now, so we only saw each other a couple times a year.

"You guys still close?"

I nodded. "He's my forever friend." Even at eight years old, James was comfortable enough in his skin to enjoy predominantly girly activities. While most boys in my class either ignored me or pulled tendrils of my unruly curls when the teacher wasn't looking, James and I spent every recess perfecting the Macarena, Humpty dance, jiggy, tootsie roll, rump shaker, and more.

"Nice. It would be great to see him."

I imagined James's reaction to seeing me with my new "boyfriend." After he verbally spanked me for not calling him the night Perry and I met up with Sidney and Will for the first time, he would die. I chuckled, wondering how long he would buy the charade. I estimated less than a minute.

"Want to let me in on the joke?" Will asked.

"We're here," I said, pulling up to my childhood home. Saved by the driveway. With shaky hands, I turned off the car and removed the keys from the ignition.

A couple minutes later, we were out of the cold and nice and warm inside my parents' heated house. My mom greeted Will with enthusiasm while I averted eye contact by hiding behind Will's and my jackets and racing to the hall closet.

When my mom asked, "How did the two of you hook up after all these years?" my heart beat frantically. I'd never pull this off. I color-coordinated all the coats to keep myself occupied until Will excused himself to use the bathroom. The last thing he said before we got out of the car was, "I really need to use the bathroom." I knew it was coming. Any second now.

"We'll tell you everything you want to know, Mrs. Lane, but do you mind if I use the bathroom first? Your daughter refused to stop for a pee break."

"Hey," I called out, my head still inside the closet. "We both agreed we could hold it."

"Go on. It's—"

"No worries, Mrs. Lane. I know where it is," Will said. "My house growing up was exactly the same, remember?"

My mom laughed. "Oh, yeah."

As soon as I heard Will's footsteps get farther away, I took a deep breath and turned to face my mom. I could feel her blue eyes boring a hole in my back.

The instant we made eye contact, she threw her arms around me and whispered, "Will Brady?" into my ear as I inhaled the familiar floral scent of her dark chocolate-brown hair, regularly highlighted to cover the gray.

I whispered back, "Surprise." Then I pulled away and gave her a sheepish grin. Usually, the scent of garlic from my mom's roasted chicken made my mouth water, but the guilt-and-anxiety cocktail I was drinking rid me of an appetite.

Her mouth was slack. "How did *that* happen?"

Before I could respond, my father entered the hallway. "My girl's home."

"Hi, Dad," I said, reaching out to embrace him.

"Guess who her date is?" My mom bounced on her toes like a teenager instead of a woman approaching fifty. She could probably recite verbatim every word I'd exchanged with Will in my life up until now because I ran home from school and told her—the words spilling out of me until my cheeks turned blue from forgetting to breathe. Knowing her glee was based on a lie stung my insides.

My dad scratched the small soul patch he'd sported my entire life. "It's not Perry?"

My mother interrupted, "No. It's Will—"

As Will joined us, I said, "You remember Will Brady, right, Dad?"

Rendered temporarily speechless, my dad's blue eyes opened wide before he recovered. "Of course I do. Blast from the past," he said, patting Will on the back. Even my dad knew if given a choice between one night of passion with Will Brady or Brad Pitt, I'd have picked Will, and he used to threaten to invite the entire Brady family over for dinner for a sing-a-long whenever I misbehaved or whined too much.

"And we're all hanging out in the hallway because?" Jordon asked, before biting into the Klondike Bar he was holding. Spotting Will, he did a double take. "Will Brady. What's up, man?"

"Hey, Jordy," Will said with a smile before shaking his free hand.

"Why are you eating ice cream, Jordy? Dinner's almost ready," my mom said.

Poor Will—trapped in a twenty-square-foot space with the crazy Lanes. What must he be thinking? I reluctantly glanced at him and opened my eyes wide in silent apology. Seemingly unfettered, he motioned to my parents. "Thanks so much for inviting me to your home. It's great to be back in the 'hood."

While they reminisced, I excused myself to the bathroom and prayed Will wouldn't refer to me as Sidney by accident while I was gone.

By the time I got out of the bathroom, my father, Jordy, and Will had relocated to the family room while my mother finished up making dinner in the kitchen. When she turned down my offer to help, claiming she was almost done, I poured myself a glass of red wine and sat down next to Will on the couch. "Everything good here?"

"Perfect." He took a sip of his own wine and clasped his free hand with mine as Jordy studied us with blatant curiosity from his favorite reclining chair. My dad danced over to my mom, who had joined us, and she placed her glass of wine on the coffee table before moving her hips in perfect rhythm with his. They were both completely unself-conscious about their audience as they danced together.

Will observed them with a small upturn of his lips. Then he leaned over and whispered in my ear, "What are we listening to?"

"'Spring Love.' Don't you just love Stevie B?" I asked with the best poker face I could adopt given the proximity of Will's mouth to my ear and his thumb absently stroking mine.

Will nodded. "My absolute favorite," he deadpanned, but I could tell he was trying not to laugh. Shaking his head in what I assumed was astonishment, he said, "Were your parents always so...?" He let his voice drop off, leaving me to guess the end of his statement.

I turned away from Will to watch my parents dance together under the gold contemporary-style ceiling lamps of their family room the same as they would beneath the laser lights at The Limelight circa 1985. "Always." My parents were nothing like the moms and dads of my friends growing up, but they were my family and their eccentricities were what made them unique. If it made Will uncomfortable, so be it—one of the reasons I gravitated toward creative types: they tended to be less judgmental of my parents' quirks.

Expecting him to roll his eyes, shake his head, or at the very least release a chuckle, I was completely taken aback when, not taking his stare off my parents, he uttered the words "They're awesome" instead.

Their "awesomeness" lasted about halfway through our first course when my mom looked pointedly across the kitchen table at me and Will before saying, "I think I speak for all of us when I ask how *this* happened." She wiggled her finger at Will and me.

Her question didn't take me by surprise since it had been asked whenever I brought a new guy home to meet my parents. This time was only different because I never had to lie before and because...well, because the "new" man in my life was Will freakin' Brady. "It's a funny story," I said just as Will responded, "Kind of a funny story." We glanced at each other and laughed until Will urged me to take the floor.

"I went to a party thrown by Anne Marie's boss a few weeks ago and Will was there. We got to catching up and hit it off." I smiled shyly at Will, unsuccessfully fighting the blush prickling beneath my skin. We had agreed on the ride up to keep the tale as simple as possible to avoid tripping ourselves up on small details. I wished I could blame my discomfort on my poor acting skills, but it was so much more. I had no doubt my mother was about to unearth something better left in my teenage diary.

Sidney

"Wow. How rich *are* your parents?" Perry asked in awe, his eyes wide, mouth slack as he took in my parents' estate from within the four doors of my Audi.

After parking my car on the spacious paved driveway, leaving enough room for other cars to get in and out, I unlocked the doors and stepped outside. Stretching my arms over my head, I replied, "Pretty effin' wealthy." Bellows and Burke was one of the most profitable law firms in the country and the only one of significant size to avoid layoffs after the market crash of 2008. That was before my time at the firm, but my father mentioned it often. The success of the firm coupled with the "old money" handed down on my mother's side meant finances were not one of my family's problems.

Perry exited the car after me, still transfixed by the house. "Wow," he repeated while running his fingers back and forth through his hair. "It looks like the mansion in *Dynasty*."

I jerked my head back. "How old are you, Perry?"

"Twenty-five. Why?" he asked, flipping his duffle bag over his shoulder.

"Because *Dynasty* was before your time."

"I watch a lot of old shows for inspiration. John Forsyth was the man."

I sighed and resisted the urge to roll my eyes. If Perry was dumbstruck by the front exterior of the house, wait until he saw the inside. And the pool and tennis court in the back. I'd called it my home from the age of thirteen until I moved out permanently after graduating law school, but seeing the imposing Venetian-style house through his eyes, I could understand his reaction. "Do you want to come inside or would you rather we set up a tent for you out here?" I asked, partially amused but mostly annoyed by his paralysis.

"Huh?" Perry said, finally tearing his eyes away from the house to look at me.

I pointed toward the front door. "Shall we?"

He shrugged. "I'm ready when you are."

I opened the front door and called out, "Anyone home?"

"I'm surprised we don't hear an echo," Perry said as he paced the stenciled hardwood floors of the entryway and glanced up at the sweeping staircase.

"It should be traditional but not boring, and please go easy on the wreaths," my mom said to a girl around my age who was furiously scribbling notes on a clipboard.

"Hi, Mom," I said, figuring she was too deep in decoration-mode to notice her only child standing there.

My mom finally looked our way. "Sid, dear. You're here."

"My mother is the queen of stating the obvious," I said to Perry before making more formal introductions.

"Why don't you take a walk-through and jot down some ideas?" my mom said to the girl. "We can discuss them after I get my daughter and her boyfriend settled in." After the girl scurried away, my mom smiled at Perry and me. "Let's go to the sitting room, have a drink, and get to know each other. You can leave your bags here for now."

When Perry whispered, "Sitting room?" I nudged him, hoping he'd get a grip.

As we followed my mom to the sitting room, she called out, "Harvey. Your daughter is here." When he didn't respond, she repeated, "Harvey. We're in the sitting room" in a commanding voice.

A few moments later, my dad joined us and bristled at my mother. "Have you forgotten I see our daughter every day at the office, Barbara?" Pecking my cheek, he said, "Good to see you again, Sid," before facing Perry. "And you are?"

Extending his hand, Perry said, "Perry Smith. Good to meet you."

Motioning to one of the two matching gray suede couches, my mom said, "Sit."

Perry and I sat side by side on one and my parents sat across from us on the other.

His computer on his lap, my dad said, "I've been going through the Swift contract. Did you notice the discrepancy in the indemnity clause?"

I glanced at my watch. "Under two minutes and he's off," I said, with a knowing look at Perry, who was too busy gawking at the partitioned wood ceiling to catch it.

"Forget work, Harvey. I want to know how these two met," my mom said, clapping her hands together.

My dad snorted and shut his laptop. "Fine. How'd you meet this one?" he asked gruffly before taking a slow sip of brandy.

I placed my gin and tonic on the dark wood coffee table. "He was my waiter at Carmines and slipped his phone number onto my bill." Raising my palms up, I said, "And here we are."

"Here we are," my dad repeated, looking as unimpressed as I'd hoped he would.

"It was a little more involved than that, Mr. and Mrs. Bellows." Taking my hand, Perry said, "Shall we tell them the whole story?"

I blinked. *The whole story?*

"Don't be embarrassed, Cherry Bomb."

Choking on her Pimm's, my mom parroted, "Cherry Bomb?"

"Whatever do you mean?" I asked with a laugh, followed by a warning look at Perry that screamed, "Drop it now." Perry might have fallen asleep before I could tell him how we supposedly met, but it was at Carmines—final answer.

Patting my thigh, Perry said, "Cherry here..." He laughed. "I call her Cherry Bomb because of her gorgeous red hair and her explosive personality." He turned to me and, ignoring my horrified expression, continued his ridiculous story. "Your daughter saw me act in the Off Broadway production of *Sheer Madness*. Impressed by my performance..." He chuckled. "...or maybe it was my biceps— my part was too small to really display my acting chops—she stayed after to get my autograph. When she asked where else she could find me, I told her I worked part time as a waiter at Carmines." Looking almost apologetic, he explained, "I'm the quintessential struggling artist, you see. I live in a rent-stabilized residence exclusively reserved for actors, but I need the extra income for the many other expenses involved in trying to get ahead."

Leaning forward in interest, my mom said, "For instance?" while even my father appeared mesmerized by Perry's narrative.

"I like to get new headshots twice a year, and trying to perfect my audition video for agents costs a pretty penny too. My manager is great, but an agent can take me to another level, you know?" My dad nodded. "Sure I do. We work with actors every day. Don't we, Sid?"

I opened and closed my mouth like a guppy. "Uh-huh," I said as my head spun. How was this happening? My dad was supposed to hear the word "waiter" and promptly leave the room.

"Anyway, I never expected to see Cherry here again." Perry grinned at me. "So imagine my surprise when she showed up a few nights later at Carmines. She pretended it was a coincidence, and I let her think I believed her." He kissed the top of my head.

My mom downed the rest of her cocktail. "Unheard of. Our Sidney going to such lengths to meet a fellow?" The liquor clearly going to her head, she whooped, "I'll be damned."

"I have that effect on women," Perry said, draping his arms around me. As I stiffened against him, he squeezed me tighter.

"I can't wait to hear more about you over dinner," my mom said before beaming at me. "I'm glad Sidney finally found someone worthy enough to bring home to her family. It's been too long."

"I might be able to help you with that agent search. And we do creative agreements if you need legal representation," my dad said.

Perry smiled wide before whispering, "This is going well," into my ear.

All I could do in the presence of my parents was nod agreeably, but as far as I was concerned, things could not have gone worse if choreographed by Satan himself.

Chapter 7

Robyn

"Remember when Jordon used to follow Will and the other older boys around the neighborhood? All the big boys with their multiple gear bikes and little Jordy on his one speed. Adorable." My mom reached over and ruffled my brother's thick head of wavy black hair.

Shifting away from her, Jordy said, "I recall no such thing."

Pleased to mock my baby brother, I teased, "Poor scrawny Jordy." He was three years younger than Will and had looked every one of those years when we were kids.

"Not so scrawny anymore," Jordy said, flexing his impressive muscles.

"Seriously, dude," Will said. "When did you get so big?"

"As a certified personal trainer, it's kind of my job." With a sheepish smile, he said, "Plus, I was sick of getting my ass kicked at bars."

My mom turned her bright eyes on me. With a hand on her heart, she said, "And you."

I knew it was coming and my heart stopped. "Please don't, Mom," I begged.

Dismissing my plea, she continued, "If someone told a teenage Robyn that one day Will Brady would be her boyfriend, she'd want to grow up immediately. Dreams really do come true." Dabbing her eyes with a napkin dramatically, she said, "I think I might cry."

I could hear Will's intake of breath and, feeling like I was pushed out of an airplane, I tightened my fist around my fork as if it were a parachute. Will was never supposed to know I had his senior picture in my hope chest along with Josh Duhamel's and Johnny Depp's. But as long as my mother exhibited enough diplomacy to describe my feelings for Will back then as your average teenage crush and not what it really was—a full-on obsession—I might survive it.

"I'll never forget the day Robyn ran into the house to announce a new family had moved a few doors down across the street. She must have only been about nine, because I still recall the way her pigtails bobbed up and down as she danced around the kitchen in glee because the boy in the family was so cute and looked to be around her age. I swear, from the day you moved in until the day you left for college, she talked about you nonstop." She beamed at me. "And now, all these years later, you guys are dating. Better late than never, right?"

My mother's shocking admission on my behalf resulted in a deafening silence, and my beating heart threatened to explode inside my chest. I struggled to find my voice until I felt Will's foot jab my leg under the table. I couldn't look at him.

"I honestly had no idea. It's too bad because I always thought she was cute too. Better late than never, indeed." His lips gently brushed against my cheek.

He was a typical attorney—quick on his feet—and it was sweet of him to play along, but I still couldn't face him. I stared down at my plate of cucumber and tomato salad, waiting for my body temperature to return to normal.

"Remember how jealous you were of his girlfriend? What was her name?" my mom asked.

"I don't recall," I mumbled. Of course I remembered Adrienne, the feisty redheaded cheerleader Will dated in high school for a couple of months. His taste hadn't changed much.

"Adrienne," Will said.

"Right, Adrienne!" my mom chirped.

I looked frantically around the room for an escape route. My spot at the table was the farthest from the front door, and I'd have to squeeze past Will to get to the back patio. Realizing I was trapped in this hell, I scrutinized the remaining piece of tomato in my salad. Such a vibrant shade of red. Almost too pretty to eat.

"I think you might have been the last guy Robyn crushed on before her silly infatuation with actors and musicians began, but if anyone could make her do away with her stubborn insistence on only dating people with SAG cards, it would be you," my mom said.

I looked up from my plate. "Not everyone I've dated had a SAG card, Mom. What about Terry?"

There was no recognition on my mom's face. "Which one was Terry?"

Answering for me, Jordy said, "The photographer."

"Speaking of Terry, what happened to *Perry*?" my dad asked.

Time stopped for a beat as my mind went blank. I was so worried about creating a believable "meet cute" for me and Will that I forgot to come up with an explanation for ending things with Perry. "It didn't work out," I said plainly, only afterward realizing I wouldn't be able to use the same excuse for Will.

"Good riddance," my mom said in unison with my dad.

Will's laugh quickly turned into a cough when I kicked him under the table.

"How do you really feel?" I mumbled under my breath. My pulse raced, but I squashed the temptation to defend Perry. On the bright side, my folks' harsh response served to minimize the guilt I felt over lying to them. Clearly, Perry was better off elsewhere. I wondered what they were doing right now and felt a pang of homesickness for my boyfriend. I hoped Sidney's family was more welcoming towards him. If all went according to Sidney's plan, her parents would barely acknowledge Perry's existence. She was so lucky.

Conversation blessedly shifted to another topic, and forty minutes later I had recovered, at least temporarily, from what would undoubtedly go down as one of the most embarrassing moments of my life. I just hoped Will wouldn't mention it again when we were alone.

After the table was cleared and the dishwasher was full, my mom leaned against the refrigerator and pointed at Will, who was still sitting at the table. "Did Robyn tell you about the Lane family tradition, Will?"

"She has not." He walked over to me and took my hand. "But clearly there are a lot of things your daughter hasn't told me about. Right, Robyn?" Ignoring my fingernails digging into his palm, he kept his eyes on my mom. "Tell me about this tradition."

"Do you sing?" my mom asked.

"If you can call it that," I mumbled.

Will drew me close to him and whispered, "Keep that up and I might cry."

Clearly thinking she had one over on me, my mom grinned. "A lawyer who sings. Imagine that. I told you so."

"Wait until you hear him, Mom." I smiled teasingly at Will and he winked at me. With any luck, my parents' discouragement of my dating choices would backfire after they did. They might even welcome Perry with wide open arms. Well, probably not Perry, but at least musical types in general.

Sidney

"What was *that*?" I hissed as Perry followed me to the guest room where he'd be sleeping. Thankfully, my parents were way too conservative to let my boyfriend sleep in the same room as me unless we were engaged. I'd shared a bed with far less attractive men than Perry—mostly during my wild and not very discerning stage after breaking things off with Jake—but I had no desire to spend more time in Perry's company unless I was boinking him. After being in his company for the last three hours, I reckoned he must be fabulous in bed for Robyn to put up with his enormous ego. Since I wasn't to know, I wanted him as far away from me as possible after lights out. And he snored. I could not tolerate a bed partner who snored, even one who managed to do it in perfect pitch.

"What was *what*?" Perry said, almost banging into me when I stopped at the room my mother reserved for him down the hall from mine.

I glared at him before turning on the light. After he joined me inside, I closed the door behind us. "That bizarre story you concocted. About me asking for your autograph." I folded my arms across my chest.

Perry took in the room he'd call home for the next few nights. "It will do," he said with a cheesy grin before sitting on the edge of the white four-poster full-sized bed and tapping his large feet against the black-stained hardwood floor.

I bent down and picked a piece of lint off the gray and white spotted area rug before leaning against the antique dresser. "I'm so glad you approve. Now answer my question."

"What about it? Your parents totally bought it."

I clenched my fists. "So not the point. I had a story. They asked how we met and I responded. It was asked, answered, and done. Why'd you mess with it?"

"Because your version was boring." He yawned as if emphasizing his point.

How he could still be tired after napping for half of the ride was beyond me. He'd never survive as a lawyer. "Not everything needs to be exciting." Certainly not the origin of our fake relationship, which was supposed to be of no interest to my father whatsoever. "It's too late now, but moving forward, follow my lead. Can you do that?"

"Follow my lead," he mimicked in an authoritative raspy female voice.

"You follow *my* lead. Not the other way around," I corrected. "And that sounds nothing like me."

"Whatever you say, Mrs. McAndrews," he said with a laugh before flopping onto his back. "If you're through with your lesson, I'm going to catch up on my beauty sleep. I worked until closing last night. Wake me up before dinner? Do I need to put on my Sunday best?"

Before I launched myself on the bed and strangled him to the edge of consciousness, I left him alone.

An hour later, the four of us were eating dinner at the stone table in my parents' kitchen. Since the first guests would arrive tomorrow afternoon for Christmas Eve, tonight would be the only informal dinner we shared as a family. I hoped my mom would be busy fussing over last-minute details for the following day and my dad too sidetracked with work to make it an extended affair. An "eat and run" scenario would be ideal.

"Where in the city is your rent-stabilized residence located?" my mom asked Perry. She took a bite of quinoa salad and wiped her mouth with a napkin.

Perry sipped his French Chardonnay. "Hell's Kitchen, ma'am. The backyard of Broadway."

"Drop the formalities and call me Barbara. We're practically family, after all," my mom said, causing me to choke on the corn tortilla in my mouth.

While I attempted to dislodge it from my throat, Perry patted my back. "You okay, Cherry Bomb?"

Once I got my bearings, I muttered, "It went down the wrong pipe."

"Good thing Perry was around to save you," my mom said.

"Sid would rather spend all day doing document review than meet a client near Times Square," my dad said with a chuckle.

"Perry doesn't know what document review is, Dad." I raised my hand to preempt his next words. "Please don't bore my boyfriend with an explanation."

My dad gave me a wounded look. To Perry he said, "I bet she refuses to go to your neck of the woods."

"We both prefer spending time at my place," I said.

"Sidney's practically moved into my studio." Perry spooned more salad onto his plate. "This is delicious, Barbara."

My mom's face brightened at Perry's compliment, while my

dad placed his fork on the edge of his plate. "That explains why you've been late to work so much lately."

My mouth opened and shut without a word. "I'm always on time in the morning, if not early," I argued. I was never late to work because I didn't want to give assholes like Michael Goldberg any ammunition to use against me.

Perry placed his hand on top of mine. "Sorry about that, Mr. Bellows. I try to get her out the door, but she clings to me like static every morning. She says she misses me too much when she's at the office."

I removed my hand from under his, desperate for a subject change. "Will Lauren be here tomorrow or Friday?" Lauren was one of my cousins, and I knew from Facebook she and her husband were arriving on Christmas morning, but it was the first thing out of my mouth.

Ignoring my question, my mom said, "Has Sidney seen you perform much?"

I said, "We haven't been dating long—"

Interrupting me, Perry said, "My luck finding professional gigs has been a little thin lately, but I've been standing in for the singer of a cover band every Tuesday night. Sidney comes to the bar every week. She says it's because she loves my voice, but I think she wants to make sure I behave myself." He winked at me.

My mom's mouth dropped open. "Sidney hasn't been the jealous type since Jake. This must be serious." The color drained from her face and she frowned at me. "I shouldn't have brought up the ex. I'm sorry."

"Your daughter and I have no secrets from each other. I know all about Jake," Perry said.

As my face burned the color of my hair, I kicked Perry under the table. Was this what he considered following my lead?

When my mom stood up and brought her dishes to the sink, I allowed myself a small breath. Dinner was almost over. Once my parents retired to their rooms, they'd leave us alone for the rest of the night. Perry could watch television in his room or listen to his music collection. I wanted to call Will and see how things were going with Robyn.

My mom turned away from the sink. "I have an idea. *It's a Wonderful Life* is on television tonight. How about the four of us watch it?"

"I'm sure Dad has work he needs to do tonight. Right?" I turned to my dad, certain he'd never choose an old movie over work.

He stroked his chin. "A two-hour break wouldn't kill me."

I gripped my wineglass like a vice. What was happening here? I brought home an artist whose resume wouldn't even qualify him as an actor on the D-list, and not only was my mom encouraging our relationship, but my dad was willing to lose billable time to watch a movie with him—a film all of us had probably seen at least ten times. "I think the movie is three hours long. Besides, Perry has that script he needs to rehearse for an audition. Don't you, hon?" I widened my eyes at Perry.

Perry nodded. "Cherry's right."

I smiled. *Thank God.*

"But it can wait until later."

I was going to kill him in his sleep.

Robyn

I couldn't look at my family while Will sang "Stayin' Alive." It was my father's turn to come up with the theme for the night, and he had chosen "songs from the decades—movie edition." I'd thought if they saw that a white-collar businessman at a Lane dinner was like a "one of these things is not like the others" quiz, they'd reconsider their nagging about my taste in men. But observing Will have the time of his life belting out lyrics into the microphone—hips thankfully in perfect time to the music because even Will Brady couldn't make bad dancing sexy—my heart hurt at what they must be thinking. He was so confident despite knowing he sucked, but what if one comment or cold shoulder from my folks destroyed his easy self-acceptance?

With one last note and a move from "The Hustle," Will concluded his performance and silence choked the family room. I brought my hands together and clapped quietly in a desire to move on with as little fanfare as possible and make a smooth transition to the next performance. My subtle appreciation was drowned out by my family's rambunctious applause, wolf whistles, and stomping feet. I glanced at my parents and brother in awe as they rose from their seats in a standing ovation.

Slapping Will congenially on the back, my dad said, "Without a doubt the most original performance this family room has ever witnessed." He clapped. "Nice job."

"Seriously, you've got moves to rival Travolta," my mom agreed.

"It's a good thing I've got rhythm since your daughter informed me I can't sing to save the human race." Will smiled playfully at me before kissing the top of my head in what I assumed was one of the "small acts of affection" we'd discussed on the drive here.

Jordy wrinkled his nose. "Even an immortal being wouldn't be safe from your voice, but I agree with my mom. At least you can dance."

"It's not about how good or bad you are. It's about having fun," my mom said before pointing at me. "Right?"

"Right," I said with a nod. I smiled up at Will.

"My turn." Jordy said. "Up for a duet, Will?"

While the two of them pondered their next song and my parents laughed over a private joke, I eased myself onto the couch. Will's performance didn't have the desired response of turning my parents against him, but as I took a long sip of wine, I realized I wasn't at all disappointed.

Many hours and countless songs later, I was exhausted and led an equally pooped Will back to my bedroom. "That went well," I said, turning on the light and placing my suitcase against the closet door.

Standing at the edge of my room, Will yawned. "What did you think would happen?"

"You're the first guy I ever brought home who couldn't..." My cheeks heated up.

He raised his eyebrows. "Sing?"

I nodded. "Even though my parents beg me to expand my dating horizons, I honestly wasn't sure how they'd react to you." I shook his comical performance of "Ghostbusters" out of my mind. "I was genuinely shocked they took it so well."

"I wasn't going to say anything, but when you went to the bathroom, they threatened to sell me into slavery for daring to be tone deaf." He rolled his eyes. "What did you expect? They're not the ones who care how well I can sing—you are."

With a teasing smile at him, I said, "I don't care either. I'm dating you, aren't I?"

Will's grin was replaced by a serious expression.

I whipped my head back at the sudden change. "What's the matter?"

He opened and closed his mouth without saying anything before blurting out, "What *is* the deal with all of the creative types?"

My eyes widened in surprise and I said, "What do you mean?" before removing the lavender shams from the pillows on my full-sized canopy bed to avoid eye contact. Of course, I knew exactly what he meant and only requested clarification to delay my requirement to respond.

Pointing at the bed, Will said, "May I?"

I slid over to give him room to sit next to me on the edge. "I used to have a rocking chair in here, but my parents must have relocated it to another room after I moved out." I hoped he'd ask more questions about the décor in my bedroom and drop the subject of my love life.

"Your parents seem to think you have a very particular type. And the corporate Wall Street guys and other white-collar types aren't it. Is that true?"

"Yes, it's true." I twisted a strand of hair around my finger.

"Why?"

"I don't know." I stood up, suddenly angry at the line of questioning. "Why do you like redheads? I can't help who I'm attracted to any more than you can."

Will snorted. He clearly wasn't buying it.

Exhaling loudly, I said, "Creative guys are more easygoing and fun. They don't have set hours for work locking them into a nine-to-five monotonous existence. I never want to be a boring married couple. I want to *do* stuff—not just come home, eat dinner, watch the boob tube, and go to sleep just to repeat it again the next day." I placed my hands on my hips. "You satisfied?"

This was my token answer, but there was more to it I'd never admit to Will. At high school dances, all the popular guys like Will avoided the dance floor as if they'd catch rabies, and I imagined them laughing at my inability to stop my hips from moving whenever and wherever a song with a decent beat came on the radio. Then I met a cute guy at a party in college who told me I moved like no one was watching and it was the sexiest thing he'd ever seen. He was a drama major and became my first boyfriend. After we broke up, I sat a few seats away from a guy at a performance of *Hairspray* who approached me at intermission to ask why I was crying. If I didn't shed tears after a musical, it meant it didn't move me at all. I was positive he was making fun of me, but he asked me on a date instead. He was a music major and became my second boyfriend. My third boyfriend was a guy who stopped me in the university library to tell me how much he appreciated my colorful wardrobe. He was an art major. Musicians, actors, and artists made me feel sexy and accepted for who I was like no "regular" guy ever had. And even though as a teacher, I lived on the outskirts of their life, I felt welcome in their world.

Will shook his head at me. "I'm not knocking entertainers, but why are you generalizing all guys with 'professional' jobs as rigid and unable to have fun?"

Shrugging, I said, "It's just been my experience" before sitting down again.

Will arched an eyebrow. "According to your parents, you don't *have* any experience with anyone except actors and artists and wouldn't know." He sighed. "I didn't mean to upset you. Forget I said anything." Bumping his shoulder against mine, he said, "I'm crazy tired. Where am I sleeping?"

I smiled timidly. "I guess now would be a good time to mention you'll be sleeping with me."

Will's eyes opened wide.

"My parents are very liberal—we're all adults, and it's not like they think I'm a virgin." I swallowed hard as warmth flooded my cheeks. It was like I wore a chastity belt from the way my body responded to the topic of sex in Will's company. "I hope it's all right."

"I'm not sure how Sidney would feel about it." He scratched his jaw. "Best not to say anything for now. I don't want to upset her over nothing."

Perry wouldn't delight in these sleeping arrangements either, but I didn't see a way out. "It would raise suspicion if I asked them to make up the bed in the guest room." I bit a decorative gold bead off my holiday-inspired painted nails.

"Yes, I can imagine your folks would be surprised if you didn't want to share a bed with your boyfriend, especially because of your epic crush on me in high school." Will raised and lowered his eyebrows suggestively.

Punching him in the arm, I said, "Stop it," before standing up and giving him my back.

"Don't be embarrassed, Robyn. I'm flattered," he said softly.

I bravely faced him with a disbelieving look. "You're telling me you didn't know?" Even though I'd only confessed my feelings for Will to my mom and James, I was paranoid I wore my crush like a permanent tattoo. Some girls knew how to play it cool. And then there was me...at least back then.

He shrugged. "I might have had an inkling from all of that." He pointed at my face. "All the blushing, but it's not as if you threw yourself at me or did anything remotely forward."

I wondered if he even remembered the night we kissed. For him, it was just another game of Spin the Bottle, but for me, it was a dream come true. It happened at a party my sophomore year when the upperclassmen upped the ante on the more middle-school appropriate game by implementing the rule that if the same two people got each other back to back, they had to kiss for real—with tongue. As an inexperienced fifteen-year-old, I was intimidated by the prospect of kissing an older boy or smooching anyone in the public eye. But Will was playing, and I'd have never forgiven myself if I sat out of an opportunity to kiss him. Eleven years later, and I could still summon how nervous I was. When Will spun the bottle ten minutes into the game, I gasped out loud when it stopped and pointed at me. It felt like an out-of-body experience as I met him in the middle of the circle, and I couldn't even look at him in the moment before he delivered a chaste kiss to my lips. My stomach quaking with nerves, I slid back to my spot and took my turn. I held my breath as the bottle spun until it stopped in front of Will again. He smirked as if predicting the probability of kissing a high school sophomore would be less than mind-blowing to an experienced junior like him. I had only made out with two other people in my life, but my hunger to feel Will's mouth on my mine for real instead of in my dreams took over and I was determined to prove him wrong.

For me, the kiss was magical. It was like our lips were created to be conjoined, and when Will brought his hands up to stroke my cheeks mid-smooch, I thought I'd died and gone to heaven. I'd promptly removed myself from the game—I wanted the last lips on mine of the night to be Will's—and excused myself to the bathroom to splash cold water on my face. Will never mentioned it, and I'd heartbreakingly assumed it had no effect on him whatsoever.

He probably forgot all about it. "If you knew how I felt, would it have made a difference?" I asked, immediately regretting my boldness. I wasn't Rachel Berry, Will wasn't Finn Hudson, and this wasn't *Glee*. In real life, guys like Will dated girls like Quinn Fabray and Adrienne, not me.

His silence confirmed this, and I frowned before I could stop myself.

"I don't know, Robyn. You were pretty and all, but I never gave dating you much thought. You were Snow White. I was seventeen. I wanted to date someone who would..."

I answered for him. "Put out?"

He smiled at me guiltily and shrugged. "I was a teenage boy."

Shaking my head at him, I said, "You said yourself my nickname had nothing to do with my purity. I might have been a naughty schoolgirl, but I guess you'll never know."

As his eyes scanned the length of my body, I held my breath until he met my eyes. "My loss, I'm sure."

A little while later, we lay side by side in my bed on our backs. We were both wearing shorts and t-shirts, although I tried not to notice that my shorts were "shorts" shorts and Will's were of the "boxer" variety. When my mother said the teenage version of me would want to grow up immediately if she knew the twenty-something model would share a bed with Will, she wasn't exaggerating. Only if I told sixteen-year-old Robyn it would all be a farce to trick my parents into believing we were a couple, she wouldn't believe me and might actually cry herself to sleep. It was almost comical and before I could stop myself, I giggled.

"What's so funny, Snow White?"

I turned onto my side with my back facing Will. "Nothing." I stifled another laugh.

"You do that a lot, you know."

"Do what?"

"Humor yourself."

"I'm very funny."

He said, "I agree," and I could almost hear him smile.

I grinned into my pillow. "Thanks for being so great today. I was worried, but you're good at this." I swallowed hard. "Pretending to like me, I mean."

"It's not hard." Silence filled the room for a moment until he clarified, "Pretending to like you, I mean."

Even with my back to Will and the lights off, I blushed. "Goodnight, Will."

"Night, Snow."

We didn't speak after that and for the next few minutes, I was fully aware of the sound of my breathing and worried it was keeping Will awake. This had the unfortunate result of my breathing harder and silently willing myself to fall asleep. Even without looking at Will, I knew when he was no longer awake from the rhythm of his breaths and finally felt my body relax as well. Just as I was about to drift off, I sat up abruptly. I hadn't texted Perry all night. I knew he wanted to remain in character as much as possible, but I missed him. Hoping it wasn't too late, I removed my phone from the dresser and sent him a text asking how things were going. While I waited for his return text, I checked my email. There was one from Lance. I gasped when I read the subject line: Budget cuts?

Hey Robyn,

I hate to be a buzzkill, and I planned to wait until January to bring this up, but I'm freaking out and you're the only one who would understand. I was in the teachers' lounge yesterday and overheard Mrs. Johnson and Mr. Philips whispering about budget cuts in elective studies like music. Have you heard anything about this? From one music teacher to another, can we talk?

Lance

So much for sparing him from the stress I was under. I bit back a sob as a wave of exhaustion washed over me. The day felt way longer than twenty-four hours. Unprepared to respond, I closed out the email and placed my phone next to me on the bed. I tried not to give too much credence to the rumor when I'd only heard it from Lynn, but the band teacher telling me he overheard two other members of the school staff discussing budget cuts was more difficult to dismiss. I glanced over at Will, who was sleeping soundly, and debated waking him up to vent. But what good would it do? Despite his physical proximity, he wasn't my boyfriend. It would be a stretch to even call him a "friend." My phone beeped a return text from Perry as if confirming my decision not to wake Will.

"The Bellows are like the Quartermaines from General Hospital. *Sidney's dad actually drinks brandy in the afternoon. Too bad none of the soap operas are filmed in New York anymore because I'd be perfect as the prodigal daughter's boyfriend from the other side of the tracks. Don't you think?"*

I laughed quietly and typed my response. *"A few of the shows were set in the Philadelphia suburbs. And I agree you'd be great."* Right as I pressed "send" I received another new one from him.

"How are you?"

I frowned and wrote him back. *"Tired, but having a good time. The parental figures are not at all suspicious about Will."* It would have made sense to tell Perry about Lance's email, but considering how little comfort he'd provided when I first broached the topic of budget cuts, I didn't bother.

"I hope he's keeping his hands to himself."

I looked over at Will, who appeared to be in a deep sleep and free of all the worries that clogged my brain space, both personal and professional. I wrote back, *"No worries. He's on his best behavior. I hope Sidney is being a good hostess and things are going according to plan."*

Perry responded in less than a minute. *"It is! Sidney's parents love me. I miss you, but things are going so well."*

My heart felt lighter knowing at least Perry was having a good time. Maybe Sidney's plan would work after all. I wrote back that I missed him too and fell back against my pillow. This time, sleep came quickly.

Chapter 8

Sidney

When my alarm went off at seven thirty the next morning, I immediately bolted out of bed and changed into my workout clothes to run around the property. It was Christmas Eve and I wanted to burn some calories to make room for the next two nights of gluttony. After slipping a pair of suede earmuffs on my head, attaching my iPod to an armband, and confirming the laces of my Brooks sneakers were double knotted, I let myself out of the house without checking to see if anyone else was even awake. I wanted to finish my run before Perry woke up so I could keep him out of trouble, but I had a feeling he'd sleep until noon.

While I ran my four-mile path, I passed gated fences which led to neighboring estates like my parents', as well as still-undeveloped land on the market for potential buyers or real estate investors. My feet pounded against the well-paved streets, and I could see my breath in front of me thanks to the arctic temperature outside. Preferring a treadmill at the gym to running outside, I fought my desire to turn around after only two miles. I was glad I didn't quit when, just as I reached the bottom of the driveway at the end of my run, I came up with the perfect plan to avoid extended time with my parents over the course of the afternoon. I would tell them I had last-minute shopping to do at the mall and drag Perry with me. The way he'd behaved the night before was unacceptable. It was as if he was infected with a disease that caused him to take everything I said and respond with the complete opposite. He was like a wild animal, and if I couldn't control him, I needed to put him on a leash.

I'd ditch him as soon as we arrived at the mall so we could do our own thing. There *were* a few belated items I needed to pick up and I also wanted to check my work email without my dad hovering over me. Perry could organize a flash mob in the food court for all I cared, as long as he stayed out of my way and had some distance from my parents. We'd conveniently get home from the mall with just enough time to clean up for dinner. The Bellows' Christmas Eve celebration was a more intimate version of Christmas—only one third of the guests, most blood relatives of either my mother or father.

Breathing heavily as I entered my house, it took me a few moments to notice the uncharacteristic morning chatter coming from the kitchen. After stretching my calves and hamstrings in the foyer, I followed the noise and stopped short at the sight before me—my parents and Perry were sitting around the kitchen table, drinking coffee and gabbing like old friends. My parents were dressed in casual day-wear, but Perry was wearing a pair of plaid pajama bottoms and a t-shirt, and he had a significant case of bedhead that, annoyingly, he wore well. He was waving around his coffee mug, clearly in the midst of an anecdote, and had my parents' rapt attention.

I stood at the edge of the room dumbfounded, one foot on the slate floor of the kitchen and the other still planted on the glass mosaic tile of the hallway, until Perry noticed me and smiled big.

"There's my honey bunny. How was your run, Cherry?" He stood up and pulled me in for a kiss which, thankfully, was closed mouth, or else I might have been tempted to bite his tongue.

Ruffling his hair for show before slowly removing myself from his embrace, I shivered. "It was cold. But now I feel better about eating whatever I want for the next two nights." Darting my eyes between my parents, I said, "You guys are up and about early."

"I have so much to do today. First, I need to go over the menu for tomorrow with the caterers and confirm they have enough vegetarian options, and then I need to double check the seating chart," my mom said.

My dad nodded. "Yes. Those two items will certainly take you all day," he said with a chuckle before continuing to type on his laptop. As my mom went to swat his hand, he grabbed it and kissed her palm. All was forgiven.

"Sidney mentioned I'm on a gluten-free diet, right?" Perry asked.

As my mouth dropped open, my mom glared at me. "She most certainly did not."

Turning away from my mother, I smiled gently at Perry, hoping he'd see the daggers shooting out of my eyes. The idiot had neglected to tell me about his dietary restrictions, but I couldn't very well admit as much to my mother since it would raise a serious red flag and suggest we'd never shared a meal together. "You sure I didn't tell you, Mom? Isn't that why you made vegetarian corn tortillas and quinoa salad last night for dinner?" Senility was an unlikely culprit, since my mother was only fifty-six, but she might blame a lapse in memory on party-planning stress and let me off the hook.

My mother sighed. "The menu last night was mere coincidence, Sidney. We have gluten-free options for tomorrow night, but now I have to speak to the caterer about tonight." She shook her head in annoyance.

"I'm sorry to add extra work for you," Perry said, frowning in my mother's direction and widening his eyes to pools of blue.

"No worries, dear," she said with a sweet smile before turning to me and adding, "Not *your* fault."

Raising my hands in defeat, I said, "I'm sorry. Dad has me slaving away at the office. How am I supposed to remember everything?"

Looking up from his computer, my dad said, "Leave me out of this. And don't blame it on work either. I haven't seen you with your computer all weekend."

I rolled my eyes. "We only arrived yesterday and you all

wanted to watch *It's a Wonderful Life* last night." With a loud exhalation, I said, "Dinner's not for another ten hours. Plenty of time. Want me to pick up some gluten-free dishes at Trader Joe's? I need to run some errands anyway." I glanced at Perry. "How do you feel about going to the mall with me?"

"I'm here for you, Sidney. Whatever it takes," he said.

"Great." As the words slipped off my tongue, I realized Perry had answered my question using an Indian English accent. "Are you rehearsing for something?" Was Perry's manager so useless that he encouraged him to waste his time auditioning for roles he'd never pull off, no matter how convincing his accent was? Perry—blond, blue-eyed Perry—would never pass for Indian unless he was playing the adopted son of Indian parents or the show was being performed exclusively to a blind audience.

"No. Perry's been giving us examples of all of the voices he learned in acting school." My mom clapped her hands together and said, "Brilliant" before pursing her lips at me. "And the answer is no, Sidney. You cannot pick up dishes at Trader Joe's. I'm not serving prepared meals on Christmas Eve. The caterer will have plenty of time to arrange a few extra dishes for Perry."

"Don't go to any trouble for me, Barbara," Perry said in an apologetic tone—no accent this time.

Waving him away, my mom said, "It's no trouble. Can you do a Scottish accent? Do Sean Connery." She looked at me with wide eyes. "Has he done his accents for you? He's wonderful."

"My favorite was the old Jewish man ordering a bagel with schmear. Priceless," my dad said laughing. "They taught you well at the Portland Actors Conservatory."

I furrowed my brow in confusion. When had my father had an opportunity to discover where Perry went to school? Even *I*, his fake girlfriend, didn't think to ask. The only reason I even knew where Will went to school was because the first thing fellow lawyers asked each other, after where they practiced, was where they got their Juris Doctorate. While I continued to contemplate how many rounds of twenty questions my parents had time to ask Perry during my forty-minute run, Perry answered, "Thank you. I like to think I'm a triple threat since I can sing, act, and dance. I've been compared to Matthew Morrison." He beamed proudly.

"You're better looking than him. You know who Perry looks like, Sidney?" Before I could respond, my mom said, "Zac Efron. Now *he's* a hottie." Then she blushed, something I hadn't seen her do since...*ever*.

"You're so sweet, Barbara," Perry said, lightly tapping my mother's hand. "I just need a guardian angel to toss some fairy dust over my head and give me some of his luck."

My dad shook his head sympathetically. "You need a good agent is what you need. Let me ask around the office." His eyes lit up. "Actually, there are several people coming tomorrow you should meet." Turning to my mom, he said, "Doesn't Marshall work for Take 3 Talent now?"

A finger to her chin in contemplation, my mom said, "I think so—"

When Perry opened his mouth to respond, I realized this conversation could go on for hours if I didn't do something. Batting my lashes at him while simultaneously running my fingers along his defined bicep, I said, "Maybe we should take our showers so we have enough time at the mall. It's going to be packed with eleventh-hour shoppers."

Perry said, "Sure" and rose from the table.

"Perry probably needs less time to get ready than you. Why don't you go on and we'll keep him occupied?" my dad said to me while motioning for Perry to sit back down.

"Great idea, Harvey," Perry said, returning to his seat. "Give me a shout when you're about thirty minutes out and I'll come up. I want to hear more about this Marshall dude first. You really think he'd talk to me?" he asked my father.

With a boisterous laugh, my dad said, "It's my party. He has no choice."

"This is great." Standing up again, Perry pulled me into a hug so tight, I could smell the fresh, sweet scent of his laundry detergent. It smelled like Robyn, and I wondered if she did his wash with a bird resting on her shoulder. Separating from me, he said, "I'm having the best time. I'm so glad you asked me."

Planting a fake smile on my face, I said, "Me too," wishing it were the truth.

Robyn

I woke up the next morning in a panic. I'd had a dream in which the new principal of my school was the Evil Queen from Snow White and she canceled the music program. I'd never dreamed about fairy-tale characters before and blamed Will for reviving the Snow White nickname. I gasped in remembrance. *Will.* I'd been sleeping on my side facing the window, but unless I'd also dreamed the last few weeks, he was right next to me. I sat up and braced myself for a visual I never dared to imagine I'd see in real life—Will Brady sharing my bed. I slowly turned my head and there he was, sleeping soundly with no evidence of bad dreams like the one I'd been having. For the benefit of my younger self, I took a minute to observe him. He was a nose breather, unlike Perry, whose faint snores from sleeping with his mouth open often woke me up. Will's lips were textbook perfect—arched Cupid's bow on the top and full lower lip. I'd dreamed about kissing the beauty mark above his top lip way before Jake Gyllenhaal made it sexy. I continued to study him for a moment before shaking myself out of it. Watching someone sleep was creepy even when you were dating him. Doing it to a random guy, even if the guy was Will Brady, sunk to a whole new level of disturbing.

I groaned to myself before stepping off the bed as stealthily as I could. I grabbed fresh underwear, a pair of magenta corduroy pants, and a lavender t-shirt and took a shower. When I returned to my bedroom, I was relieved to find the room empty since I wasn't prepared to see Will in his languid waking-up state. I noted with a blush that if he woke up like Perry, he'd be relieved to find the room to himself. But I couldn't remember Perry ever making my bed like Will had. Before heading downstairs, I emailed Lance back to tell him I'd heard the rumors too but was trying not to panic. I also suggested we get together after the holiday and brainstorm solutions. I knew there were foundations in place to assist struggling music programs. Maybe they'd help us.

A few minutes later, I joined Will in the kitchen. "Good morning."

"Back at you," he said with a sheepish smile. "Hope it's okay I made my own breakfast. I was starving and no one was around." He pointed to the bowl of Cheerios in front of him at the kitchen table.

I waved him off. "Of course, it's fine." With my back to him as I removed a gallon of orange juice and a container of yogurt from the refrigerator, I asked, "You sleep all right?"

"Great. You have a comfy bed," Will said with a yawn, and I looked over in time to see him stretch his arms over his head. He gestured toward his computer. "I don't expect any work emergencies, but I need to at least stay on top of the emails."

I sat across from him at the table and sipped my juice. "One perk to being a music teacher is the lack of homework over the major holidays. With the winter concert out of the way and several months until the spring concert, my break is a holiday in its truest sense." Of course, if the rumors Lynn and Lance heard were true, I might find myself on a permanent holiday soon. I swallowed down the ache in the back of my throat with a spoonful of yogurt.

"Lucky you," he said with sincerity. "I think we're the first ones up." Even though Will hadn't showered yet, he'd thrown on a pair of black sweatpants and a hoodie. He probably assumed my parents would be weirded out if he came down in boxer shorts. If he were more familiar with my parents, he'd know they wouldn't even notice. I, on the other hand, would, and I was hoping for a blush-free day.

The scent of coffee was decidedly absent, which meant no one had been downstairs yet. "Jordy can sleep all day. My parents are more unpredictable, but they seem to be asleep as well." I swallowed a spoonful of yogurt and glanced up at Will, who was studying me curiously. "Is something wrong?"

He shook his head. "Is your hair wet?"

As I ran a hand through my long hair, droplets of water fell to the surface of the kitchen table. "Yes. It takes a while to dry because it's so thick."

Will's eyes opened wide. "You don't use a blow dryer?"

"Nope."

His mouth formed an O. "Wow."

I snickered. "What's so fascinating about letting my hair dry naturally?"

"I don't think I've ever dated anyone who wasn't high maintenance about her hair. Sidney even has that iron thingie."

"A flatiron?"

He shrugged. "I guess."

I patted down my hair self-consciously. "Sidney has great hair."

"So do you."

Caught off guard, I choked on a response but was saved when his phone blessedly pinged a text message.

"Speak of the devil." As he typed a response, I read the coupons on the back of the cereal box until he looked up. "Sidney says 'hi.'"

"Tell her I said 'hi' back." I watched Will tap on his phone, completely engaged in his conversation with his girlfriend. I wondered how much Sidney missed him when they were apart. Then I pondered whether Will was homesick for her. Was he silently counting down the hours until he saw her again? I missed Perry, but I wasn't exactly pining over him. I thought back to leering at an unaware Will while he was sleeping and felt sick to my stomach. What kind of horrible girlfriend was I? "Don't think you need to hang out with me all day if you have people to see." Distance from Will would do me good.

Will pushed his phone to the side and cocked his head at me. "Are you trying to get rid of me?"

I smiled timidly. "Not at all," I lied before scooping up the last of my yogurt and walking my dishes to the sink.

He laughed. "Good. What's the plan for tonight?"

I sat back down. "We always celebrate Hanukkah on Christmas Eve. Just a traditional dinner. It's really informal. I hope it's okay."

"Of course. But I've been texting some of the guys from high school and a bunch of them are planning to go to Billy Murphy's tonight. You game for meeting them after dinner?"

"Sure. I should text James." I needed to catch him up on the boyfriend swap and beg him not to cause a scene when he saw Will and me together. I jumped out of my chair. "Be right back."

I raced up the stairs and after closing my bedroom door behind me, I scrolled for James's name on my phone. He answered on the first ring. "Thank God. I was going crazy with Robyn withdrawal."

"You could have called me first," I said with a chuckle as I realized how much I truly missed my oldest and dearest friend.

"Yeah, sorry. Yesterday was hectic, but I was about to call you. I swear."

Twirling a tendril of still-damp hair around my finger, I said, "You free tonight? A bunch of people from high school are going to Billy Murphy's."

"Like who?"

I cleared my throat. "I have to tell you something and you might die."

"Please don't joke about my mortality, Robyn."

"I'm serious. You might want to sit down for this."

"I'd rather do the Whip and Nae Nae with my favorite dance partner."

I squeaked out a laugh as my heart exploded in my chest. "James."

"Relax. My butt is officially in a chair. Spill."

"Guess who's in my kitchen right now?"

"Lisa Lisa? Brenda K. Starr?" James loved to tease that my

parents' list of Facebook friends would be really impressive if it were 1985.

"Will Brady," I whispered.

"I didn't hear you. Will to Power?"

Raising my voice one level, I said, "Will Brady."

"Will Brady? Did you say Will Brady is in your kitchen?"

I nodded until I realized he couldn't see me through the phone. "Yes. And he slept in my bed last night."

"YOU SLEPT WITH WILL BRADY LAST NIGHT?"

As James's scream pierced my eardrums, I held the phone away from my ear. "Only in the literal sense. We slept together, but we didn't *sleep* together. Keep your voice down. I don't want him to hear you." I opened my door a crack and peered down the hallway. There was no sign of Will, so I closed the door again.

"Why is this news to me, Robyn Taylor Lane?"

Wincing at the use of my full name—inspired by another eighties music icon, Taylor Dayne—I said, "I'll tell you everything. Try not to interrupt me until I'm finished."

James miraculously remained silent as I relayed the whole story. I left out the part where I ogled Will while he slept.

When I was finished, James said, "You're right, I'm this close to a heart attack." He whistled through his teeth. "Wow."

"I know, right?" It was freeing somehow to finally confide in someone who would truly understand the enormity of the situation. James used to hate playing "If you could have sex with anyone in the world, who would it be?" with me, because while he switched things up through the years—sometimes it was Orlando Bloom, for a while it was the substitute gym teacher, and then his crush on John Stamos was legendary—my answer was always Will Brady. He'd never admit it because I called dibs, but I knew James also crushed on Will for a while too.

"Are you still in love with him?"

"Of course not. And I wasn't 'in love' with him. It was an innocent crush. I moved on years ago, and I'm taken. But guess what? Perry might land an agent out of all this." My lips curled up at the thought. Noting James's silence, I said, "You there?"

"Shh. I'm enjoying a moment of silence for Perry. You have great taste in men, Robyn."

I chuckled. "Tell that to my parents."

"I'm sure your mom agrees Perry's one gorgeous piece of man beef. She just wishes he came dressed in a Brooks Brothers suit instead of black t-shirts and jeans that fall dangerously low on his hips."

"I'm going to have to tell them the truth at some point."

"Not if you fall back in love with Will."

"It wasn't love, James. And Will already has a girlfriend anyway." Whether it was "serious" yet was irrelevant.

"Psst. Sidney's got nothing on you."

"You've never seen her. She looks like Adrienne."

"No way."

"They both have red hair." Aside from the hair, they actually looked nothing alike, but I'd bet Adrienne used a blow dryer and flatiron too.

"You can have red hair if you want."

"Not happening."

"Good. You're gorgeous, sweetie. If Will Brady doesn't want to park his car in Robyn Lane, he should have his license revoked."

"Thanks. But it doesn't matter anyway. We're just pretending." At the sound of knocking on my door, I said, "Come in" and smiled at Will. Pointing to my phone, I mouthed, "James." Into the phone, I said, "Billy Murphy's later then?"

"Is he there?" James whispered.

"Yes."

"One more question and I'll let you go."

Pacing the room, I said, "Shoot."

"Does he sleep in the buff?"

I gulped, remembering my genuine struggle to keep my eyes from wandering in the direction of Will's boxer shorts the night before. Facing the wall, I said, "Probably between eight and nine. I'll text you." I ended the call and when I turned back around, I almost banged right into Will. He was holding a change of clothes and a toiletry bag. "Is now a good time to shower?"

An image of Will with water dripping down his naked body flashed before my eyes, and I bit back shame. "Sure. Let me get you some towels."

Chapter 9

Sidney

"Here," Perry said, placing a large coffee cup next to me.

"What's this for?" With one last sip, I finished off the Americano I'd bought for myself. Then I moved the fresh cup closer to me before continuing to type out an email to my paralegal. I didn't expect her to read it on Christmas Eve, but at least it would be off my plate.

I heard Perry say, "You guys using this?" and a moment later, a chair squeaked as he sat down across from me at the small table in the Starbucks I'd been hiding in for the last thirty minutes. "Peace offering."

"Are we at war?" I pressed "send" on the email and looked up at Perry. I was hoping the time-out from my fake boyfriend would last longer than a half hour.

He shrugged. "You tell me. You didn't speak to me at all on the ride here, and then you ran off on your own the second you got out of the car. I circled the mall three times before finding you here."

"I was taught if I didn't have something nice to say, not to say anything."

He tousled my hair. "Sweet Cherry Bomb. What could I possibly have done to annoy you now?"

Wiggling away from him, I hissed, "Why don't you ask me in an Irish brogue? Rumor has it you're great at accents." I went back to reading my emails with half concentration.

"Are you always this uptight, Sidney Bean?"

I clenched my jaw. "Stop it with the nicknames, Perry. I'm not in the mood."

He snorted. "Are you ever? For Will's sake, I sure hope so. Unless he's into the frigid type," he muttered.

Slamming my laptop shut, I said, "I'll have you know I rock Will's world. Frigidity is *not* a problem."

Perry smirked. "I see I've hit a nerve."

Suddenly too exhausted to argue, I rested my head in my hands and mumbled, "This whole boyfriend swap is not going as I planned."

"And clearly you blame me. Why?"

I raised my head as my annoyance got a second wind. "Why do you think?"

"I haven't a clue." Appearing bored, he glanced around the cafe.

I followed his eyes, noting how many of the female patrons were gawking at him. "Is it necessary to suck all the energy out of every room you're in?"

He whipped his head back toward me. "What are you talking about?"

"All of your stupid stories. First last night and now this morning. My mom is acting like a schoolgirl in puppy love and my dad has made you his pet project. The whole idea of the swap was to avoid my parents taking any interest in you whatsoever."

Perry scratched at his thick hair. "I thought you didn't want to bring Will because you were afraid your dad would either insult or recruit him. Aside from name dropping all of his famous clients over the years, your dad's so fascinated by me, he's barely mentioned work." He paused. "You're welcome."

Perry was correct. As far as he was concerned, the plan was working. I pressed my fingers to my temple. I had no desire to make Perry my confidante, but maybe if he understood, he'd stop being such an infuriating pain in the ass. If Snow White liked him, he must be a decent guy. "I wasn't completely honest with you guys about my motivations for the swap."

Leaning forward with interest, Perry said, "Secrets. I like 'em."

I rolled my eyes but went on to explain why it was so important to me to keep my parents out of my personal business. "Every moment of my working life is documented within one sixth of the hour, and all my father needs to do is review my billable hours to be privy to every move I make during the day. I like being a lawyer, and having my last name in gilded lettering on the frosted entryway to the firm adds to my ambition and desire to be brilliant at it. *Working* with my dad I can live with. But if I give my parents any leeway into my personal life, it's over. They'll suffocate me. That's the real reason I didn't want to bring Will home with me. He's the only thing I have that's all mine and if they meet him, it will all be ruined." I choked back a tear. "Do you understand?"

Perry's eyebrows squished together. "Not even a little bit. Will isn't here. I am. Mission accomplished. You can keep Will as your dirty little secret."

Shaking my head, I argued, "My dad doesn't know it's not real and wasted no time putting his mark on *my* territory. He was supposed to be bored by you, not impressed." I smirked. "And don't even pretend you're not loving every second of it."

Perry snickered. "In what universe would an actor turn down a generous offer for an introduction to an agent?"

"You don't get it. My parents love you, which means they'll wonder why I never mention you again after this weekend. They'll ask how things are progressing between us, and do you want to join us on a family holiday to the Berkshires? And when I tell them we've broken up, they won't let it go. It took them years to recover from losing Jake. You're the first boyfriend I've brought home since him. I thought they'd ignore you."

"Impossible," Perry said, looking smug, but then his facial expression softened. "I get it, and I'm sorry, but it's too little too late. What do you expect me to do now?"

I frowned. "Stop being so..."

Perry licked his lower lip. "Irresistible? Charming?"

"Maddening is more like it." I sighed with exaggeration. "Can you just not be so friendly with my parents? They're not your future in-laws."

"I wasn't expecting to be added to the will." He rubbed his hands together. "Although, the things I could do with some of the Bellows money..."

I glared at him.

He chuckled. "Sorry, Cherry, but I'm not going to hide in a corner all weekend to avoid your family liking me, especially if it means missing out on a career opportunity. Maybe you should have been honest from the start about the role you wanted me to play, but the truth is, I never would have agreed to come along if I knew you expected me to shy away from the spotlight. It's not who I am."

"Not the spotlight. Just my parents." I held my breath.

He stood up. "Text me when you're ready to go." Then he turned his back, completely oblivious to the fact that every woman in the room, including me, was watching him as he walked out of the coffee shop.

Except I was pretty sure the rest of them were staring at his ass while I was already planning my next move. I'd tried to reason with him—I'd practically begged—and he refused to play nice. As far as I was concerned, Perry had declared war.

Robyn

"Thanks for coming with me," I said to Will over the loud din of the Gallery at Market East. "One of my New Year's resolutions each year is to buy all my Christmas and Hanukkah presents before Thanksgiving, or at least before Christmas Eve, and yet, here I am."

"You're in good company," Will said, lifting his chin toward the crowd of people we were following like sheep. "The trick to making New Year's resolutions is to choose ones that can be implemented immediately. You're setting yourself up for failure if you set goals almost a year ahead of time."

"An expert at New Year's resolutions, are you?" I teased,

bumping my arm against Will's playfully.

As we shuffled along as quickly as possible given the traffic, Will said, "Yes, Grimm's fairytales and New Year's resolutions are my areas of expertise."

"Just Snow White though, right?"

He turned to me and grinned. "The only one that counts. Where to first?"

"The place I'm most likely to find something for everyone. I bought the big stuff online, but I completely forgot about the stocking stuffers."

"I know just the place, but if we want to make it home for Hanukkah dinner, we need to make our New York City aggression work for us." Grabbing my hand, he said, "Follow me." Not releasing his strong grip, he weaved us through the crowd past Foot Locker, Old Navy, and Burlington Coat Factory, until we arrived at our destination—Big Kmart.

A few minutes later, I held up a treble clef picture frame. "James would love this."

Will nodded his approval. "You can put a picture of you guys from high school inside," he suggested.

"Great idea. I already know which picture I'll use."

"Which one?"

"One year, we dressed up as Cheri Oteri and Will Ferrell as the Spartan cheerleaders from the *Saturday Night Live* skit. I still have a picture of us in my bedroom here." My heart warmed at the memory. "It was outdated, but we liked to be retro." Many kids stopped dressing up for the holiday in high school aside from weekend Halloween parties, where the girls dressed as scantily as possible. The theater kids, like James and me, wore our costumes to school on Halloween every year until graduation and spent weeks brainstorming ideas. One year, we were Elton John and Kiki Dee and did a performance of "Don't Go Breaking My Heart" in the hallway. Another year, we were Judy Garland and Mickey Rooney.

"I remember that."

I cocked my head to the side. "The costume or our retro

tendencies?"

He laughed. "Both, actually."

"Did you think we were weird?"

Will's eyes opened wide. "No. I—"

When my phone rang, I grabbed my cell from my purse and said, "Sorry" to Will.

He shook his head and whispered, "No worries" before examining a baseball-shaped photo frame.

I didn't recognize the number. "Hello?"

From the other side of the phone, I heard, "Miss...Miss Lane?" followed by a sniffle.

"Yes, this is Robyn Lane. Who's this?" I asked gently, since whoever it was on the other end sounded like she was crying.

"It's me, Aimee. I'm sorry to bother you." She breathed heavily.

Frowning into the phone, I said, "It's no bother. What's wrong?" Although I wondered how she got my number, I was more concerned by the reason for her call.

"I went to the doctor yesterday. My mom said it wasn't nice to call you on your holiday, but I didn't listen. Don't hate me."

"I could never hate you." At that, Will turned around, his eyebrows drawn together. I shrugged helplessly and stepped to the side to avoid other shoppers overhearing the conversation. "What did the doctor say?" My stomach tightened in the realization it was probably bad news if Aimee was crying, but I held out hope she was overreacting as children tended to do.

"I have pulps on my vocal chords and need voice therapy." The sounds of sobbing reverberated through the phone. "I won't be able to sing in the spring concert."

I assumed she meant "polyps," which meant she was right about missing the concert. In a worst-case scenario, she might never be able to sing again. And I was the naïve music teacher who told her she probably just needed to rest her voice. I moved the phone away from my ear and muttered, "Crap," but as Aimee continued to cry, I knew I had to do something. "Listen to me,

Aimee," I said, as an idea brewed in my noggin.

"Yes?"

"I know how much you love to sing, and the very last thing you ever want is for someone to say you can't." *Way to state the obvious, Ms. Lane.*

"Uh-huh," Aimee said sadly.

I pictured Aimee on the other end of the phone, convinced her life was over, and willed myself not to give into her sadness. "I'll need details from your mom, but if you're in voice therapy, you're probably right about not singing in the spring concert this year."

"I know!" she wailed.

I silently prayed what I was about to say would provide a modicum of relief. "I love to sing too. And when I was your age, my favorite part of school was the concerts. Like you, I was chosen for a lot of solos. Now, as the teacher, I can't sing with you guys, and I miss it so much."

"I'm sorry, Ms. Lane."

I was touched by her sympathy for me during her own struggle and even more determined to provide her a diamond in the rough. "Not your fault, sweetie, but thanks. Anyway, I might not be able to sing, but I get to do the next best thing. You know what that is?"

"No," Aimee said, blowing her nose into the phone.

As enthusiastically as I could, I said, "I get to direct the show. Which means, I decide what songs to sing and who sings them. *And* I come up with dance routines and everything. It's really hard." It wasn't a lie. I did miss performing, but producing the concert was equally fun in a different way.

"You're good at it."

Her compliment tickled my heart, but it wasn't about me. "Thank you. It's not an easy task to do all by myself, and I could really use help. Do you think you'd want to be my assistant?" I crossed my fingers.

I heard her gasp. "For real?"

The knots in my belly unraveled marginally at the hint of cheer in her voice. "Yes. I can't swear you won't miss singing, but I do promise you'll have fun. Assuming your mom, dad, and Principal Hogan are on board, what do you say?" I'd known Aimee's parents for several years now and was positive they'd agree, and Principal Hogan always said yes as long as you showed him respect by asking first.

"Yes."

"Good. Now please try not to let this ruin your Christmas, okay? You have my word I will talk to your parents after the holiday and get this all sorted out."

"Thank you, Miss Lane. I'm glad I didn't listen to my mom."

"Me too," I said with a laugh. "Merry Christmas, Aimee."

"You too. Bye."

After we hung up, I let my head fall backward and breathed a sigh of relief.

"Nice job."

I faced Will and smiled timidly.

"I only heard your side of the conversation, but whatever you said to your student seemed to have worked," Will said, beaming at me.

I tossed the photo frame for James in my basket, and as we continued walking up and down the aisles, I summed up the phone call for Will. When we reached the café, we sat down at an empty table. I finished my story over the Snapple iced teas Will bought us.

He shook his head in awe. "Talking down a hysterical child— not a job for the weary. Did you always want to be a teacher?"

I shrugged. "You know what they say: 'Those who can, do; those who can't, teach.'"

Will's eyes darkened. "No offense, but I wanted to pummel your boyfriend when he said that."

Tapping my hand on Will's across the table, I said, "Perry was only teasing. You don't know him like I do."

"If you say so," Will said unconvincingly. "For what it's worth, I thought you had an incredible voice in high school. And based on last night's performance, you still do." The night before, I'd sung "Raindrops Keep Falling On My Head" from *Butch Cassidy and the*

Sundance Kid for the sixties, the theme from *Mahogany* by Diana Ross for the seventies, and "Fame" from *Fame* for the eighties.

"Thanks," I said, trying to ignore the flip of my belly. As a teenager, I used to daydream about Will watching me perform or even walking past the auditorium while I rehearsed and being so mesmerized by my singing voice that he fell in love with me on the spot.

"And for the record, I didn't think you were weird."

I squirmed, remembering asking him the question before Aimee called. "It's okay. I was."

Will shook his head. "You were quirky."

Cocking my head to the side, I said, "Isn't 'quirky' a nice way of saying 'weird'?"

"Not when I say it. You were adorable." Locking his eyes on mine, he said, "You still are, Snow," before looking away as if regretting his words.

My lips parted, but I was at a loss for a response. If it were ten years ago, I'd be crossing my fingers Will's next words would be "Will you be my girlfriend?" But he already had one of those, and I had someone too. And besides, calling me "adorable" didn't mean he was attracted to me. It could mean he wanted to adopt me like a rescue dog. Clearing my throat, I said, "What about you? Do you like being a lawyer?"

Will nodded. "So many aspects of law fit my personality. I've always been very analytical, I love solving puzzles, and writing is a strength too." He raised an eyebrow at me. "And despite popular opinion, not all attorneys are boring, rigid workaholics."

It was never my intention to insult Will, and as I sunk lower into my chair in shame, I stammered, "I didn't mean—"

Smiling wryly, Will raised a hand to stop me. "As you know, I also have a thick skin. Quite useful since everyone hates lawyers. And bad singers."

I giggled.

"But honestly, my firm strikes a good balance between work and home. I don't always leave the office at five, but it's not unheard of either. I make it to my seven o'clock cycling class every Wednesday night like clockwork. And I rarely work weekends or miss out on vacation time. I might not make as much money as I would at other firms, like Sidney's, but I wouldn't change it for anything. You're not the only one who likes to *do* things." He grinned again to show me he was playing.

I leaned forward, wanting to learn more about the real Will as opposed to the boy I'd placed on a pedestal all through my childhood. "For instance?"

"Besides the usual—spending time with friends, movies, sporting events, concerts—I went skydiving last year, hiked Mt. Kilimanjaro the year before, and went on safari in Africa the year before that. Here's one that might surprise you—I took an improv class two years ago."

My chin almost hit the floor. "No way."

He smirked. "Yes way. At the PIT Comedy School."

Logic suggested I shouldn't be stunned by Will's proclamation considering what a ham he was on the dance floor, but I was reeling anyway. "Any particular reason you took the course?"

Will shrugged. "I wanted to try something outside of the box. I was also considering a writing class at Gotham Writer's Workshop, but I was lost for what to write about. At least in improv, someone else assigns you the topic."

"True. Were you any good?" I guessed he was—as long as there was no singing involved.

"Let's say I'm better at improvisation than I am at singing and worse than I am at dancing. I'd rate myself a solid six. But it was fun, and now I'm a champ at getting uptight judges to crack a grin every once in a while."

"You're full of surprises, Will Brady."

"I aim to keep you on your toes, Snow White. And by the way, I think I was Austin Powers the year you were Cheri Oteri, so I can be retro too." In a British accent, he asked, "Do I make you horny?" while waggling his eyebrows.

"Yeah, baby, yeah," I replied with a chuckle. Afraid Will could read my mind and know I was only half-joking, I stood up and tossed his empty iced tea bottle in the trash can. Perry's face flashed before my eyes, and a wave of guilt washed over me.

When I sat back down, Will leaned his elbows on the table, his eyes sparkling with interest. "You never did tell me how you came to be a teacher. I would have guessed you'd have gone into show business like Perry."

"Honestly, it never even occurred to me to perform professionally. Maybe it was because my parents openly discouraged it, but I always did it for fun. I had the time of my life with James performing in high school." My heart soared in remembrance of the many late nights after school with the other theater kids singing and dancing over delivery pizza. "And I was in an a cappella group in college too. I think if singing was what paid my bills, it would lose something. But by teaching music and directing the entertainment for the school, I get to share my passion with a whole new generation." My stomach dropped as fear of the school shutting down the music program overcame me once again.

Wrinkling his brow, Will asked, "What's wrong?"

I told him about the rumors and sighed dejectedly. "For all I know, it's baseless prattle, but after getting Lance's email, I can't help being concerned."

Will wrinkled his nose. "How much do you think the music program costs?"

"According to my research, it's only about two hundred dollars per student annually, but I don't know how much of the total school's budget it accounts for. Did you know there's a direct correlation between exposure to music and language development in children under ten?"

Shaking his head, Will said, "I did not."

I nodded eagerly. "It's true. An article I read also claims music education decreases students' involvement in delinquent behavior and improves their self-image. Some students even score better on their SATs." I stopped talking as I caught Will's amused grin.

"Sorry. I got carried away."

"No apologies necessary. You're passionate about it."

"Anyway, I vowed not to worry about it until January." I glanced inside Will's basket. "What do you have in there?" I could tell it was a DVD but not what the title was.

Kicking the basket behind him and out of my sight, Will said, "Nosy much?"

I rolled my eyes. "I don't want to know anyway. Just making polite conversation." I pretended I didn't notice the upturn of Will's lips as he stared me down.

"I'll show you if you want."

"Never mind. I've lost interest." My lips twitched and I changed my answer. "Okay."

Will grinned wide. "You're so easy," he said before his cheeks turned pink. Then he reached down and placed the DVD on the table in front of us.

I narrowed my eyes. "The complete series of *How I Met Your Mother*. Why the secrecy?"

"No reason except I like teasing you."

"Nice." I smirked. "We should probably get back to shopping, huh?" I motioned toward my basket, empty aside from the picture frame for James.

Will nodded. "I'll pay for mine now since I actually need to check out a few more stores. How about we meet in front of Toys 'R' Us in..." He glanced at his watch. "Is an hour enough time?"

Since he hadn't mentioned needing to buy anything before, I had my suspicions he was itching for alone time—possibly to call Sidney—and I swallowed back my disappointment. Then again, I wanted to buy him a gift and didn't know how I'd manage to keep it a surprise if he was glued to my side. This break would give me the opportunity I needed. I'd call Perry too. I feared I was enjoying my time with Will entirely too much. I was counting on the sound of Perry's voice and a few sweet nothings exchanged between us to remind me of what was real and what was pretend. "Perfect. Just text me if you need more time."

Chapter 10

Sidney

By the time the sun set on Christmas Eve, the temperature had dropped into the twenties, but my mother was too proud of her outdoor living room to let frigid weather deter her from showing it off. Instead, heating lamps surrounded the closed-off area and papier-mache lighting fixtures hung from the wrought aluminum ceiling. Feeling victorious to the bone, I waved a lazy hand at Perry across the space and gave him a smug grin. I was certain no one else on the patio could read into my smile as anything more than a woman beaming happiness in her boyfriend's direction. But we both knew the truth—I had won the evening's battle. Actually, "won" lacked the oomph required to describe what I'd accomplished. I had killed it.

After Perry stormed out of Starbucks, I spent the next hour conducting research and devising a plan to obtain the upper hand for our client, an agent attempting to keep an A-list actor locked into a contract. The agreement was not set to expire for another two years, but the actor was trying to get out prematurely. After I shared my notes with my father, he was way too busy to focus on Perry. And my mom was so occupied with the caterers, she didn't have time to drool over him either.

From where he sat on a white wicker sofa, my dad said, "We are golden." He continued to flip through the black binder of articles I had pulled for him from various gossip magazines regarding the actor's extracurricular activities, which could potentially support a claim of breach of contract. He placed the binder on one of the many crafted wood coffee tables decorating the room. "Your research and strategic points are the perfect ammunition. You're a genius, JB."

I chose to ignore his use of the grating nickname. "That's why you pay me the big bucks," I said, while glancing over at Perry, who was holding court with my father's sister and sisters-in-law. For a moment, I wondered what Perry had said to make my aunts laugh so robustly, but I quickly lost interest. As long as they weren't laughing at my expense, who cared? I turned back to my dad, who was now typing furiously into his phone.

Sensing me watching him, he said, "I'm emailing opposing counsel now—the schmucky one."

I scrunched my face. "The schmucky one?" As far as I was concerned, they were all schmucks. Mid-yawn, I looked over at Perry again. The ladies were now following him into the house— probably back to the damn piano. Even though I'd been in and out of my father's home office most of the night aside from when we were eating dinner, Perry's singing had traveled throughout the house. I'd heard him belting out "Baby, It's Cold Outside" with my Great Aunt Ruth and "Do They Know It's Christmas" with my Aunt Eileen and Uncle Gil, who were probably regaling him with stories of attending the Live Aid concert in 1985. My extended family's endearment to him was annoying, but at least they wouldn't have as frequent access to me later to harp on our "split."

As my father continued to jabber on about how our adversaries wouldn't know what hit them, my phone rang—Will. "Hi," I said, trying to keep my voice neutral so my father wouldn't think I was flirting with another man while my boyfriend was organizing a sing-a-long with my kin less than a hundred feet away. "Hold on a second," I said into the phone. To my father, I said, "I'm going to take this call."

My dad whispered, "Is it work-related?"

"No." I snapped my mouth shut. "I mean, yes." Not knowing which answer was more likely to sidestep more questions from my father, I continued to stutter, "No, well, kind of."

"Which is it?" My dad blinked at me in confusion before waving his hand in dismissal. "Never mind. Tell whoever it is you'll call him back. Unless it's a client."

Turning my back on my father, I mumbled into the phone, "Can I call you back, Will?" Or maybe I'd initiate sexting instead. Our communication so far on this trip had been entirely too tame. After he said "Yes," I faced my father again.

"Who's Will?" he asked.

From behind me, Perry asked, "Yeah, who's Will?" before snaking an arm around my waist.

Even though my first instinct was to pull away, I knew leaning into his embrace made for a better show. In his current state, my father was blinded by work, but someone else might have been watching, and I didn't want to raise suspicion. "I thought you were keeping my aunts busy," I said with a high inflection to suggest I was happy to see him.

"I missed my girlfriend," Perry responded, a little grin starting to curl its way around his mouth. "I thought we could do a duet. Maybe 'Little Drummer Boy/Peace on Earth' as a tribute to the late David Bowie. I know your voice isn't great, but you can sing backup."

"Who said my voice wasn't great?" I asked.

Not looking up from his phone, my dad said, "I did."

Perry laughed. "Well?"

Only to prove them both wrong, I said, "Fine. Let's go." I was getting tired of working. It was a holiday, after all.

Before I could take a step, my dad put out his arm to trap me in place. "Can you do it later or tomorrow, Sidney? We should finish this."

"No rest for the weary, eh, Mr. Bellows? Why don't you take a break and join us?" Perry asked.

With barely a glance at Perry, my dad said, "I'm afraid not." Of course, the glee with which he expressed the words suggested he couldn't be happier.

Darting my eyes between an eager Perry and my singularly focused father, I unmasked the true reason Perry had joined us outside. It had nothing to do with a desire to sing with me and everything to do with winning back my dad's attention. "You heard the man. Work beckons. But you have fun without us," I said.

"If you say so." Perry shrugged and walked away.

I smiled at his back. Like I said, I killed it.

"Sidney," my dad barked. "Focus."

After all our local relatives went home and the visiting ones retired to their guest rooms, I was finally able to make my exit as well. At my mother's insistence, my parents and I were always the last ones standing at all events hosted in our residence. If it were up to my father, he'd force me to work through the night, but my mother insisted Santa Claus wouldn't come in if we were awake, and my dad humored her grudgingly. Anxious to confront Perry in private, I faked patience while he thanked Barbara again for the wonderful gluten-free dishes she'd added to the menu and kissed both of her cheeks goodnight. I didn't even complain when he grabbed ahold of my elbow and didn't let go until we reached his room.

Standing in the hallway with his body relaxed against his bedroom door, Perry batted his long eyelashes at me. "Thank you for a wonderful night, Cherry Bomb. I had a great time." He leaned in and closed his eyes.

I slapped his cheek with enough force to show I wasn't playing his game, but not hard enough to hurt or be construed as physical abuse toward a fake boyfriend. "Get over yourself."

Perry opened his eyes. "One of those chicks who doesn't kiss on a first date. I should have known." He frowned playfully.

I rolled my eyes and changed the subject. "Did you enjoy yourself tonight?"

Entering the room, Perry said, "I did. After a few martinis, your snobby relatives are a fun bunch. Did *you* have a nice time?" He sat on the edge of the bed and kicked off his shiny black leather shoes.

I followed him in and closed the door. "You put in a good effort, but you're up against a champion fighter. It's best you accept your loss and move on."

Perry scrunched his face in pretend confusion. "What did I lose?" Chuckling, he said, "Besides a few pounds. For a middle-aged broad, your Aunt Eileen can cut a rug."

Crossing my arms across my chest, I said, "You almost had me going there for a while with your lame attempt to get my father's attention."

"Is Will aware of how crazy you are?" He stood up and began unbuttoning his shirt as if I weren't standing there.

I averted my eyes, but not before I caught a glimpse of chest hair. For some reason, I'd imagined Perry with a smooth, hairless chest. Even though it was against my better judgement, Perry was one of those men all straight women pictured naked whether they wanted to or not. "Don't bring Will into this. You're just upset I'm winning."

"What are you talking about?" Perry asked with wide eyes.

"You refused to voluntarily cool it with my parents, so I took matters into my own hands and cornered my dad with work. If you noticed, neither of them doled out any attention your way all night." Of course he'd noticed.

Perry's eyes narrowed, followed by the upturn of his lips, and then his torso began to shake.

"What?" I said as my body temperature rose in confusion.

Ignoring me, Perry continued to chortle, until I pushed him. "What the hell is so funny?"

He stopped laughing and shook his head at me. "I had no idea we were in a battle, but I surrender. Happy now?"

I had gotten what I came for, but it didn't feel right. He was giving in too easily. "You have nothing else to say?" I asked skeptically.

"Actually, I do."

I smirked. "Go on."

Perry sighed. "While I was engaging in holiday cheer with your aunts, uncles, and cousins, you were working. On Christmas Eve. You looked pathetically sad and I felt sorry for you. So...being the nice guy I am, I took pity on you by playing my role as a flaky actor and trying to help you escape your dad's claws so you could enjoy the holiday instead of working. But it seems your definition of 'winning' is slaving away at work with your dad and 'losing' is having a good time. So you're right, you win."

I opened my mouth, certain a biting response would find its way off my tongue, but nothing came out.

Gesturing toward the door, Perry said, "You can let yourself out."

He turned his back on me, making it clear a response was unwelcome, and I was relieved because I had nothing to say.

Robyn

"I'm stuffed," Will said, patting his stomach. He sat on the edge of my bed and continued to rub his tummy in small circles. We'd finished Hanukkah dinner and excused ourselves from the table to get ready to meet our friends at the bar.

I stood in front of him and gave his leg a light tap. "You mostly ate stuffed vegetables. It's like Chinese food. You'll be hungry again in thirty minutes."

"Even if I can't eat again until New Year's Eve, it will be worth it." His eyes glowed. "Those sfinz things were like crack. I couldn't stop at just one." He shrugged sheepishly. "Seriously, I was expecting potato pancakes, which would have been fine, but what we just ate..." He pointed downward as if we could see the kitchen through my hardwood floor. "That was insane."

Will at the dinner table was like a little boy with a new train set. It was endearing. Watching him spoon more and more food onto his plate made me hungry, and I wound up eating way more than I usually did. Although when I thought about it, Perry fanboyed my mom's cooking too and it never rubbed off on me. I brushed the thought aside in favor of a mini history lesson. "What you just experienced was a Sephardic Hanukkah meal. Potato pancakes is an Ashkenazi tradition, but it's more well-known." I walked over to my vanity and fiddled with my large collection of bangles before slipping on my Pandora charm bracelet instead. I'd keep the jewelry simple tonight.

"Maybe I should know more about your background since we're supposed to be dating and all."

When I felt Will's breath against my neck, I whipped around in surprise. I hadn't heard the bed move when he got up.

He smiled apologetically. "Didn't mean to scare you."

"You didn't," I stuttered. I tucked a hair behind my ear and took a timid step back. When the knob from my dresser pressed against my back, I jumped again.

Will chuckled and put a hand on my shoulder. "Easy, partner."

Even though I hadn't technically done anything wrong, I felt deserving of a scarlet letter for the schoolgirlish way I was acting. Poor Perry deserved better. I walked back to my bed to put some distance between Will and me. "What were you saying about my background?"

"Only that I should probably know more about you if my friends are supposed to believe you're my girlfriend. Until this weekend, I didn't even know you were half Jewish."

"We really don't need to lie to your friends. It's not like they hang out with my parents after work." Putting on a charade in front of more people seemed like more work than was necessary.

"It's a small town. You never know when they might run into each other. And besides, I haven't practiced my improv skills in a while." He grinned. "It will be fun, Snow."

I shook my head at him. "If you say so." I wasn't sure I'd describe pretending to be a couple as fun but let it go. "I wouldn't worry too much about not knowing my life story. Even real couples don't know everything about each other immediately," I said. I jumped again when I heard a knock on my open bedroom door.

Jordy leaned against the wall, his broad frame blocking the "Without music, life would be a mistake" poster I'd hung a decade ago. "What do you mean 'real couples'? Are you guys not a 'real' couple? What am I missing?" He glanced from Will to me with furrowed brows.

My shoulders tightened and a bead of sweat formed on my upper lip. How long had my brother been standing there? For a moment, I debated confessing everything to him. It might be nice to relieve myself of the guilt. But it wasn't fair to burden another person with my secret. He was waiting for an answer, his arms crossed as he continued to gaze at us with focus. I opened my mouth even though I had no idea what I was going to say.

Will approached where Jordy was standing. "You're not missing anything. I haven't had a chance to tell my high school friends I'm dating Robyn. And your sister here..." He looked at me with bright eyes. "She's worried they won't believe us since we didn't hang out much in school. I told her it doesn't matter what they believe since it's the truth." He tapped me on the nose playfully before facing Jordy again.

Jordy nodded in understanding. "I bet my sister still can't believe it herself. Considering..." He winked at me.

I glared at him. I had no interest in rehashing the details of my high school crush. It was painful enough the night before. I was also more comfortable giving my brother the look of death than making eye contact with Will. Once again, he'd saved the day as if it was in his job description.

Will glanced at his watch and back up at me. "We should get out of here soon. Almost ready?"

Still speechless, I answered with a nod of my head.

"Have fun," Jordy said.

"Thanks," Will and I said in unison.

Jordy stepped out of the room, and I closed the door behind him. Will and I looked at each other with wide eyes. I was still shaking with residual fear of getting caught, but when Will burst out laughing, I joined him. When I collected myself, I said, "That was too close for comfort."

"You were right," he said.

"About what?"

He grinned. "I'm hungry again."

I took calming breaths through my nose as we walked from the crowded parking lot toward the entrance of Billy Murphy's, a neighborhood bar in East Falls, about ten minutes from Bala Cynwyd. We'd barely escaped my house without exposing our cover, and now we had to convince Will's friends from high school he was actually dating Snow White. When we reached the front door, Will took my hand. "You ready for this?"

In my mind, the music from 2 Unlimited's nineties "jock anthem" cued, and I responded in kind, singing, "*Dun dun dun dun dun dun dun dun dun dun dun dun dun,*" accompanying it with a raising-the-roof dance move. When Will broke out into a huge grin, I smiled back. "Let's do this."

The moment we entered the dark bar, the scent of buffalo wings wafting through the air, someone shouted, "Robyn!" and I was assaulted by strong male arms. James lifted me up in the air and swung me around before placing me back on the floor. He grabbed both of my hands with his and took me in from the tips of my taupe ballet flats up the length of my royal blue stretch jeans to my yellow top and finally to my face. "Stunning." Then he smiled into my eyes before pulling me into a hug and squeezing tight. "Yay, Robyn's here." He released me and scrutinized Will. "No need to be jealous. I'm still gay." He laughed and slapped Will on the back.

Will grinned and shook his hand. "If you weren't, I'm pretty sure no one else would have a chance with her. Right, Snow?"

I shrugged. "Probably not." I beamed up at James's ever-gorgeous olive-skinned mug. His shaggy almost-black hair flopped charmingly across his forehead over soulful brown eyes. And his full lips broke into a radiant smile that, in addition to showcasing his straight upper teeth and adorably crooked bottom ones, held all the secrets of our childhood, tween, and teenage years. Even better, his head was affixed to a lean toned six-foot body. A romantic pairing for us was never in the cards, but lucky for me, James was as beautiful on the inside as on the outside, and his mere presence was enough to make my jitters all but disappear. I planned to stick close to his side.

"You two make a handsome couple," James said with a wink before glancing behind us into the bar. "Don't worry. Your secret is safe with me."

I had told Will I'd come clean to James because keeping secrets from him was impossible. At least I assumed it would be if I ever tried.

As I spotted some of Will's buddies from high school by a table perched against the seventies wood paneling wall, a surge of shame washed over me and I whispered, "It's not too late to change your mind, you know. You sure you want to do this?"

"One hundred percent." He grinned and motioned to his friends. "Shall we?"

"Let's." Then I shared a stolen moment with James, who smiled at me and squeezed my hand in silent encouragement.

An hour or so later, I was no longer nervous under the assumption the scariest moments of the night were behind me. After initial surprise at the news of our unexpected pairing, Will's friends quickly accepted it and moved on. While they reminisced their high school glory days as the cool popular boys—not purposely calling attention to themselves, but drawing observation anyway by virtue of their quiet confidence and ability to entertain each other—James and I reverted to our music-geek personas, taking turns at the jukebox and making an ad hoc dance floor.

Lost in the beat of "Can't Stop the Feeling," my eyes closed as the rhythm took over and stripped all the stress from my body more effectively than any massage or facial ever could. With each wiggle of my shoulders, hips, and butt to the music, my worries melted away. I didn't think about the possible eradication of the music program, Aimee's polyps, or the ramifications of pretending my high school dream guy was my real adult boyfriend. I simply danced. When the song ended and I opened my eyes, the first thing I noticed was Will watching me from across the room, and I froze in place, wondering what he was thinking. My fantasy superpower back in high school was the ability to read Will's mind, and apparently it was a magic I still craved ten years later.

As the first notes of "Moves Like Jagger" echoed from the jukebox, he gave me a slow smile, and no longer paralyzed, I moved to the beat and bravely motioned with a "come hither" gesture for him to join me. Since I fully expected him to wave me away, I was shocked when he accepted my invitation.

As we danced together, I teased, "I thought you'd be too cool to dance in an Irish pub."

Moving in closer and placing his hands on my hips, he whispered, "I think I proved myself to be less than cool last night, don't you?"

I shivered from his breath in my ear but skillfully parlayed the spasm into a dance move. "You're full of surprises."

"I hope that's a good thing."

"It is," I said as the music stopped and we locked eyes. Lost for breath, I counted the seconds until the next song came on. It was a slow one, and I took a step back from Will, anxious for him to look away so I could breathe again.

But Will had other ideas and pulled me toward him. "Might as well put on a good show."

I nodded before placing my hands on his shoulders. I had thought sleeping in the same bed as Will was difficult, but it was nothing compared to slow dancing with him. I noticed he'd used my vanilla-scented body wash—it smelled better on him. My head was close to his heart, which I could feel beating underneath his shirt, and I grasped for something to break the silence. Lifting my head away from his chest, I glanced up at him and questioned, "What happens when they turn seventy-one?"

Will cocked his head to the side and his lips parted slightly. "What?"

I gulped. "He says in the song he'll love her until they're seventy. Then what? They could have a few good decades left." It was an honest question and one I'd asked myself each time I heard the song, but from the stunned expression on Will's face, I suspected his earlier definition of quirky where I was concerned had just expanded to include full-fledged "weird."

But then the tips of his mouth turned all the way up until his smile practically swallowed his face. "Could you be any cuter?"

I sucked in my breath. By my calculations, Will had now called me "cute" or some thesaurus equivalent of the word at least three times. But what did it mean to him? Knowing it shouldn't matter and hating myself for caring too much, I forced myself to mention the unmentionable. As heat coursed through my veins, I said, "Sidney's cute too."

He laughed. "Nah. Sidney's not cute. She's sexy and sharp, but she's not cute."

The unintentional jab didn't surprise me as much as jolt me back to reality, and I begged the song to end already. Of course, Will Brady would date a sassy, sexy lawyer and not a cute Snow White schoolteacher. And who was I to complain anyway? My steady boyfriend was a gorgeous actor whose hotness factor left tongues wagging in his wake wherever he went. But still...it hurt.

"You're sexy too," Will said, his voice throaty.

My mouth dropped open and I looked up at Will, who regarded me with a sad smile. As the song blessedly ended, I dropped my arms to the sides.

Will cleared his throat. "I probably shouldn't have said that."

Red-faced, I pointed at the bar. "Drink?"

He nodded and as we approached the bartender, I intentionally avoided eye contact with James, who I could feel staring at me from somewhere to my right.

I accepted the bottle of Magic Hat Number 9 Will bought me, mostly as a prop to assuage the awkwardness I was feeling. I could take a sip when I was lost for something to say or when looking down the head of the bottle was easier than peering into Will's green-speckled eyes.

A voice from behind said, "Come outside with me," and before I could respond, James pulled me onto the bar's empty outdoor deck.

Hugging myself to keep warm, I questioned, "Since when do you smoke?" even though I knew the outdoor-only activity had nothing to do with why James had dragged me outside on a cold December night.

James draped his coat over my shoulders and smiled. "Frostbite is a small price to pay to find out what's really going on between my BFF and her new bae." He waggled his eyebrows.

Snickering, I said, "With your cool lingo, you'd fit in perfectly with my students. Will's not my real bae, remember?"

"You can fake being a couple, but you can't make chemistry where it doesn't exist."

Rolling my eyes, I said, "Your point?" When he glanced over his shoulder to make sure no one was in earshot of our conversation, I braced myself for his response. Apparently, I wasn't the only one who noticed something weird was happening between Will and me.

Facing straight ahead, he said, "There was some serious heat radiating off you guys when you were slow dancing."

I shrugged. "He thinks I'm 'cute.'"

"Cute is good, Rob."

"Yeah, well, *Sidney* is sexy." I groaned. Jealousy was not an attractive trait.

Bumping my shoulder, James said, "You're sexy too."

Biting my cheek, I mumbled, "That's what he said," before jerking my head back when James was suddenly standing in front of me, his forehead almost kissing mine. Startled, I asked, "What?"

He smiled into my eyes. "Will thinks you're sexy *and* cute. Will Thomas Brady *likes* you. And I think I saw an extra bulge in his jeans while you were dancing. How does it feel?"

A blush heated up my face as I instinctively imagined how Will's bulge would feel. Certain James could read my mind, I said,

"Stop it," and punched him in the arm. We broke out into a fit of laughter until I regained my bearings. This time it was me who skimmed the area to make sure no one was listening. "Will is with Sidney. He seems to really like her. And I'm dating Perry, remember?"

James sat down on one of the black metal chairs and stretched out his long legs. "You said it wasn't serious."

I stood before him, too antsy to sit down. "Which couple are we talking about?"

He crossed his arms over his chest. "Let's put aside Will and Sidney for now. Although if I were Sidney, I'd be a smidge worried about the way my boyfriend was looking at another girl." He made a *tsk-tsk* sound.

My stomach rolled uncomfortably.

"Let's talk about you and Perry. You've been with him almost a year. Shouldn't you be ready to take it up a notch by now?"

I grimaced. "You sound like Will."

James tapped a finger to his lips. "No comment." He studied my face. "I worry you're wasting your time with him. We're almost thirty."

"I never considered it wasting time if I was enjoying myself. Life is short. And I'm not going to dignify your last statement with a response." I shuddered for emphasis even though his words had hit home. Unlike many of my single girlfriends, I wasn't plagued by the "when" in terms of getting married and raising a family, but serious about Perry or not, I questioned whether I should be in a long-term relationship with one guy when I was clearly struggling with unresolved feelings for someone else.

"And then you die. Although I can list far worse ways of going than all tangled up in Perry."

James always had a way with words. "I think you missed your calling. You should have been a writer instead of a teacher." We were like twins from another mother. Both of us had music in our hearts but chose a career path in education. James taught English as a second language at the high school level. "Enough about me.

How are things going with Spencer?" Spencer was James's long-term partner.

"Spencer is splendid, thank you."

"Glad to hear it." Even though I desperately wanted to change the subject, I also genuinely cared about the status of James's first serious relationship. But I was also freezing. "Can we go back in now?" When he nodded, I handed him his jacket and led the way inside and over to where Will and his friends were standing at the bar.

With narrowed eyes, Will glanced from James to me as if he knew we'd spent the last five minutes dishing about him. "You guys need a drink?" he asked.

I shook my head while debating whether I should stand closer to Will like a "real" girlfriend would. I looked to him for guidance, and as if reading my mind, he reached out his hand and pulled me so I was leaning with my back against his chest with his hands resting on my shoulders. I took a sip of my now lukewarm beer and tried to ignore the curious glances Will's friend Leon, a tall guy with nearly platinum hair and pale blue eyes, was throwing in our direction. Back in high school, Leon had a reputation as a player, the label assigned when he dated a girl for several months and dumped her as soon as she'd slept with him—every virgin's nightmare. The statute of limitations had probably expired on that particular crime by now. Still, I'd always wondered what Will got out of their friendship.

Pointing at Will (and technically me since I was leaning against him), Leon asked, "Didn't you say your girlfriend was a redhead?"

I hoped it was Leon's intoxication, evidenced by his bloodshot eyes and pronounced Philly accent (his "didn't" sounded more like "ditint"), that made him think it was appropriate to ask about a former girlfriend in front of a new one—pretend or not. But I wouldn't bet on it.

"It didn't work out," Will said, stealing my line—the one I'd borrowed from Sidney.

Leon frowned. "Too bad. Wasn't she the one you said gave great—"

"We broke up," Will interrupted in a loud voice, but anyone over the age of thirteen could probably have completed Leon's sentence. My body tensed against Will's and he made a show of squeezing my shoulders. I couldn't tell if he was playing the role of the gallant boyfriend or if he sensed my actual discomfort. Either way, I was grateful my face was hidden from his sight since I was certain it looked like I'd dived headfirst into a bowl of tomato soup. If I'd wanted details on Sidney's oral skills, I would have asked him thirty minutes before when he'd announced how sexy she was.

Since I was his girlfriend in name only, I had no right to be so uncomfortable. Then again, since a bona fide new girlfriend might genuinely be upset under the circumstances, I could probably get away with expressing my discomfort by later claiming it was all part of the act. Only, I knew if Will really *was* my boyfriend, I wouldn't care what someone said about one of his exes because I'd be secure in what we had. The only reason I was upset now was because I was insecure and I wasn't his girlfriend; Sidney was.

Pulling myself out of my head, I gave James a "whatcha gonna do" look and a half shrug.

James scrunched up his lips and gazed straight ahead to where historical photographs decorated the wall. "Robyn, what did you used to call your ex, Perry?" He scratched his cheek, appearing to contemplate, and then his face lit up. "The Phoenix. Right? Because he could go on and on and—"

"James." My mouth dropped open, but quickly snapped shut when I felt the involuntary tickle of a laugh in my throat. I inched away from Will, who had let go of me like I was a hot potato.

"What?" James asked, playing dumb.

He was so wrong, yet I wasn't sure I'd ever loved him more. "Can we change the subject?"

James shrugged. "I was merely pointing out that Will wasn't the only one with a ..." He cleared his throat. "...skilled ex."

"Thank you for sharing another one of Perry's winning

attributes with us," Will muttered.

I felt Will's stare and reluctantly met his gaze. I couldn't gauge his expression—sadness, resignation, disgust? Was he concerned Perry was practicing his superior stamina on Sidney?

"It makes complete sense to me," said Oliver, interrupting my thoughts. He was another regular fixture by Will's side during high school. But it was a friendship I understood, especially after getting to know Will better over the last couple of days. Oliver was as good-natured as Leon was crude. And even though he was also in the drama club, he managed to avoid the "theater-kid geek" stereotype.

Will and I broke eye contact and faced Oliver. At the same time, we said, "Huh?"

Oliver smiled. "You two as a couple. I can see it. I was there the night you guys kissed for the first time. At least I assume it was the first time." He raised a dark eyebrow.

I gasped out loud and quickly clapped my hand against my mouth. I wasn't prepared for someone to mention *The Kiss* on the assumption that no one remembered it besides me. My hands shook and I placed my near-empty bottle on the bar as a safety precaution. I couldn't look at Will.

"You remember *their* kiss from ten years ago? Kind of creepy," Leon said, pointing the bottom of his empty Yuengling bottle at Oliver with a smirk.

Oliver ran a hand through his light brown hair. When he smiled, a dimple greeted us from each cheek. "I thought Snow White was hot. I was hoping I'd be the one to kiss you," he said to me.

My mouth dropped open. Oliver always waved hello when he passed me in the hallways and even stopped by my locker from time to time. And he invited me to his parties, but I never interpreted his attentiveness as romantic interest. He was cute too, with light brown eyes the same color as his hair and, of course, those dimples. "How come you never asked me out?" I asked quietly.

He shrugged. "I could tell you weren't into me."

I didn't bother to refute the statement since he was right. How could I appreciate Oliver's appeal when I was too busy pining over his out-of-my-league best friend?

"Dude. Stop hitting on your buddy's girl," said Leon, rolling his eyes at Oliver.

"I'm not hitting on her." Oliver glanced at Will. "I'm not."

"I need some fresh air," Will said. Without another word, he removed his beer from the bar and walked to the porch.

"Way to go, asshole. Now he's pissed." Leon motioned to the bartender for another round while Oliver and I exchanged confused glances.

"If he's upset, it's not about my 'true confession.' Not Will's style," said Oliver before taking a sip of his beer.

James tossed me my coat before motioning toward the porch. He whispered, "Go."

I walked outside and closed the door behind me, hoping when I opened my mouth, a coherent sentence would magically fall from my lips. But before I could say anything, Will said, "Snow." I wondered how he knew it was me since he was sitting down and facing the other direction.

Reading my mind, he said, "It's your perfume. It smells like a sugary lemon. It's nice." He turned around to face me. "Sit."

I grimaced as my butt hit the cold surface of the chair. I didn't know what to say.

Will frowned. "I'm sorry about what Leon said. Please don't think I go around objectifying my girlfriends. He left out the context of the conversation."

I snickered. "Yes. Only the most high-brow philosophical discussions would result in your touting your girlfriend's *talents*," I teased before darting my eyes toward the wood floor of the porch. "It doesn't matter what I think."

"It matters to me." He took a sip of his beer. "I'm also sorry I reacted so badly to James's comment about Perry."

"Is it because you're worried about Sidney spending the holiday weekend with 'The Phoenix?'" He'd already proclaimed his trust in Sidney on the drive from the city, but it was the most logical explanation for why he was so upset. I couldn't allow myself to think there might be another reason he hated Perry so much.

Will scraped his fingers through his hair and studied my face in silence before standing up. "Mind if we get out of here soon?" Without awaiting my response, he opened the door and motioned for me to go in before him.

I instinctively opened my mouth to respond before his words registered. I stammered. "Um, sure. Let me say goodbye to James first?" The sentence came out like a question even though there was no way I'd leave without telling James.

Focusing on something behind me, Will said, "Whatever you need," and backed up an inch.

I took a step forward and touched my hand to his shoulder. "Is something wrong?"

Flinching, he said, "I'm just beat, Robyn," before scanning the restaurant again. "I'll be with the guys. Come get me when you're ready, cool?"

I nodded, and as I stared as his retreating back, it dawned on me this was the first time since we'd arrived in Philly that he'd called me Robyn instead of Snow.

"You look like you're about to cry," James said, breaking me out of my trance.

I took a deep breath to calm my nerves. "Something's not right with Will." I told James what transpired. I kept my voice down and barely moved my lips. In case Will was looking, I wanted him to think we were saying our goodbyes.

James pursed his lips. "The guy is so jealous, the green in his eyes is blinding."

"Of Perry being with Sidney, right?" It was the obvious explanation. Sidney was sexy, and I'd observed the way Will's eyes glowed when he talked about her. But I hadn't imagined some of the tender glances he'd thrown my way. Had I? I held my breath, hoping, wishing...for what? I didn't even know what I wanted.

"Something like that." He smirked. "More like, *nothing* like that. He's jealous of Perry because Perry is your boyfriend, obvi."

"I don't know, James." I scratched my head as my stomach churned in a cocktail of conflicting emotions.

James drew me into a hug and rested his head on mine. "You're the Andie to his Blane."

I laughed as I pulled away. "I love you, James."

"Back at you, *Snow*. Talk to him and call me immediately afterward."

I gulped. "I will."

Chapter 11

Sidney

Shutting the door of my room behind me, I squeezed my eyes shut, hoping to erase Perry's smug expression from my mind's eye and the image of him laughing in my face. Why on Earth Robyn dated him voluntarily was a mystery. I'd been his fake girlfriend for less than forty-eight hours, and I couldn't stand the sight of him. December twenty-sixth couldn't come soon enough—he'd be out of my life for good. I'd deal with the aftermath of my fake breakup when the time came. For now, I'd focus on the big picture. Perry's repugnant disposition was an unforeseen bump in the road, but the boyfriend swap was working in the one way that mattered. My parents were none the wiser regarding Will and therefore not a threat to our relationship. The coils in my belly settled down at the thought.

I hoped Will was getting along with Robyn's family and wondered if the Lanes were anything like the Bellows. I doubted it. I wouldn't be surprised to learn that instead of providing a fancy catered dinner, the Lanes dragged Will to a shelter to feed the homeless. Amused at the thought, I glanced at the clock on my nightstand. It was late, but not obscenely so. I called Will back, but it went into voicemail after four rings. After leaving a brief message, I hung up and got ready for bed. I wasn't sure if my heavy eyelids and aching limbs were a result of spending the day working with my father or plotting against Perry, but either way, I was knackered.

After turning the light off in my room, I curled under the covers and closed my eyes underneath my Morgan Lane silk charmeuse "To The Moon and Back" sleep mask. I inhaled the lavender-scented fragrance of my freshly washed pillowcase and breathed in and out slowly through my nose, assuming sleep would come quickly, but it didn't. I wasn't a stranger to insomnia and had a full-range of exercises to get me through the sleepless nights. I didn't count sheep, but I did add up other things—victories at work, guys I'd kissed, etc. When those failed, I would visualize myself at the gym and tally the number of bicep curls or push-ups I did in my mind. But even as my body cried for shuteye, my mind wouldn't shut down. Hating to waste waking hours lying in bed, I removed my eye mask, turned on my bedroom light, and started up my computer.

The search screen on Facebook was my first stop, and my fingers keyed the letters on autopilot as if it hadn't been years since I'd spelled out the name of my last serious boyfriend: Jake Harrington. Holding my breath, I clicked "enter" and waited for the results to come up. My Jake was the top result because of our mutual friends. I brought my head closer to the screen in anticipation but quickly pulled it back as his profile picture stared back at me. The photo was of a guy bouncing a little boy on each of his knees—identical twins. Thinking it might not be Jake, I scrutinized the photo more carefully. Wavy sandy-brown hair that curled around his ears reminiscent of a Hollywood teen idol from the 1970s—check; greenish gray eyes with premature lines around the edges—check; golden complexion as if he belonged on a beach— check. It was definitely Jake. But who were the little boys? An only child with no nieces and nephews, I had no idea how to gauge the age of anyone under ten, but they appeared to be somewhere between one and two years old. I supposed it was possible Jake could have gotten hitched and sown his seed in the last three or so years, but my best friend Lisa would never have kept something like that from me. She was friends with Jake in high school and connected us by email the first week of college and we'd hit it off.

They'd stayed in touch after we broke up. If Jake had gotten himself a ball and chain, wouldn't Lisa have let me know? Then again, as far as Lisa was concerned, and everyone else for that matter, I'd broken up with him and never looked back. Maybe Lisa didn't keep me posted on Jake's life because she didn't think I'd care, and she knew I'd tell her so.

I tried to picture Jake as a father. Once, before we broke up, I'd told him I'd be up all night finishing a paper. This was when I was a law student at Colombia and he was still at Cornell getting his Masters. Jake drove from Ithaca to the city—a five-hour drive—with a Turkey Hill B.L.T. on ciabatta with melted cheese from Collegetown Bagels and corn nuggets from Glenwood Pines in a cooler. These were our go-to study foods as undergraduates and the gesture was sweet on so many levels. Only I'd been too focused on making law review to appreciate it, and after a snack and a short break for sexy time, I pushed Jake to go home so I could finish my assignment. I wasn't a heartless wench during the entirety of our five-year relationship, but I'd reached that threshold eventually. If Jake's performance as a boyfriend was any indication, he'd make a great dad, and, although it pained me to think about it even after all these years, a loving husband too.

Suddenly craving the sound of Lisa's voice and nostalgic for someone who knew me before there was a JD at the end of my name, I sent her a text: *"You up?"* Then I tried to justify how texting someone well after midnight was acceptable. As a pastry chef for a Michelin-starred restaurant in Chicago, Lisa was accustomed to late hours. And, if not, hopefully she'd put her phone on silent so I wouldn't wake her.

Before I could add to my list of defenses, my phone sounded to the ringtone of Destiny's Child's "Independent Woman" and Lisa's name flashed across my screen. Either she'd been awake or I was about to be on the receiving end of a tongue-lashing from my very tired and angry best friend. "Merry Christmas," I said gleefully into the phone.

"There are only three reasons you'd text me this late. Someone died, you're working late, or you're drunk. You wouldn't be so giddy if someone kicked the bucket, so I'm guessing it's one of the others." She didn't sound pissed—thank goodness.

"That would depend on whose leg did the kicking," I said dryly.

Lisa chuckled. "Ah, yes. I forgot who I was talking to. So which is it?"

"None of the above, actually. I can't sleep and thought you might be up. And you are."

Lisa yawned. "Just barely. I spent hours preparing pies and was about to settle in for a few hours before I have to wake up and put them in the oven. I want to get to my dad's early enough tomorrow to witness my nephews' faces when they see the Christmas tree."

"How is Frank these days?" Frank was Lisa's father, and after a brief stint as a deadbeat dad after her parents' divorce, he'd rediscovered his paternal instincts with the help of his second wife. Lisa and her younger sister eventually forgave him for those lost years and now alternated spending the major holidays with him and their mother, who was also remarried.

"Typical Frank. Trying to fix me up with his newest protégé."

"Is this one promising at least?" Mr. Salinger was old-fashioned and wanted both of his daughters married by thirty. He didn't seem to connect the fact that his own first marriage, at the age of twenty-three, had ended in divorce. The owner of a meat-distribution company, Frank liked to keep his matchmaking attempts close to home and pushed Lisa into many dates with his employees. None of them had led to a second date, probably because the so-far incompatible men likely only agreed to the first date to avoid termination.

Sounding weary, Lisa said, "I'll find out tomorrow. Frank invited this one, a new vendor specializing in halal goat, beef, and chicken, to dinner."

"Good luck with that," I snorted, picturing a guy wearing a bloodstained butcher's coat sitting at the head of her dining room table with a freshly slaughtered cow in front of him.

"And what about you? How's Will? You're still seeing him, right?"

"Yes, we're still dating. But I brought someone else to the Bellows' Christmas spectacular this year."

Lisa gasped. "It's not like you to cheat, Sid. Why not let him loose if someone else is tickling your fancy? And, yes, I am using 'fancy' as a euphemism."

Laughing, I said. "I'm not screwing around on Will." Even if I was bored with Will, as maddeningly perfect as Perry was from a purely superficial standpoint, I'd rather practice my swiping skills on Tinder than fornicate with him. "I borrowed someone else's boyfriend for the week."

"Come again?"

I explained the boyfriend swap to her. "Spending time with this guy is the equivalent of listening to the theme song of *Orange is the New Black* on repeat."

"Yikes." Lisa hated the song too, so I knew she'd get it.

"I don't want to talk about him though. Other than him grating on my nerves, the swap is working, at least on my end." Since the idea had been my creation, I wanted her to know the plan was solid—as solid as Perry's pecs.

"What *do* you want to talk about?"

Jake. "Nothing specific. Just stuff. Any gossip to share?" *For instance, Jake. Is he married with children?*

"I've got nothing. Ask me again tomorrow. At least I'll be able to shed light on Meat Guy."

"Meat Guy? He sounds like a porn star."

"If he has a mustache, I'm going home, and I'm taking my pies with me."

I yearned to ask her what she knew about Jake, but my lips wouldn't cooperate. She didn't need to know I stalked him. I could say I saw his picture under "people you might know" on Facebook and noticed the twins. It wasn't really lying as much as avoiding unwanted follow-up questions. I'd been so certain I made the right decision when I let Jake go, and I only looked back sometimes—like now. It wasn't that I had regrets; I was just curious. So why couldn't I ask the question? It was four words—is Jake a dad? I rolled my eyes up to the ceiling and let a stream of air out of my mouth. "So, I—"

"I love you, Sid, but do you mind if we table this conversation until tomorrow? I have to wake up in about five hours."

I leaned back against my headboard and closed my eyes. "Sure thing. Get some sleep. Merry Christmas to the Salinger clan and give my best to Meat Guy."

"Will do. Don't kill Perry."

"I won't. Just superficial wounds, I promise."

After we hung up, I stared at my home, noting the absence of a return call or text from Will. Maybe he instinctively knew I was obsessing over an ex-boyfriend and was avoiding me as punishment. I put my sleep mask back on and set my mind on falling asleep. Once I applied myself to something, it was rare I didn't succeed.

As long as "something" was not asking my closest friend a simple four-word question.

Robyn

Once safely parked in my parents' driveway, I turned the engine off, unbuckled my seat belt, and looked at Will. He was staring at his phone. "We're home," I announced.

As if in a daze, Will lifted his eyes away from his phone and blinked at me. "Oh, right." He freed himself from the seat and placed the device in his back pocket before opening the passenger door.

Tucking my hands in my jacket pockets as we walked up the driveway, I pretended not to notice the tension in the air. The car ride home from the bar was silent aside from the stupid comments I'd made while tinkering with the radio in a desperate attempt to make conversation. Adding to my tally of pathetic dialogue, I said, "I think the temperature dropped at least twenty degrees since yesterday."

With a groggy smile, Will said, "Accuweather calls for a brutal Christmas. Al Roker agrees, but I'm still hoping Bill Evans will give us a reprieve."

Chuckling, I said, "You're sure up on your television meteorologists."

"Only NBC and ABC. I couldn't tell you about CBS."

"I think it's John Elliot." When Will regarded me in surprise, I said, "I only know because Perry was stuck in an elevator with him once." I winced at the mention of Perry's name since it seemed to be a sore subject and concentrated on unlocking the front door of the house.

Sarcasm dripping from his voice, Will said, "Let me guess, Perry kept him *so* entertained with his pitch-perfect singing voice that John barely noticed he was trapped."

"Of course not," I said quickly. According to Perry's telling of the story, he *did* make John laugh with his impersonations of various anchors and reporters, but I didn't think providing further details on the matter would go over well with Will.

After hanging up our jackets, I motioned toward the kitchen. "Want water?"

Will grinned sheepishly. "I'm kind of starving. Any chance we can eat leftovers from dinner?"

I was so thrilled to see him smile again, I'd have offered to drive him to get hoagies if it was what he wanted. "Sure." Happy at least a smidgen of tension had been lifted, I forced myself to shrug off concerns about what we'd talk about while snacking. As Will followed me to the refrigerator, I was taken aback by sounds coming from the family room. "Is anyone down here?" I asked.

One at a time, the members of my family popped into view— first my mom, then my dad from next to her on the couch, followed by Jordy from the reclining chair. It was like a Whac-A-Mole game, but without the light and sound features. I glanced at my watch.

"What are you guys doing up?" Jordy was a night owl, but my parents rarely stayed downstairs past ten. What if Jordy only pretended to believe Will's explanation earlier and had told my parents he suspected we were lying about the whole thing?

"We were watching a movie," my dad replied at the same time my mom said, "Binge-watching on Netflix."

Peering at the flat-screen television through the open space connecting the kitchen to the family room, I said, "You're binge-watching movies on Netflix? On Christmas Eve?" I glanced at Will to see if he thought it was weird too. He was smirking as if in on the secret. I mouthed, "What?" and he shrugged in response.

Jordy cleared his throat. "We watched a movie first and *now* we're binge-watching *Fuller House.* Too wired up about Christmas to sleep."

"Sure." I nodded as if I actually believed he'd pass a lie-detector test with that explanation. But I couldn't make sense out of why they were all waiting up for us like we were sixteen and on our first date. Maybe they really *were* too keyed up about tomorrow to fall asleep.

"But enough about us. How was *your* night?" my mom queried, stepping into the kitchen and glancing eagerly between Will and me.

No, they were definitely waiting up for us. I scratched my head and frowned at her. "It was fine. Right, Will?"

"It was better than fine," Will said, snaking an arm around my waist. "Drinks with friends. Dancing with my girl. No complaints here."

I whipped my head toward him. How did he recover so quickly from the most awkward drive in history to seamlessly assume the devoted boyfriend role? I had a feeling he underestimated his talents in improvisation. From where I stood, he was a solid nine and a half.

"Who else was there?" Jordy questioned.

"Leon and Oliver from Will's class," I said.

"They asked about you," Will added.

"Really?" Jordy beamed. If my crush on Will hadn't lessened with time, neither had Jordy's hero-worship of Will's friends.

"And James was there too," Will said.

My mom clapped her hands together. "Wonderful. What does James think of you two dating?" She glanced pointedly at me.

"We're holding a summit to discuss it after the New Year," I muttered, rolling my eyes. Over the years, James and my mother had engaged in plenty of discussions about my taste in men right in front of me as if I weren't there. Wanting to change the subject almost as much as I wanted my family to go upstairs, I removed the Tupperware of leek patties from the refrigerator and placed them on a paper towel. "You okay with heating these in the microwave?" I asked Will.

Reaching out to grab one, Will said, "No need. I'll eat it cold."

I slapped his hand away. "No, you won't. That's disgusting. It'll take one minute to warm."

When Will pushed his lips together like a scolded little boy, I shook my head at him and smiled. "You'll thank me later."

Will tucked a wavy strand of my hair behind my ear and locked eyes with me. "You're sexy when you boss me around."

As heat caressed the back of my neck, I dropped my gaze toward the tips of my ballet flats. Was this part of his act, or was he torturing me for the fun of it?

The sound of Jordy clearing his throat jerked me out of my trance. "Banter involving my sister in the context of sex is my cue to go to bed," he said.

"I'm beat too," my dad said. Looking around the kitchen in a daze, he added, "I have no idea why I'm still down here to begin with."

"That makes one of you," I said to my mother, who was beaming at Will and me like we were a musical duo whose Freestyle single hit the top one hundred on iTunes.

Still grinning, my mom said, "Fine. We're leaving. Have fun, you two." On her way out, she tousled my hair and whispered, "He's a keeper" in my ear.

I gulped. I was pretty sure Sidney thought so too.

Realizing I wasn't even hungry, I left Will in the kitchen to finish his feast and went upstairs to get ready for bed. Not that I believed for a hot second I'd be able to lower the volume on the confusing thoughts in my head. Could James be right? Was it possible Will had developed feelings for me? Being with Will was one of those dreams I never imagined would come true. It was up there with performing on a Broadway stage or directing my students in a concert before the President of the United States. But that was when I was a kid. I was a grown woman now.

I'd been so certain my crush would make things really awkward between Will and me, at least on my end. I'd imagined myself unable to string two words together, much less talk and laugh as effortlessly as we had these last few days. But at the start of the trip, there had been clear unspoken boundaries—Will was dating Sidney, I was with Perry, and any romantic gestures we shared were faked for the sake of my family. Thirty-six hours later and the boundaries had become blurry—I could no longer tell when Will was pretending and when he was being real. Was this because he'd developed an attraction to me, was it a case of temporary short-term impairment due to drinking, or had I dreamed up all the tension between us? Perhaps it was one sided.

And what about Perry and Sidney? I'd been happy with Perry before Will Brady reentered my life. Hadn't I? I sat down on the edge of the bathtub, closed my eyes, and concentrated on Perry and all the reasons we worked so well together. He was fun and we both liked to dance. But Will was fun and he liked to dance too. And he was good at it. Perry was more my type in terms of occupation, obviously, but Will had a creative side as well. Maybe we weren't as different as I thought. It wasn't as if Perry and I (or any of my past boyfriends for that matter) spent all our time at Broadway shows, dance parties, or sing-a-longs. We engaged in non-artistic activities like going out to dinner and to the movies often too. I opened my eyes and aggressively brushed my teeth. As I took my frustrations out on my toothbrush, I hoped my gums wouldn't bleed, but I also thought it would serve me right if they did.

Maybe James was right. While I burned away the months with Perry, I wasn't getting any younger. He was a good time, for sure, but would he be there for me if I needed him? Perry thought a night out could cure all ailments, and sometimes it could, but how about when it couldn't? Would he stick around? And, more importantly, would I want him to? If the deer-in-headlights reflection staring back at me in the mirror was any indication, it was clear I had no idea. If nothing else, this boyfriend swap experience had given me a lot to think about. James had urged me to talk to Will, but for now, I would leave it alone and get through the remainder of the holiday the best I could. I nodded at myself in the mirror to seal the decision and returned to my bedroom where Will was sitting on the edge of the bed in the process of removing his socks.

"Do you even remember kissing me?" I asked, gasping the second the words slipped off my tongue. Apparently, the pact I'd made with myself to let it go was sealed in non-stick spray.

Will looked up at me with a surprised expression. "Of course I do. Why would I forget?"

I shrugged. "I figured I'd gotten lost in the shuffle with the hundreds of girls you've kissed since."

Will raised an eyebrow. "Hundreds?"

My eyes widened. "Thousands?"

Will shook his head and smiled at me. "I don't know how I got the reputation of being the Wilt Chamberlain of the Philadelphia suburbs, but I don't think I've reached the three-digit numbers in women I've kissed. But if I have and just forgot, I do remember kissing *you*."

Feigning nonchalance, I said, "Was just curious," before pretending to pick something off my closet floor.

"Is that all you wanted to know?"

I closed my eyes and breathed in and out deeply before turning around to face him. "Did you think it was a good kiss?" Although I wished I could crawl into my closet and dig a hole to China, I fought to keep my eyes on him and live up to the boldness of my question.

The corners of Will's lips turned up slightly and he nodded. "I thought it was a great kiss. Did you?"

What I wanted to say—the truth—was that it was one of the best kisses I'd ever had. I wasn't so far gone as to have thought about it every day over the last ten years, but whenever I'd think about Will, my pulse instinctively raced in memory of the seconds right before, during, and after the kiss. In slow motion, I'd recall his face coming closer and closer to mine as we met in the middle of the circle and how I closed my eyes at the first brush of his lips against mine. If I tried hard enough, I could still remember how it felt—tender yet intense. "Yes, I did."

Will's face lit up for half a second, but the brightness disappeared before I could capture it in my mind and was replaced with an unreadable expression. "I'm exhausted. Mind if we call it a night?" He scooched to the top of the bed and slipped under the covers. "Goodnight, Snow," he muttered, his eyes already closed.

Further discussion was off the table for the night, which was probably a good thing. My first instinct had been to leave things alone, even if my mouth had refused to cooperate—why did I have to bring up the stupid kiss? With any luck, or a Christmas miracle, things would be back to normal in the morning.

Chapter 12

Sidney

Perry was gesticulating wildly toward my Aunt Eileen, no doubt regaling her with some whimsical anecdote about his life as a struggling actor. I snuck up behind him, stood on my tippy toes, and kissed the nape of his neck. "Merry Christmas, babe." As much as I preferred my time without Perry to my time *with* him, there was only one more day and a single sleep ahead of me before this nightmare of a holiday would be over. I could play the part of the doting girlfriend for twenty-four hours. It was preferable to being recruited by my dad to put in pre-Christmas billable hours. *One more day.*

Aunt Eileen beamed at me. "Perry wants to direct a group performance of 'Do They Know It's Christmas?' later and said he'd upload it to his YouTube channel. Isn't that exciting? We'll be famous," she yelped before clamping a hand on Perry's shoulder.

My first thought was: *Perry has a YouTube channel?* My second thought was: *Of course he does.* My last thought was: *My father would take down the video faster than Perry could unhook a co-ed's bra.* The year before, a Canadian law firm posted a video of the flash mob their attorneys had performed at the Toronto Eaton Centre mall during the holidays. It went viral and there was some buzz at B&B about organizing something similar. My father and Stan called a special meeting, making it clear that any employee who thought making an ass out of himself on social media reflected well on Bellows and Burke could hand in his resignation now. While firing his sisters wasn't an option, there was nothing to stop him from cutting them out of his will. "My sweetie's got lots of brilliant ideas up his sleeve. Don't you, gorgeous?" I said before planting a kiss on his perfectly scruffy cheek. If I didn't know better, I'd think Perry hired a professional to groom his five o'clock shadow.

Without looking me in the eye, Perry said, "If you say so." Glancing at his almost-empty glass, he muttered, "I need another Bloody Mary," and with a parting wink at Aunt Eileen, he walked toward the bar on the other side of the room.

I stared after him with my mouth ajar. What was with the 'tude?

"He's really something, Sidney. Think about how gorgeous your children will be."

I turned my attention away from Perry's rushed voyage to refill his drink and back to my aunt. Forcing a chuckle, I said, "Let's not get carried away. We're a long way from having kids." *As in, maybe in another life.*

Aunt Eileen glanced fondly in Perry's direction while running a hand through the shoulder-length curly blonde hair she'd worn in the same style for as long as I could remember. "Still. He's quite charismatic." Skimming the room, she said, "At least you don't have to worry about competition at one of my brother's affairs." She wrinkled her nose. "Although Barbara told me one of his business colleagues is dating someone even younger than you."

"Aaron Davenport. And he left his girlfriend at home." *Or with the babysitter.*

Aunt Eileen clapped. "Thank goodness for small favors. Truth be told, I haven't liked any of your boyfriends since Jake, but Perry is so magnetic. And talented. Imagine if he won a Tony award."

A *what?* "Did he tell you he was nominated for one?" Perry had proven to be prone to exaggeration, but blatant lying seemed out of character even for him. And why did she have to mention Jake?

Aunt Eileen's jade-green eyes bugged out. "No, he didn't.

That's amazing news. I'll have to congratulate him later," she said before scurrying off toward Uncle Gil.

I shook my head like there was water in my ears, trying to make sense of the preceding conversation and how much liquor my aunt had ingested to believe Perry—who had never even been in a real Broadway show—could possibly be eligible for a Tony nomination. Whatever. I followed him to the bar, where he was talking to my dad. I inhaled deeply through my nose and let it out slowly, reminding myself this wasn't real and no matter how keen my father was on Perry, it would be over soon. My parents survived the Jake breakup; they'd live through the impending disappearance of Perry from my life too. I wouldn't make a big deal out of it, but when the time was right, I'd say, "It didn't work out." Then I'd strategically change the subject to something neither of them could resist, like which attorneys at the firm were assigned "Super Lawyer" status and the new trends I found for party planning on Pinterest.

I came up from behind the two of them and tapped Perry on the arm. "Please don't tell me you're dissing my vocal skills again. I might be persuaded to prove you wrong with a little ditty later."

"We weren't discussing you at all," Perry said dryly.

"I was urging Perry to try the Glenfiddich 1937. He said he's more of a Tito's vodka man, but I told him the Scotch would take the edge off," my dad said.

"I'm not sure even the finest Scotch could heal what currently ails me." He gave me a pointed look and then turned back to my father. "Career-related stress."

"Well, hopefully you'll make some connections tonight." My dad glanced over my shoulder. "I see someone I need to speak to." With a pat on each of our shoulders, he said, "Enjoy yourselves," and excused himself.

The tension in the air was as thick as San Francisco smog. I opened my mouth to tell Perry we should make the best of the night, but before I got the words out, he walked away. I closed my mouth as fast as I could, but not before I made eye contact with

Aunt Eileen. She frowned at me and mouthed, "Everything all right?" before jutting her head toward Perry. This was the second time she'd seen Perry run away from me, and I didn't enjoy being made a fool. I grinned and waved her off.

An hour or so later, I had made my rounds, greeting some of my father's business associates and doing my best to charm the hopefuls to send some business to Bellows and Burke. The hot hors d'oeuvres had been released and the guests, particularly those who were imbibing too quickly to consider their calorie intake, flocked to the catering staff as if the trays contained weapons and they were contestants in *The Hunger Games* desperate to kill before being killed. With most of the guests enveloping the waiters, it was easy to spot Perry standing off to the right, conversing with our family accountant and her husband.

I joined his conversation of three and said, "Merry Christmas, Jill. You too, Rod," before leaning in to give them both a kiss. "I see you've met my boyfriend, Perry."

"Yes, he's been telling us about his health coverage through SAG," Jill said with bright eyes.

"Hearing it from a real actor's perspective is quite eye opening," Rod agreed with a nod.

I rubbed Perry's elbow with two fingers. "In a good way, I hope." This was his opportunity to make up for blowing me off earlier.

While slickly removing himself from my light grip, Perry responded, "Aside from losing sleep wondering whether I'll meet the minimum earnings required to remain eligible, it's a dream." Smiling warmly at Jill and Rod, he said, "If you'll excuse me, I see a tray of lamb sliders with my name on it, but I hope you'll stick around to hear me play the piano later."

"We wouldn't miss it," Jill said.

"Great," Perry said before glaring at me and walking away.

Jill and Rod gave each other curious glances, and we stood for a moment in silence. Hoping they didn't notice the smoke coming out of my ears, I unclenched my fists and held my head up high. "I should make my rounds before my father accuses me of shirking my hostess responsibilities. Enjoy yourselves."

I let out an audible sigh of frustration before quickly planting on a smile for the benefit of my similarly aged but married cousin Lauren—Aunt Eileen and Uncle Gil's daughter—who, from the way she was frowning at me, had witnessed the scene with Perry. "We had a bit of a tiff last night and he's holding a grudge," I confessed. Rolling my eyes, I said, "Typical man."

Lauren shook her head in sympathy. "Todd is the champion of passive-aggressive behavior. I find it's pointless to apologize more than once. Eventually, or as soon as he realizes he won't have sex again if he keeps up the silent treatment, he lets it go as if nothing happened." With a knowing raise of her eyebrows, she said, "I have a feeling Perry will get over this once he tosses back a few more of those cocktails and wants to get frisky with his beautiful girlfriend."

I kept my back as straight as possible to avoid giving into the shudder I was desperate to release at the thought of Perry getting frisky with me. "I'd better instruct the bartender to add an extra shot to all of his drinks then, eh?"

"Atta girl." Lauren clinked her glass against mine and rejoined her husband.

I glanced at my watch, wondering if it was a good time to call Will when from behind me, I heard a deep voice say, "I've been trying to get your attention all day."

I blew a stream of air through my lips and braced myself for impact before facing Aaron Davenport. In his early forties, Aaron was handsome with short chestnut-brown hair, light blue eyes, freckles, and a slim but fit build. He used his connections in the entertainment industry more than his good looks to get in the pants of beautiful, young, and ambitious aspiring actresses who were too inexperienced and naïve to doubt any of his promises. My knickers, however, might as well have been surgically attached to my body as far as Aaron was concerned, but so far, he hadn't given up despite my continuous (but polite) refusal to "give it up."

"Merry Christmas, Aaron," I said with a bright smile before

accepting his Hollywood-style two-cheek kiss. Although I'd be tempted to take a shower to wash his slime off my body, he was a client, and it was my job to put on a good show. Aaron was the owner of a voice-over company originally based solely in New York City. He'd met my father a decade earlier when he took over a small studio in LA and hired Bellows and Burke as outside counsel in the deal. B&B later assisted when Aaron acquired offices in Chicago and Minneapolis. His moral compass was questionable, but my dad and Stan didn't care as long as he paid his bills.

Aaron darted his eyes the length of my body before eventually landing on my face. "What's shaking, Jaws?" He'd nicknamed me after the famous fictitious shark after I handled time-sensitive contract negotiations on his behalf and ripped opposing counsel a new one.

"I've been meaning to call you, actually," I said while trying to keep the crab puff I'd swallowed earlier from coming back up.

"Finally changed your mind about letting me take you out?" Aaron said, raising his thin eyebrows. "Harvey wouldn't mind. I'm practically family anyway."

"Which would make it virtually incest," I protested while shaking my head in practiced amusement. Turning the conversation to a more business-appropriate topic, I asked, "Have you pondered expanding AD Voice Over into Canada next?" The latest issue of *Business Insider* included an article about the Great White North becoming a new hotspot in the industry, and I considered it part of my job to stay on top of trends in entertainment.

Aaron's eyes twinkled. "You're so sharp, Ms. Bellows," he said, looking me over appreciatively again. "I'm considering Vancouver or Montreal for my next business venture. Care to help me choose? We can visit both in the name of 'research.'" He winked at me.

"I'm sure Ashley wouldn't appreciate me encroaching on her man." Before he could argue, I added, "And I'm afraid my boyfriend wouldn't be thrilled either. He already has a jealous streak."

"He doesn't seem very green-eyed to me."

As a vision of Perry's annoyingly penetrating eyes flashed before me, I replied, "He's not. His peepers are blue like a pair of jeans after the first wash...wait, what are you getting at?"

Aaron gave me a lecherous grin and pointed to where Perry was standing only a few feet away, surrounded by women. "I think he might be okay with swinging."

I grimaced. "Those are my relatives. And most of them were already in menopause when he was born."

Aaron shrugged. "I've been observing you guys all day, and let's just say he seems more interested in engaging in couch aerobics with them than more high-intensity activities with you."

Knowing Aaron was "observing" us sent creepers up my back like the Boogey Man's fingers, but I ignored the sensation. The fact he noticed Perry's cold shoulder toward me was more upsetting. "We argued last night and he's stubborn," I said as casually as possible while trying to make eye contact with Perry. When he looked my way, I blinked at him three times as quickly as I could.

"Wow. You must have really bruised his ego. It *does* happen to everyone, you know. Even young guys like Perry." He chortled obnoxiously.

"I don't know what you're talking about," I lied while contemplating the wisdom in calling Aaron out on how inappropriate it was to attack my boyfriend's ability to achieve an erection. I was his legal counsel, not his sorority sister. But I had more vital things to ponder. For instance, why Perry refused to acknowledge my signal for help. I'd told him about Aaron after he woke up from his nap during our drive from the city. I said if I blinked at him three times in a row, it meant I needed to be rescued. Hoping Aaron would be too busy checking out my breasts to catch me in the act, I kept my stare on Perry, willing him to notice me. After what felt longer than the line for the ladies' room at a bar on St. Patrick's Day, he laughed and angled his head in my direction. While my face was in his line of vision, I blinked once, twice, three times and held my breath.

I knew he saw me—both times. I was already tempted to kick

him where it hurt, and if he ignored me one more time, I'd have his balls on one of my mom's Flora Danica china platters. Our eyes met, I blinked—hard—blinked again, and...dammit...he dissed me again—this time to dance with my Great Aunt Edna.

Enough was enough. With my fists clenched, I took a step backward and said, "Excuse me, Aaron. I have an urgent matter begging for my attention." Before he could say anything, or possibly while he was saying it (I didn't wait around to find out if he bothered), I hoofed it over to Perry and broke up his dance routine. "Apologies, Aunt Edna, but I need to borrow Perry for a minute." Without awaiting a response from either of them, I grabbed ahold of Perry's left hand and dragged him out of the room. When we were in the hallway, I checked left and right for nosy catering staff before opening the door of the service pantry, pushing Perry in, and then closing the door behind us. The combined smell of cedar and dust tickled my nostrils.

"What's your problem?" Perry asked, his eyes shooting deadly bullets into mine while he shook out the hand I'd been holding. I hadn't gripped it that hard—wimp.

"*My* problem?" Stepping closer to him, I repeated, "*My* problem? What's *your* problem?" I poked a finger into his chest.

Nearly tripping over a precariously located stepladder, Perry smirked at me. "No complaints here. I'm having a gay old time."

I rolled my eyes. He probably *was* gay and Robyn was acting as his beard. In fact, many of the actors I was attracted to were gay, like Matt Bomer. Not that I was attracted to Perry. "You were having such a wonderful time, you failed to rescue me."

Cocking his head to the side, Perry said, "From what?"

I wasn't buying the dumb act. "Aaron. I blinked at you three times. Make that nine times."

Perry's mouth dropped open. "Oh. I wondered why you were blinking so much. I thought you might be having a seizure."

"And you were so concerned, you pretended not to notice? It's a good thing you're not a doctor or you'd have broken the Hippocratic Oath."

"I decided it was more likely you had a hair in your eye." He kicked at an economy-size package of Charmin toilet paper rolls.

"You're so full of shit, Perry. You've been intentionally evading me all day for no reason."

His eyes bugged out. "Everything's a battle with you. You're pissed when I'm friendly, you're pissed when I ignore you. I'm just trying to follow your lead like you asked."

"I've been trying so hard to be nice all day."

Perry crossed his arms over his chest. "Well, maybe I'm sick of how hard you need to try to be a nice person. Seriously, you at your kindest is like Robyn with a bad case of PMS."

My skin bristled with irritation under his cocky gaze. "Well, I'm sick of you comparing me to Robyn all weekend. Robyn is so sweet. Robyn can sing. Robyn, Robyn, Robyn." I rubbed my nose to hide my flaring nostrils.

Perry smiled. "I get it," he said plainly.

"Get what?"

"You're jealous."

"Jealous? Of Robyn? *Pfft.*"

"You are. Robyn gets a piece of all of this," he said, with a sweeping motion down the length of his body, "and it's killing you."

"You're gross."

"You're so used to being in control you can't stand that I won't bend for you." He stared me down before flicking his tongue across his lower lip. "But I bet you wish I'd bend you over right now."

Waving my hand in protest, I said, "You're such a pig," and turned my back on him.

"What? You don't like it rough? Is Will a *gentle* lover?" Perry asked condescendingly.

I faced him again. "Leave Will out of this. And he's plenty rough when I want him to be." The room suddenly seemed very small and my body flushed with warmth.

Smirking, Perry sat on the top step of the ladder and asked, "And how often is that?"

"Why are you so interested in my sexual preferences? It's

nothing *you'll* ever need to know." I smiled victoriously, thrilled to have turned the tables. And then my lips curled back down when I realized I'd singlehandedly proven Perry's accusation that I craved control.

Perry raised himself to a standing position and shoved past me. "You couldn't handle me, Cherry Bomb."

To his back, I said, "The hell I couldn't," before placing a hand on both sides of his waist and turning him around to face me. "And I can prove it to you." Before my mind or conscience could process that what I was about to do would affect not only me and Perry, but also Will and Robyn, I launched myself at him, latching on to his mouth like I was drowning and his lips were my life preserver.

Robyn

My brother had bought me an iTunes gift card every Christmas since I'd owned my first iPod Nano. Even though the contents of the envelope he'd handed me were no surprise, I was no less appreciative. "Thank you," I said, drawing him into a hug. When we separated, my eyes met Will's. In an instant, I was no longer in my parents' family room, but back in my childhood bed, curled in Will's arms as he spooned me from behind. The red sangria I was holding slipped through the fingers of my right hand and *splat* onto the multi-colored area rug. The splash of the liquid from the full glass seemed to reach all four corners of the rectangular-shaped room, and everyone grew silent as all heads turned toward Jordy and me. "My fault. Sorry, I'll clean it up," I said before racing into the kitchen, hoping my thick mane of hair covered the mask of embarrassment I was now wearing.

"I'll take care of it. And besides, the red will blend into the rug," my mom yelled after me. "Just refill your glass and bring me the pitcher."

With shaky hands, I opened the refrigerator with the public intention of doing as told by my mother. Fortunately, it also served the added benefit of cooling off my heated face—and if I was being honest, certain parts of my body—from the memory of waking up to Will's beating heart against my back, his rhythmic breathing in my ear, and his long fingers laced with mine. We'd closed our eyes for the night on opposite sides of the bed, but either I'd leaned my body against his in my sleep or he'd reached for me at some point, perhaps mistaking me for Sidney. It was no doubt an innocent, unconscious maneuver to start, but my failure to extricate myself from his embrace after I'd taken several waking breaths wasn't so chaste.

Knowing I'd raise suspicion if I didn't get my head out of the stainless-steel Kenmare soon, I filled my glass and rejoined Will and my family, which included my paternal grandparents—Nana and Pop Pop Lane. Will and my dad were discussing the holiday playlist. The song selection for the Lane Christmas was something my dad took very seriously. Most families probably listened to back-to-back Christmas albums in their entirety—maybe Harry Connick Junior, Elvis Presley, or even the soundtrack from *Love, Actually*—but we did things differently. Each year, my dad created a new playlist by selecting individual songs from some of his more than two-hundred holiday albums. Every guest was asked to contribute one song and the goal was to stump my dad by choosing a tune he didn't own or even recognize. It was probably nineteen hundred and something the last time Kevin Lane admitted defeat.

My dad draped an arm congenially across Will's shoulder and announced, "Will's ready to give his song choice. Think you can astound us with your selection?"

Will tapped his fingers together and took a slow glance around the room, stopping when his eyes met mine. He smiled sheepishly. "Robyn warned me the odds were about a million to one, but you can't win if you don't play."

"Atta boy," my mom called out in encouragement.

After emptying his glass of sangria, Will said, "Drum roll, please."

Everyone obliged, and I couldn't contain my smile at how

seriously he was taking this.

Will cleared his throat. "My contribution is 'I Want An Alien for Christmas' by Fountains of Wayne." He seemed to hold his breath awaiting the family's response.

At first, no one said anything, and I wasn't sure how my father was going to handle it. This was his stage and the rest of us were just players, but after a moment, he clapped Will on his back. "Well, I'll be damned. You did it. No guest to the Lane family Christmas has contributed an original song in this decade until now."

Will's mouth dropped open. "Really?"

My dad slowly shook his head. "Not really." Pointing at me, he said, "But you were close. Your girlfriend already chose the same song."

When everyone glanced my way, I shrugged. "Sorry."

"At least we know he didn't cheat," Jordy said.

"It was a great effort, Will. Better luck next year," my mom said before refilling his glass.

Will walked over to me and smiled softly. "I can't believe we both chose the same song." He'd been companionable to me all day, appearing to have recovered from whatever had plagued him the night before. Unless it was part of his performance. He could probably give Perry a run for his money in terms of staying in character.

"Great minds," I said. "Although you did better than most. Typically, guests—even repeat ones—pick songs we've included many times before. They don't even try. Not only did you make an honest effort, but you would have won if I didn't get to my dad first."

"You're saying it's all your fault then?" Will teased, his hazel eyes twinkling. "Maybe I should hold back your present."

"A gift? For me?" I hopped on my toes as excitement danced under my skin. I wasn't expecting anything from Will. His mere participation in this farce already went above and beyond.

"Yes, a gift. For you," he said, mimicking the eager tone of my voice. "Do you want it now?"

Nodding, I said, "I'll give you mine now too." I reached under the tree to where I'd left his gifts the night before and placed them on the floor by my feet. I wondered if he bought my gift at the mall when we'd separated, like I had for him.

Handing me a small box wrapped in mauve-colored paper and tied with a white ribbon, he said, "Merry Chrismukkah, Snow."

I gasped. "You bought me something from Pandora?" A minute ago, I'd been pleased with what I'd chosen for him but not so much anymore. I tentatively removed the box from his hand.

"I noticed your bracelet. Sidney has the same..." Will's face turned red as he realized his faux pas, and he coughed. He glanced at my family before turning back to me. "Pandora is the only commercial you don't fast forward. I figured you were trying to tell me something." He raised his eyebrows, clueing me into his lie to cover up his almost mistake. "Open it."

Of course, we'd never watched television together, and my eyes widened in awe at how fast he thought on his feet. I did as he asked. With shaky hands, I slid the ribbon off the box, ripped through the paper, and removed the lid. My heart jumped into my throat. It was a sterling silver tiara charm with "Snow White" engraved on the ball. When I lifted my gaze from the box, I felt Will's eyes boring into mine and swallowed hard. "This is amazing. Thank you." Since my family was watching, I knew limiting my gratitude to a verbal expression would seem weird. I stood on my tippy toes and placed a soft kiss on his mouth. I allowed my lips to linger a few seconds like a real girlfriend would before drawing back. Will's face had reddened, and I felt the heat of his blush down to my toes.

"Apparently, Snow White *does* wear a crown," he said, breaking the awkwardness.

I chuckled and held the charm up for the others to see. "Isn't this great? You guys remember my nickname from school, right?" My family responded with collective approval of the gift choice.

"My turn," Will said, bending down to pick up the two packages I'd purchased for him.

I chewed on my fingernails knowing how lame my gifts were

compared to his.

When he opened the first one—Off Track Planet's *Travel Guide for the Young, Sexy, and Broke*, I joked, "Two out of three ain't bad." The gift was inspired by our conversation at the mall about what Will liked to do in his free time. He was young and sexy, and even lawyers appreciated a good bargain.

"Maybe you guys can plan a vacation together," my mom suggested.

"Great idea, Mrs. Lane," Will said. "I love it, Snow. Thanks so much."

Sensing his internal conflict over whether to kiss me again, I pushed the other gift toward him before he had a chance. "Next one."

His eyes twinkled as he removed the trucker hat from the box and read the inscription. "This is awesome," he said, placing the cap on his head. He repeated the words on the cap: "I've Got Rhythm."

"You sure do," my mom agreed.

"I almost bought you a t-shirt with the quote, 'I sing way too much for someone who can't sing,' but I liked this better," I confessed.

"Me too," Will said. Pulling me into a hug, he mumbled, "Thanks, Snow" into my hair.

I'd debated buying Will Christmas presents because I feared it might make him uncomfortable, but I took the risk because I wanted to do something nice for him. Racing against the clock to find the perfect gifts with the hour we had apart brought me joy, as did the expression of happiness on his face when he opened them. I knew I wouldn't experience the same pleasure giving Perry the gifts waiting for him at home—a royal blue cashmere sweater and tickets to see *Finding Neverland* on Broadway (again).

I looked over at Will, who was examining his new hat like it was a valuable collector's item, and felt a heavy ache in my heart. In that moment I knew I had to end things with Perry regardless of whether I ever saw Will again after this week. The relaxed and low pressure nature of my relationship with Perry had felt right before and perhaps it was at one time, but I couldn't go back. Even if I wanted to, it would no longer be the same.

As if reading my mind, Will tipped his hat at me and winked. Not wanting him to see the sadness in my eyes, I flashed a quick smile before kneeling in front of the tree to find the gifts I'd bought for my grandparents.

About a half hour later, all the presents had been exchanged and we snacked on appetizers—a shrimp cocktail and a sushi platter—our lame attempt at the Seven Fishes tradition.

"What is it you do, Will?" my nana asked, and I wondered what took her so long to spark up conversation with him. Her blue eyes had followed him since she and my grandfather had arrived early in the morning. No matter where he was standing or with whom, Nana was always within earshot of his conversations, and I figured she had her hearing aid juiced to the highest volume so she wouldn't miss a word.

"I'm a lawyer," Will said, angling his chair in her direction.

Nana bit the top off a jumbo shrimp and swallowed it down. "You mean you play one on television?"

Will wrinkled his forehead. "Um, no. I'm a real attorney."

My Pop Pop leaned forward in his bridge chair. "Like on *The People's Court* or *Judge Judy* though, right? You don't work at a real law firm," he stated matter-of-factly as he scratched at the thin layer of silver hair on his head.

When Will glanced at me in amusement, I covered my eyes with a hand and sighed. "Will is a lawyer at a real law firm," I said, dropping my hand to my side. My Nana's mouth opened and anticipating her next words, I continued, "And, no, it's not a reality show."

"That was my next question," Nana confirmed. "It must be because you can dance," she said, motioning toward Will. "You know what they say about men with rhythm."

I clamped a hand against my mouth to stifle giggles.

Pop Pop stood up. "You mean to tell me that Robyn Taylor Lane, my granddaughter..." He paused to point at me. "...is dating a regular person?"

"Didn't think I'd live to see it," Nana mumbled.

Will's lips quivered and his face turned red. "Your middle name is Taylor?"

"Yes. What of it?" I asked, folding my arms across my chest. Of course, I had an inkling where this was going but held out hope I was wrong.

Will's chest heaved up and down. "Nothing."

"Stop it," I said with a punch to his leg.

Glancing at my parents, he said, "The name choice was inspired by Taylor Dayne? Am I right?"

"You bet," my dad confirmed. "Did you know 'Love Will Lead You Back' peaked the year Robyn was born?"

"Priceless," Will mumbled under his breath.

Chapter 13

Sidney

I could feel Perry's breath against my mouth as we continued to kiss. His fingers deftly lowered the zipper of my little black dress, and I dropped my hands from his hair. My eyes still closed, I blindly reached for his belt buckle.

The sound of boxes crashing brought me back to earth. I opened my eyes. "What the..."

A woman, probably a few years younger than me, stood before us in a black and white catering uniform. Her brunette hair was pulled back in a bun and her heavily painted red mouth contrasted with the paleness of her skin as she looked upon us in shock. "I'm so sorry," she stammered. "Mr. Bellows asked me to bring out another bottle of Crown Royal. I saw you two and knocked down some cereal boxes while trying to make a quick escape." She turned her back on us, knelt, and began picking up boxes of Corn Flakes and Lucky Charms—my dad's favorite "healthy" and "not-so-healthy" cereals.

My breath coming quick, I glanced at Perry. His reflection mirrored my horror. The girl's timing left me both mortified and extremely grateful. If she hadn't come in when she did...I shook off the thought. Thank goodness she had. I'd find a way to give her an extra-large tip.

Perry removed his eyes from mine and tapped her on the back. "We'll take care of this. You should get back with the whisky. Don't want to leave thirsty party-goers hanging."

The girl stood up. "Are you sure?" she asked while nervously straightening out her black skirt. The color slowly returned to her cheeks.

We replied, "Yes" at the same time and remained silent until we heard the pantry door close.

In a state of shock, I pulled on the bottom of my now-wrinkled little black dress.

Perry rested his gaze at the top of my head. "You might want to fix your hair." Then he turned his back, buried his face in his hands, and mumbled, "What the hell were we thinking?"

A tsunami of guilt washed over me. I'd teased Will about keeping his hands to himself, but it never occurred to me I would be the adulteress in this situation. Even though none of my pairings since Jake had been serious, I'd never cheated on even my most casual boyfriends, much less gone after another girl's guy. Hopelessly desperate to be absolved of blame, I said, "This is all your fault. You goaded me." I smoothed down my hair—a delayed reaction to Perry's earlier comment.

"Don't even," Perry said as he faced me again, his eyes lit in anger.

"You're the one who accused me of wanting you to 'bend me over.'"

"I wasn't serious. Although, given the way you attacked me, I guess there was truth in the statement after all." He removed two cereal boxes from the dusty floor and returned them to the shelf.

My stomach dropped as I recalled the animalistic way I'd hurled myself at him. It would be magically delicious if Lucky the Leprechaun could cast a spell so this never happened. The only saving grace was that we stopped before it went too far. "I didn't see you pushing me away. In fact, you seemed very excited about it." I raised an eyebrow.

"Schuester has a mind of his own," Perry said, motioning to his privates.

"Schuester?"

"From *Glee*," he said, rolling his eyes upward as if he'd chosen the name of someone who was actually famous, like Barack Obama or Michael Phelps.

"You named your penis after a character on *Glee*?"

"Not just *any* character—the one played by Matthew Morrison. Better his last name than his first."

"What's his first?"

"Will." He gave me a wry smile.

Will. My stomach curdled as if I'd chugged sour milk. What was I going to say to Will? Even though we didn't have sex, it was still cheating. My comments about Perry being a "blond god" notwithstanding, I knew Will trusted me. He was a stand-up guy who gave as good as he got. I pictured the disappointment on his face if he knew what I'd done and felt an ache in my gut.

"What are we going to do now?" Perry asked, interrupting my thoughts. His cerulean eyes pleaded for an easy solution.

Unfortunately, I had no quick fix for him. "Why are you asking *me*?"

"I thought you had all the answers."

I bit my cheek. "I usually do, but not this time. What was I thinking?"

"Ah. A question I know the answer to."

I hadn't realized I'd asked it out loud. "Do tell," I said, even though I doubted his ability to bestow wisdom at this time.

"You had to have the last word. I said you couldn't handle me and your inflated ego wouldn't allow you to let it go."

"*My* inflated ago? Pot. Kettle. Black."

Perry shrugged. "It's the only reasonable answer to explain why you'd throw yourself at me—a guy who, regardless of his overwhelming charms, you don't seem to like."

I wasn't ready to acknowledge there might be truth in his statement. "What was your excuse, then?"

At the same time, we said, "Schuester," and chuckled. But we both knew it wasn't a happy laugh; it was the sad laugh of two desperate, guilt-ridden people.

"I don't think this is the best place to devise a game plan." The walls of the oversized pantry seemed to be closing in on me and my lungs cried for fresh air. "For now, let's go back and get hammered. We'll worry about this tomorrow."

Tapping my head, Perry said, "I knew my precious Cherry Bomb was in there somewhere." He smiled at me.

I snorted and, in spite of myself, grinned back. Things would get ugly soon enough.

As promised, Perry and I rejoined the festivities and drank back-to-back Gin and Tonics, heavy on the gin and light on the tonic. We were both blitzed by the time the formal dinner was served but managed to hide it well. Perry relied on his acting skills to feign sobriety, and I used sheer determination. On a positive note, Aaron spotted us entering the sitting room together and hadn't bothered me since.

The antique Howard Miller grandfather clock in the formal dining room pinged six o'clock, and I happily noted we were well past the halfway mark for the day's festivities. Dinner would be served, then dessert, followed by an hour of after-dinner digestifs during which the guests would begin their departures.

"This room..." Perry said as he scanned the large space, his eyes Olympic-sized pools of blue. He let his sentence drop off, but I knew what he was thinking.

My parents' estate held two dining rooms—one for cold weather and one for formal dining in the spring and summer. The winter dining room, where Christmas was held, was a Federal/Georgian style with two black marble fireplaces on opposite sides. The long dark wood table, large enough to accommodate more than forty guests, looked like something out of *Downton Abbey*. But most impressive, at least in my opinion, was the mural they'd hired an artist to paint along an entire wall. It was a Tuscan landscape in a warm orangey hue that added warmth to a room mostly occupied by those not often described as warm and fuzzy.

"I know. It's something, right?" I smiled at Perry. After we agreed our indiscretion was not up for discussion until later, we'd managed to get along. I suspected we were temporarily bonded by shared feelings of shame and nothing else, but I'd allowed myself to enjoy his company. It felt like the Last Supper before the reality of what we'd done would set in and we'd have to deal with it.

My mouth salivated at the sight of the warm crescent rolls circling the table and when the server got to me at last, I spread a hefty amount of soft butter on mine and took a bite. I closed my eyes to fully treasure the crispy outside and soft inside of the pastry. This was not a day for watching my calorie intake. The fattening dishes on the holiday menu were my most powerful motivator for pounding the icy pavement every morning when everyone else in my residence was still asleep. I also desperately needed to coat my stomach and sober up enough to nail my role as junior hostess. With my father holding court at one end of the table and my mother on the other, I was placed in the center to make sure just about everyone was in conversation-distance with a Bellows.

Marshall, a good friend and sometimes-colleague of my dad, jutted his shaved head toward Perry. "Barbara mentioned you're an actor." Marshall sat directly across the table from Perry, who was to my right.

"I am," Perry said cheerily.

"She also said you were seeking agent representation."

Perry replied, "I am."

I subtly kicked him under the table and whispered, "Expand your vocabulary" out of the side of my mouth. Perry's main purpose for agreeing to the swap was to make connections to take his career up a notch. At some point in the last three hours, I'd shocked myself by developing a smidgen of interest in Perry's future, and I didn't want him to blow it by showing a complete lack of charisma due to an alcohol-induced brain malfunction.

"My manager is great, but even he agrees having an agent on my team could make a world of difference," Perry clarified while I nodded my head in approval.

"I represent artists through Take 3 Talent. Name dropping over butternut squash soup is tacky, but if you want to talk privately over dessert later, let me know."

"My answer is a resounding yes," Perry said. He smiled wide and gave a thumbs up sign. His corniness was eye-roll worthy, but I was pleased for him. There would be at least one bright spot in this dark train wreck of a day.

Marshall leaned his muscular upper body, surprising for a man probably pushing fifty, forward in his chair while blatantly scrutinizing Perry with narrowed blue eyes. "You've got a good look—dangerously handsome, but your face is inviting and unexpectedly approachable. I bet you don't take things too seriously and are probably self-deprecating."

When everyone glanced at me curiously, I realized I'd snorted in response to the laughable "self-deprecating" comment. "Sorry." I pointed at my throat. "Tomato went down the wrong pipe."

Perry smirked at me, but Marshall smiled politely before returning his focus to Perry. "Ever done any comedy?"

Perry sat straighter in his chair and puffed out his chest. "I've done some improvisational work and a couple of comedic roles in off-Broadway productions. I'm open to both comedic and dramatic roles."

"Let's definitely talk." Turning back to me, Marshall said, "Your boyfriend might be the next big thing. How does it feel?"

Before I had a chance to reply using my own improvisational skills, Perry broke in. "I'm actually back on the market. Sid and I broke up earlier today."

I didn't even realize I'd dropped my fork until I heard metal crashing against porcelain. I lifted my butt off my seat in surprise. It figured, the second I let my guard down around Perry, he screwed me over. So much for my plan to make as little fanfare of our split as possible. Even as my head spun in embarrassment, my brain worked to recover and gain back control. I smiled sweetly at Marshall. "I thought it better to keep it to ourselves until after the holiday, but my impulsive ex here can't keep a secret to save his life."

Perry smiled sheepishly. "It's true. I'm honest to a fault."

"It's your cross to bear," I said, not even trying to hide the sarcastic tone of my voice.

"Did I hear something about a secret?" my mom asked from her end of the table.

I silently cursed the acoustic tiles my parents had installed on the ceiling to improve the sound quality in the room. "If it's a secret, Mom, best not to announce it across a table of forty people. Am I right?" I flipped my hair and smiled charmingly at everyone at the table whose eye I caught—except for Perry. I wouldn't even honor him with the evil eye. I was too annoyed at him for ruining our peace.

"It's not a secret if it's a topic of discussion at our Christmas dinner," my dad called out before gesturing for a server to refill his wine glass.

And with my father's statement, the table fell silent as all the guest—relatives, friends, and business acquaintances alike—ceased eating to stare at Perry and me.

Perry waved his hand. "It's nothing really. Sidney and I have called it quits. Irreconcilable differences."

"It's all right. We agree we're better off as friends." I stood up and said, "And now back to our regularly scheduled programming," before sitting back down and hoping the conversation was over.

"I knew something was off with you two today," Aunt Eileen said.

"How could you let him go, Sidney?" my mom cried out while dramatically fanning herself with a linen tablecloth.

"Who said it was Sidney's idea? I bet Perry broke up with her to date Jennifer Lawrence," Great Aunt Edna suggested.

"What makes you think Perry even knows Jennifer Lawrence? His most impressive gig to date was a teeth-whitening commercial." I knew it was a low blow, but my own blood relatives insinuating that Perry was too good for me was cruel too.

"And therein lies your problem," Uncle Gil stated.

"Where are you going with this?" I asked.

"You're too focused on the bottom line. You need to hone your nurturing side or you'll never have a successful romantic relationship," said Uncle Gil.

"I've never met anyone as competitive as you, Sidney," Aunt Ruth agreed.

Cousin Lauren snorted. "Remember when you raced Patrick to see who could fold the origami box at my dad's fiftieth birthday party at KOKU?"

"And then you dumped him when he beat you," Uncle Gil added.

"We were barely even dating," I protested to deaf ears as my family members continued to volley back and forth. I felt like a lab rat being scrutinized by a bunch of novice scientists.

Aunt Eileen asked, "Have you even had a real boyfriend since Jake?"

"If memory serves, she couldn't handle both law school and a love life," my dad said. "B&B thanks you for making the right choice."

"You can blame yourself if she never settles down, Harvey. She gets her competitive nature from you," my mom shouted across the table.

My stomach cramped like I'd been kicked in the gut—hard. I had no idea my family felt this way about me. It was too much all at once. Unable to hold it in any longer, I regarded Perry with my stoniest glare, but he wasn't looking at me. His face had drained of color and he darted his eyes around the table in apparent shock. As if sensing me staring at him, he turned to me with a pained expression and mouthed, "I'm so sorry." Rising from his seat, he said, "Hey now. Christmas is supposed to be about kindness toward all men, which I assume includes women like Sidney here." He gestured toward me before addressing the other guests again. "Sidney is an amazing woman who deserves your support in this difficult time. Our breakup is a private matter, but I assure you it has nothing to do with any shortcoming on her part." He sat back down.

Marshall was the first to break the silence by clapping, but soon everyone joined in a standing ovation I assumed was aimed at Perry's heartfelt speech. Everyone, that is, except me. I used the opportunity to take ownership of the one remaining crescent roll. Too bad I'd lost my appetite.

Robyn

After we'd finished dinner and dessert and my grandparents went home, the rest of us hung out in the family room, hoping a glass or two of Lambrusco would aid in our digestion of more food than any of us usually ate in two days. *Meet Me in St. Louis* aired on the muted television while the annual Christmas soundtrack played on the stereo. When Bing Crosby's "White Christmas" came on for at least the third time and none of us could complete a sentence without pausing to yawn, the night came to a close. Jordy was the first to excuse himself to bed, but when I caught Will fighting to keep his eyes open, I knew it was time to call it.

The remaining four of us climbed the stairs to the second floor and stopped in the hallway before going to our respective rooms. "Goodnight, guys. Dinner was awesome." I kissed my mom on the cheek. "And thank you both so much for my present. I love it." I embraced my dad, squeezing tightly. My parents had bought me a Roland V-Synth Synthesizer. I didn't have room in my apartment for a full-sized piano and relied on the one at work. With a keyboard at home, I wouldn't be limited to playing songs only appropriate for the under-thirteen crowd, and I might even succeed in writing an original song for something other than a school concert. I worried it was too expensive, but they'd assured me they found a good deal on eBay.

"Our pleasure, Snow White," my dad said before glancing conspiratorially at Will. I watched them share a smile.

"We hope you enjoyed yourself, Will," my mom said. "Robyn seems to think we're a tough crowd. Don't you, sweetheart?"

My cheeks warmed. "Not tough, but unrelenting. Suppose Will

wasn't a music lover. This night would have been super awkward for him." *And me.*

"Anyone who doesn't love music deserves to feel awkward," my dad said.

Will chuckled. "True story."

I'd lost count of how many times my mom had beamed at Will over the course of the weekend, but she did it again. "I like this guy."

I shook my head at her but smiled. "I couldn't tell."

Extending his hand to my dad, Will said, "Thanks so much for including me. I had such a great time." He hugged my mom, who mouthed, "Love this guy" over his shoulder.

I feared she wasn't alone in that emotion and my stomach plunged. He'd go back to his life with Sidney after tomorrow, and there was no reason for us to see each other again. I didn't know what Will was thinking, but even though nine years had passed since I watched him drive away to college, I felt the same now as I did then—heartbroken.

A few minutes later, Will and I lay side by side in silence under the girly purple and white polka dot ruffled comforter I'd delighted in as teenager and wished I could still get away with in my twenties. We only had one more sleep before we'd return to the city and our regular lives, and I wanted to say something before it was too late, but I didn't know where to start. If I admitted my high school crush on him had returned with a vengeance worthy of a sappy Hallmark movie, would he say he had feelings for me too? Or was I destined to play the part of the lovestruck teenager pining for the unattainable "it" boy through my twenties too?

Going straight to bed was probably for the best. Declaring my romantic interest in Will before officially ending my relationship with Perry was a bad omen, not to mention not very fair to Perry. There was also Sidney to consider. Actively coveting another woman's man broke the unspoken girl code. It could also put my living situation in jeopardy, since Anne Marie idolized Sidney and probably wouldn't support my trying to steal her boss's boyfriend. I groaned to myself in frustration. My Fairy Godmother was doing a crappy job of looking after Snow White right now.

The still of the room was truncated by a quiet chuckle originating from Will's side of the bed. It stopped suddenly. I wondered if he was laughing in his sleep, but then he did it again. "Did I miss something?" I asked, happy for the excuse to initiate conversation.

"I was thinking about your grandparents' reaction to you dating a 'regular' person," Will said before laughing again.

I groaned again, this time out loud. "I know. If I brought Perry or any of my exes, rest assured someone would mention before the curtain came down on the day how predictable I was for dating an actor or a musician. This time, I brought you, a lawyer and the complete opposite of my usual type, and we're lucky neither Nana nor Pop Pop went into cardiogenic shock." I'd join in Will's mirth if I found it remotely as humorous as he did.

"How do you think they'll react when you tell them you're back with Perry?"

And here it was—the opening I'd been waiting for. The time had come to tell Will my attraction to him had grown stronger after spending so much time together and regardless of what happened between us, I was going to end things with Perry. Even though it was dark in the room, I closed my eyes, hoping I'd feel less vulnerable if I couldn't see him. "The thing is—"

In a quiet voice, Will said, "He's not right for you, you know."

I opened my eyes as my heart slammed against my chest. "How do you mean?" Was he going to throw himself in the ring for my affections?

The bed shook beneath me as Will rearranged his position so he was leaning on his elbow facing me. I remained on my back. "He's not good enough for you."

Unless there was abuse involved, I didn't measure couples in terms of one person being better than the other. Two people were either the right fit or not, and while Perry might not be The One for me, I didn't think I was superior to him in any way. "I don't think you're being fair—"

"Did you ever consider your attraction to only flaky creative types is a crutch because you're not ready to settle down?"

I sat up and looked at Will. "What are you saying?" My pulse raced as if preparing for an attack.

Will mirrored my position on the bed and frowned. "Take Perry for instance. You've already mentioned you guys don't really talk about the future, and it's probably because Perry can't afford to plan beyond tomorrow. Since he's so unstable, it makes him safe for you to date because you don't have to worry about it going anywhere."

All my blood seemed to travel up my body and land on my face as my anger grew. "Thank you very much, Sigmund Freud. I knew a Juris Doctorate permitted you to give legal advice, but I had no idea it also qualified you to psychoanalyze me."

Will pushed the covers off his legs. "I shouldn't have said anything."

Staring down at my wobbling knees under the comforter, I replied, "No, you shouldn't have."

He patted my shoulder. "It was just a thought."

Flinching from his touch, I said, "For one, it's none of your business. And considering you've been married...let me count...zero times and have been dating Sidney for less than six months, I resent your insinuations." My body was shaking like I'd come in from the rain. How silly of me to think Will's aversion to Perry was based on his own desire to be with me. He was merely concerned by the extent of my emotional availability and had likely been formulating his theory the entire duration we'd been together.

"I didn't mean..."

I turned my back on his side of the bed as a signal the conversation was over. I willed myself to fall asleep, but I couldn't turn off the thoughts in my head. I also couldn't stop wondering what Will was thinking. Had I overreacted?

"Robyn?"

I lay still as a corpse, holding back the guttural sobs perched precariously at the edge of my throat.

"I know you're awake."

My brain itched to respond, but my heart was having no part of it.

"Please don't be mad. I'm sorry."

When his phone rang, he vaulted off the bed, muttering, "Dammit."

I heard him say, "Hey, Sid," before leaving my bedroom and closing the door behind him, presumably to have a private conversation in the hallway or bathroom.

Chapter 14

"Merry Christmas," I belted out in forced cheer. I heard the click of a door closing. "Did I interrupt something?"

"No. We were just..." For a moment, the only sound was Will's breathing, but then he said, "Merry Christmas back at you. Did you have fun?"

I flashed back to my time with Perry in the pantry as the knots in my stomach twisted and turned. "Typical Bellows holiday. Nothing more, nothing less." I swallowed hard at my lie. "Glad it's over. How about you?" I hoped my guilty conscience wouldn't seep into my voice. I wanted to wait until we were face to face to tell him what happened.

"Same here, I guess."

"I'm sorry I talked you into it, Will." At least that much was true. I'd been so afraid my parents would unknowingly sabotage my relationship with Will. I'd managed to do that just fine without their help.

"It's okay, Sid. I'm glad you did."

"You are?"

Will coughed. "I just mean you shouldn't feel bad. The Lanes treated me well. And I met up with some friends from high school. It was fun. No need to apologize."

I sat up. "So...it wasn't too awkward? Pretending to be Robyn's boyfriend?"

Will seemed to hesitate, but then said, "I guess I'm a better actor than you give me credit for."

"Well, that's good."

"I was wondering..." His voice dropped off.

"Yes?" I prayed he wouldn't say he was curious if I'd sucked face with Perry. I really needed to own up to the kiss in person so he'd see in my eyes how sincerely remorseful I was. Would he forgive me, or would it be the end of us? I wasn't ready to call it quits on our relationship, but I suspected it was already over and he just didn't know it yet.

"What's your favorite Christmas song? Did you ever watch *Meet Me in St. Louis?*"

I wiped my tired eyes. "Um, what?" He was talking too fast and sounded like a hyperactive second grader.

"It's just, I don't know much about..." He hesitated. "You know what, never mind. Can we talk more tomorrow? I'm beat."

His mood swing hurt my tired and guilty heart. "Yeah. Me too. I'll see you tomorrow."

"Goodnight."

"'Night." I ended the call and placed my phone on the nightstand. I sat on the edge of my bed and buried my face in my hands. Had it really been less than a day since I'd woken up that morning? I was exhausted like I'd worked an entire week—with overtime.

Our dinner table had become the setting for an episode of *Steve Harvey,* with me as the pathetic guest and my family as the experts with insight into my life love and all its dysfunctionalities. Blessedly, Perry's impassioned speech had silenced the crowd and things returned to normal by the meat course—my dad bragged about a record-breaking victory in court, my mother complained about questionable new members of the Scarsdale Golf Club, and Aunt Edna knocked a bottle of La Faraona out of a server's hand, causing the six-hundred-dollar Spanish red wine to spill all over the formal two-tone decorative tablecloth. My temporarily low-key—albeit tipsy—mother was nonplussed since the cloth was polyester and, therefore, machine washable. After dinner, Perry was forced to gently let down my aunts and uncles' pleas to direct a group musical performance in favor of discussing his future with Marshall, and I avoided Aaron's lecherous glances by pretending the catering staff needed me to oversee the cleanup. Two hours and change later, the night was in my rearview mirror and I had another Bellows' Christmas celebration under my belt. As soon as the first guests went home, I shirked my hostess responsibility and escaped to my room.

I was about to get undressed when there was a knock on my door.

"Sid. It's Perry. Can I come in?"

"I guess."

He entered my room and closed the door behind him. Leaning against one of the tall white chests on either side of my vanity table, he raised his palms in the air. "Have at me. I deserve it."

"Deserve what?" I kicked a black platform sandal off my right foot and then my left.

"What happened at dinner...what a shit show."

Truer words had rarely been spoken.

Perry continued his excuses. "I swear I wasn't trying to be an ass when I told Marshall we broke up. I figured, we're going back to the city tomorrow anyway, why not drop the charade and enjoy the night? Honestly, I had no idea your family would attack you like that." He shook his head in bewilderment. "They were like a swarm of flies."

I snorted. "More like a pack of wolves."

Shrugging, Perry said, "Anyway, I'm sorry."

I had every reason to be infuriated with him, and I wished I was. What fun it would be to take Perry to task for his actions and watch him shrink into himself in guilt. But for the first time since we'd met, I couldn't summon the anger emotion. I was angrier with myself than I was with him at this point. "It's fine, Perry. What's done is done, and if I've learned anything about you this week, it's that you don't always use the best judgment." I smiled in spite of myself. "Now that you're not my problem anymore, I can sort of see your charm."

"Are you sure it's not because we were almost..." He waggled his eyebrows. "...lovers?" His cocky grin quickly morphed into a frown. "Never mind."

I rolled my eyes. "Speaking of misguided decisions, can we discuss how we're going to handle this now so we don't have to talk about it on the car ride home tomorrow? And maybe I'll be able to fall asleep tonight?" I always slept better when I had a plan.

Perry paced the gray and white printed area rug that adorned my childhood bedroom's wood floor. "Maybe we shouldn't tell Robyn and Will. What they don't know won't hurt them, right?" He looked at me hopefully.

It wasn't as if Perry's suggestion hadn't occurred to me. If we both agreed to take the secret to our graves, no one would get hurt and we could avoid twin nasty breakups. But how happy could I be lying to Will about something as major as cheating? Each time he mentioned Robyn, Perry, or even Christmas in general, I'd feel soiled. It wasn't fair to him to continue as if nothing happened. "I can't lie to Will," I said firmly, trying to hide the regret in my voice.

When Perry regarded me with pleading blue eyes, he resembled a Siberian husky. "It will only be lying if he straight-out asks you if we hooked up and you say no. Not likely to happen."

Amused, I said, "Who's the lawyer in this room?"

"It was worth a try." He shrugged.

"Maybe they'll be okay with it," I said, even though I didn't believe myself.

Perry raised an eyebrow. "Will didn't strike me as the type of guy who'd forgive cheating. And Robyn definitely wouldn't."

I thought of something funny. "Imagine if the two of them fooled around as well and are having the exact same conversation in Philadelphia right now." On second thought, it wasn't very humorous.

Perry smirked. "Will and Robyn? Never. We're definitely the villains in this story, Cherry."

I sighed. "You're so right." I motioned toward my door to let him know it was time to leave me alone. "See you in the morning." I was exhausted.

A few minutes later, I crawled into bed and closed my eyes. Maybe if I shut them tightly enough, I could erase the faces of my family regarding me with pity for failing to create and sustain a true love connection. But I'd need earplugs to drown out their voices playing like a soundtrack on repeat saying I was too competitive, I lacked a nurturing gene, and I was too focused on the bottom line to ever be as successful in love as I was at law. The thing is, they were right.

For spring break my first year in law school, Jake planned a four-day weekend for us at a luxury ranch in Montana where we'd go horseback riding and learn to fly fish—something I'd always wanted to do—and I told him I couldn't go because I cared more about earning one of forty-five coveted spots on the *Columbia Law Review* than I did about his romantic overtures. Instead, I spent all week at home working on my personal statement for the *Review* application with my father hovered over my shoulder. Initially, Jake accepted my ambition as part of what made me "me"—he said it was a turn on—but eventually it killed us. Over the years, I had kept myself so busy chasing one win after another it left me no time to consider whether the successes even made me happy—until now. Something had to give, but I had no idea what.

Robyn

"Do you still hate me?"

I gripped the steering wheel tighter and frowned. Staring at the road, I asked, "Why would you think I hated you?"

"You've barely said a word to me since we woke up. Your parents were giving us curious looks all during breakfast."

I could hear the regret in Will's voice and winced in discomfort. "You're paranoid. They didn't notice anything." I recoiled as the bold-faced lie escaped my lips. I had spied my mom's furrowed brow out of the corner of my eye as she looked back and forth between Will and me as we sat side by side at the kitchen table without uttering a word to each other. And there was nothing subtle about her repeated requests for me to pass her this or hand her that in a relentless attempt to catch my eye. I'd managed to slide the platter of toast and the pepper shaker across the table to her all without looking up from my own plate of food. I even gave her the lamest goodbye hug in Lane mother/daughter history because of my overwhelming desire to own up to the truth—that this year's Chrismukkah was a fabrication, and Will was no closer to being my boyfriend now than he was a decade ago. If I let her squeeze me too hard, it might all come spilling out. Maybe I would tell her soon, but I needed to hold it together at least long enough for the car ride back to New York. I hadn't lied to her since I was thirteen and I told her I had a hole in my boring black rainboots so she'd buy me a new pair of bright red ones. She never found out I'd purposely bludgeoned my old pair with scissors. I dreaded the disappointment on her face when I confessed to this lie.

"Please don't be this way, Snow. I'm really sorry."

When we stopped for a light, I turned to him. "If you must know, I *am* going to break things off with Perry when I get home."

Will's eyes opened wide. "Whatever you think is best," he said in a casual tone belying his earlier strong opinions on the matter. But I caught him smile before turning to look out the window.

My skin burned with irritation. "I was planning to end it before you chipped in your two cents. But for what it's worth, your theory was wrong."

Will faced me again and frowned. "I believe you. I just couldn't think of another reason to explain your attraction to him. He's so...wrong," he said, shaking his head.

I narrowed my eyes. "Why do you care so much?" It was on the tip of my tongue to remind him that Perry would be out of his girlfriend's life soon enough too, and he should move on.

He shrugged. "I just do."

I waited for him to elaborate, but he said nothing and resumed staring out his window. I figured he had nothing else to say and focused on the road with one finger in my mouth as I chewed on a nail.

Another twenty-five minutes passed by without a word exchanged between us. Although I sang softly along to the music to calm my nerves, Will was silent. Apparently, he was all sung out from a musical weekend with the Lanes. My mind flashed back to the night before when I played "It's the Most Wonderful Time of the Year" on the piano while Will strutted around the family room belting out fake lyrics to distract us from his horrible voice.

"You're doing it again, Snow."

"Doing what?"

"Giggling to yourself."

"Oh."

"Were you laughing about my singing again?"

I whipped my head to face him with my eyes bugged out. "How...how did you know?"

He grinned. "I didn't. Until now."

"Sorry."

"No worries. I'm hoping I created enough material to keep you Lanes in stiches for the foreseeable future." He cleared his throat. "You ready to get back to the city?"

"Not really," I mumbled. My stomach churned at the thought of what lay ahead of me. I wasn't looking forward to my talk with Perry. He'd been a good boyfriend to me for almost a year, and it wasn't his fault my feelings for him weren't where I thought they should be at this point. And in another week, I'd have to face Principal Hogan and the possibility that the job I loved so much was in jeopardy as well as the music education I considered vital to every child. And let's not forget my pathetic depression over saying goodbye to Will for what might be the final time.

I was only comfortable discussing one of those items with Will. "I couldn't sleep last night, so I did some more research on budget cuts." I grimaced, hoping Will wasn't insightful enough to make the connection between our argument and my bout of insomnia. "I found a few foundations focused on helping endangered music programs at schools. Maybe a grant from one of them would be a solution."

"Your school is lucky to have you. So are your students."

I shrugged helplessly. "I won't go down without a fight. I can't." I knew Lance would help me, and even though I wouldn't wish the same panic I was experiencing on someone else, it was comforting to know we were in it together.

"If anyone could make it happen, it's you." Will reached across the front seat and tapped my thigh with his fingers before returning his hands to his own lap.

"You say that like you know me." My chuckle came out like a strangled cry.

"I *do* know you," he said, his stare on me. "Maybe more than I know my own girlfriend."

He'd looked away too fast to catch me flinch. Maybe if he'd uttered those words a few days earlier—even yesterday—they'd have filled my naïve heart with hope. But today, I felt my face flush in anger that he'd be so heartless to toy with my emotions and play with my head once again. I was beginning to think he enjoyed it. I wanted to scream myself into laryngitis or weep until I needed a prescription for Restasis for dry eyes. Instead, I focused on the open space of road ahead of me and floored the gas. It was time to go home.

Because I wanted to avoid extended conversation, I didn't argue when Will refused my offer to drop him off at his apartment in Union Square and drove straight to the car rental place. After we got out of the car and emptied the trunk, I told him I could take it from there.

Will placed his small wheeled suitcase on the concrete and tucked his hands in his jacket pockets. "Can I give you some money?"

I shook my head and removed my wallet from my purse. "It's paid for already, and besides, this was my gig, not yours. I can handle it," I said, adding the required, "But thank you" at the end.

"If you insist."

I felt his gaze on me and forced myself to face him head on. Planting on a smile, I said, "I guess I'll see you around." My heart was racing, and I made an instant decision to pick up a bottle of wine on my way home. It would go nicely with a marathon of the *High School Musical* movies. Maybe James and I could watch separately but together.

"I had a really good time with you, Snow," he said, taking a step closer to me.

Please don't hug me. Please don't hug me. As my throat closed up, I fidgeted with my purse and said, "Me too," until I found myself wrapped in his arms in the dreaded embrace and breathing in the scent of him bathed in my vanilla body wash. When we separated, Will planted a soft kiss on my forehead. I bit my lips to keep them from trembling and blinked to hold back tears. Then it was over. With a sad smile, Will grabbed the handle of his suitcase and walked out of the rental garage and out of my life.

Chapter 15

Sidney

From my small kitchen nook, I peered through the open wall at Will, who was sitting on my couch. "Can I pour you a glass of wine? I stole a few good vintages from my dad's cellar." When my voice came out an octave higher than normal, I turned my back on him and cursed at myself. Getting flustered around men was never my MO before, and it wouldn't be now either if I wasn't about to confess to cheating on the man in question.

"Sounds good. Thanks," Will said.

I poured us both a generous glass of Rioja from the bottle I'd been airing out for the last hour and joined Will in my living room. After I'd dropped Perry off earlier, I'd come home and devised a game plan for owning up to making out with Perry. That was all it was—kissing. Granted, it was a hot, sweaty, hate-inspired makeout session, but at least we hadn't slept together. I shuddered to imagine what might have gone down if we hadn't been caught. I liked to think I would have pushed Perry away before it went too far, but I wasn't so sure. I took a deep breath and handed Will a glass. "Cheers."

He clinked his glass against mine and smiled oddly. Normally when Will grinned, the green and gold flecks in his pupils actually twinkled, but not now. "Cheers," he echoed before taking a sip and darting his less-than-playful eyes around the room.

Placing my glass on the coffee table, I sat next to him and leaned my head on his shoulder. "I missed you," I said, reaching for his hand to initiate my plan. I *had* missed him, but I couldn't change the fact that I'd betrayed his trust. All I could do was use my lawyerly skills to admit my wrongdoing in a manner that downplayed the heinousness of my act. Strategic touching and a little alcohol were major players in my performance.

Will stood up abruptly and since my head was on his shoulder, it lost its landing place and dropped awkwardly to the side. Ordinarily I would give him hell about it—in a sexy, teasing way, of course—but under the circumstances, I let it slide. After straightening my head, I gazed up at him. "Everything all right?"

"Mind if I use the bathroom?"

I was taken aback by the question since he'd never asked my permission to use the facilities before, but joked, "You know where it is."

I skimmed through the latest issue of *Bloomberg Businessweek* and nursed my wine until he returned.

"Hey."

Startled, I let the magazine slip through my fingers. "Hey yourself. Come sit. I want to hear all about your Christmas."

Will joined me on the couch. "It was fine, Sid. As you can imagine, we did a lot of singing." This time, his eyes did twinkle when he smiled.

"How'd you do?" I had no idea if Will could sing, but I assumed Perry was better.

Will chuckled. "I got an F for sound quality, but an A plus for technique."

"I can vouch for your technique, if you know what I mean," I teased, nudging him playfully on his upper thigh to lessen the tension in the air.

"Funny," he said, sliding an inch away from me. "Anyway, there's not much to tell. I'm sure your holiday was more eventful."

Sucking on air, I said, "What do you mean?"

"With Perry," he said, practically choking on Perry's name. "How'd it go?"

I answered, "It was fine. Why?" and immediately regretted it. I sounded paranoid. If I asked about his holiday, of course he'd reciprocate. Composing myself, I added, "As threatened, Perry entertained everyone from my ancient aunts and uncles to business colleagues of my dad's. In fact, he might have snagged an agent."

"Is that right?" Will sneered before mumbling, "I guess it will soften the blow."

I frowned. "What blow?"

"Never mind." Will stood up again.

"Need to use the bathroom again already?" I joked, even though I was more exasperated than humored at this point. The guilt was chewing on my insides, and I desperately needed to 'fess up and accept Will's reaction, whatever it would be.

"Just restless. I was sitting in a car all afternoon." He stretched his arms over his head and then glanced behind him as if expecting someone.

I raised myself from the couch and placed a hand on his shoulder. "Is something wrong?" I wasn't paranoid—Will was acting strange.

"Not at all." He sat back down. "What else did Perry the Great accomplish this weekend? Did he get stuck in an elevator with Steven Spielberg? Or Al Roker?"

My head reared back. "Considering neither of those people were there and my parents don't have an elevator, the answer is no. You're being weird." When Will looked at me with regret in his eyes, my heart hammered against my chest. If I didn't have so much confidence in Will's sense of values, I'd think he had his own confession to make. Desperate for comfort, I took a big gulp of wine.

Will scratched his head. "Maybe I am, but I just spent three nights pretending to be someone else's boyfriend and lying to a lot of people. Under the circumstances, I think I'm handling it well. Evidently, not as well as you."

"I wouldn't say I'm handling it well either." My hands trembled. I put down my glass before it crashed onto the floor.

He furrowed his brow. "You're not?"

"There's something I need to tell you." I swallowed back the pain in the back of my throat. "It's about Perry and me."

He frowned. "What about you?"

I couldn't face him when I made my confession so I closed my eyes. I wished I could cover his eyes so he couldn't see me either. "We hated each other from day one and fought like opposing counsel in an intense trial the entire time. And then..." I felt like I was perched to jump out of an airplane, paralyzed to hurl myself over the edge.

"Then *what*, Sidney?"

"When I'd say 'yes,' he'd say 'no.' If I went left, he'd go right. If I claimed the sky was blue, he'd insist it was purple. He knew how to rattle my cage, and I walked right into it. To make matters worse, my parents loved him and he ate it up. It came to a head, we had a bitter confrontation, and before I knew it, we were kissing." I opened my eyes and faced Will, who was staring at me in shock. "But it was inspired by hate, not attraction. I'm so sorry, Will. It meant nothing and I swear to God, we didn't have sex." I cringed in anticipation of his reaction.

Will blinked at me. "You cheated on me with Perry?" He stood up and paced the room.

I rose too. "It was only a kiss. I could have kept it a secret, but I didn't want to lie to you. I don't want it to be the end for us, and I hope coming clean shows you I'm committed to giving us a go. We're so good together."

He shook his head. "I don't know what to say to this."

"Can you forgive me?" I held my breath and stared at the twitching vein in his neck.

He turned his back on me, not saying anything.

I searched my mind for words, but my brain was incapable of presenting a further defense. I swallowed back the thickness in my throat and hunched my shoulders in defeat.

After what felt like forever squared, he sat back down. The twitch was gone. He patted the spot next to him. "Sit."

It was a positive sign that he didn't storm out of my

apartment, slamming the door behind him, and I joined him on the couch with cautious hope.

He took a sip of wine and placed it back on the coffee table. "I thought the swap was a bad idea from minute one. We were playing with fire, but I agreed because it was so important to you and I wanted to make you happy."

"You were great, Will. I can't begin to—"

"Let me finish, Sid," he said in a soft voice.

I nodded and placed my fingers over my racing pulse, willing it to slow down.

Will absently tapped his foot against the surface of the wood floor. "Over the last few days, I've thought about it from your perspective and the conclusion I've reached is if you truly cared about me, you wouldn't have so easily and eagerly put me in the position you did."

My heart jumped into my throat. "I thought I was doing it for us. My parents..." I searched for my next words in the high ceiling. "We were having so much fun, and I was afraid introducing you to them would be the beginning of the end." I contemplated going into further detail, but the theory that made so much sense mere weeks before suddenly seemed dumb as dirt.

Will sighed. "I have no idea what you're talking about, but it honestly doesn't matter. If you were truly invested in our relationship, you wouldn't let your parents get in our way. But you did, and on top of it, you crossed the line with Perry."

Placing my hand on his thigh, I said, "You have my sincere remorse. I can admit when I'm wrong, even though I hate it." I released a nervous laugh. "I want to make it up to you—introduce you to my parents even." I licked my dry lips. "Unless the kiss is a deal breaker."

He smiled at the floor as if he shared a secret with the hardwood tiles. "It's interesting that Robyn's folks disliked Perry, but your mom and dad took to him so intensely. Maybe our parents know something we don't about who's right for us." He scraped a hand through his hair and looked back up at me. "If so, I don't think your parents would have liked me, Sid." With a pained expression, he continued, "Because kiss or no kiss, I already had my doubts as to whether we belonged together. The truth is, I think we can both do better."

Robyn

After dropping off the rental car, I cabbed it home and changed out of my heavy sweater and jeans into a t-shirt and my coziest pair of pajama pants—navy blue and emblazoned with images of different breeds of dogs from poodles, pugs, beagles, and more. I allowed myself a brief stint of self-pity, choosing to spend it with a mug of hot chocolate piled high with mini marshmallows and staring out the window and down at the Hudson River and New Jersey on the other side of the water. I'd save the bottle of wine for when Anne Marie got home from her own holiday later that afternoon.

My shared living space with Anne Marie on Manhattan's Upper West Side might not have been exceptional in terms of square footage, but the view from our apartment on the twenty-seventh floor made up for it. The sky at sunset was streaked in various shades of blue, pink, orange, and yellow. It was breathtaking, and I would have been happy to spend the entirety of the evening not moving if my mind didn't keep dreaming up images of Will reflected along the surface of the water. I half expected to see his shadow hovering over me, hear the sound of his laughter, or feel the flutter of my heart from his nearness, but I didn't. There was no reason to think I ever would again. It was like a repeat of the summer before my senior year of high school—watching Will move out of his parents' house for college and wondering when, if ever, I'd see him again. But unlike in high school, when the most attention Will gave me was a smile in passing in the hallways or a few words of conversation at a social event, this time, we'd been inseparable for almost a hundred hours. We'd slept together. Sure, our PG-rated slumber party was more Disney Channel than

Skinamax, but it didn't make the proximity of our bodies clad in only thin shorts and t-shirts any less real. And the accidental spooning session was etched in my memory.

I knew I was being stupid moping over a guy who wasn't mine to begin with. Will and I weren't even compatible. I wasn't a sharp, sexy redhead, and he wore a suit to work on a regular basis. Once my pity party came to an end, I'd leave the memories of my brief stint as Will Brady's "girlfriend" behind and life would resume as normal. I'd survived my unrequited crush in high school and gone on to date many guys—nice, good-looking, fun, and talented guys. And even though my time with Perry was coming to an end, I knew it wouldn't be long before I found myself interested in someone else—someone equally enamored with me and hopefully in touch with his creative side. No more lawyers. The only way I'd date a lawyer was if he were...Will. I sighed dejectedly and glanced at my watch. Perry would be here any minute.

Moments later, there was a gentle rap at my door. "It's me. I ran into Anne Marie in the lobby," Perry called out from the hallway.

"Come in," I said, lifting myself to a standing position and placing my empty mug on the dresser. I resisted the urge to bite my nails.

Upon entering my room, Perry pulled me into a hug. "There's my girl."

I inhaled the faint scent of citrus from his Acqua Di Gio cologne and frowned into his chest. I wished he wasn't so happy to see me. It made what I had to do so much harder. But I had to rip off the bandage. Perry was better off without me at this point.

"Welcome home," he mumbled into the top of my head.

"Back at you," I said. When we separated, I was surprised by the genuine smile that appeared on my face. We'd had a good run, and I had no regrets.

"It's good to be back in the city where not everyone is a rich white person."

I laughed. "I take it Scarsdale isn't much of a melting pot?"

He shook his head and sat on the edge of my bed. "How was the city of Brotherly Love?"

"Philadelphia was fine." I dropped my gaze to the floor before reluctantly meeting his eyes and letting out a deep exhalation. "We need to talk, Perry."

His face fell. "You know already?"

I jutted my head back. "Know what?"

"About me and Sidney."

"What about you and Sidney?" My heart beat rapidly in anticipation of his next words.

"You don't know?" He sat on the edge of my bed. "Forget it then."

"Seriously? What happened between you and Sidney?" I pulled him up to standing position.

Perry pinched the bridge of his nose and closed his eyes. When he opened them, he said, "Promise me you won't be mad."

I groaned. "Just say it." Did they fall in love? Wouldn't that be ironic?

"We kissed."

My mouth fell open. "You...kissed?" I repeated his words back at him, not sure how I felt about his confession.

Perry raised his hand. "Before you say anything, you need to know that Sidney started it. She threw herself at me. I...I didn't see it coming."

I narrowed my eyes. "So Sidney kissed you and you pushed her away." I had my doubts he'd be so guilt-ridden if that were the case.

He ran a hand through his hair. "In the spirit of true disclosure, not exactly. Not right away at least. I kissed her back. You know how weak Schuester is." He looked at me pleadingly.

My eyes bugged out. "You slept with her?"

Shaking his head frantically, Perry shouted, "No! No. No. No. We didn't have sex." He let out a deep breath. "But I didn't push her away, and we might have if someone on the catering staff hadn't walked in on us. I'm sorry, Robyn. Please don't hate me."

What happened next came as a surprise to both of us. My belly quivered and my throat tickled, and I laughed. I closed my mouth to get my bearings, but another giggle forced my lips open.

Perry's eyes bugged out and he stood up. "You're losing it, aren't you? Everyone has their breaking point, even you. You're hysterical and it's all my fault." He paced the length of the foot of my bed, muttering to himself.

With one hand on my mouth to stifle the laughter, I reached out to touch Perry with the other. "It's okay." I took a deep breath in and out to compose myself. I should have been angry as hell, but it was so damn funny. It wouldn't be humorous at all if my feelings for Perry were where they should have been after almost a year together.

Perry stopped moving and studied me. "You sure?"

I nodded. All that time I spent drowning in guilt for crushing on Will when Perry almost had sex with Sidney. Was *any* man immune to her charms? "I don't hate you, Perry. And at least I don't have to feel so wretched about breaking up with you now."

He grinned. "Yeah...Wait. Why are you breaking up with me?"

"Really, Perry? You're asking me that now?" I smirked.

Perry shrugged sheepishly. "Fair enough. But you were dumping me before you even knew about Sidney and me. Why?"

I sighed. "Because, honestly, I think I'm ready for a more serious relationship and we're not going anywhere. Am I right?"

He nodded. "Probably. But we had fun, didn't we?"

"We did," I said with a gentle smile.

"You didn't..." Perry made a humping gesture. "With Will, did you?"

"We didn't even kiss," I said with a smirk.

Combing his fingers through his hair, he asked, "So why now? Did your parents pressure you?"

"No. They think I'm dating Will." I grimaced as I remembered I'd need to 'fess up pretty soon, and considering my mother was as enamored with Will as I was, it wouldn't be fun.

"Gotcha. Well, I should probably go then. Unless you want to have sex one last time." He cocked an eyebrow.

Chuckling, I said, "It's a tempting offer, Perry, but one I must decline."

"I understand. I really am sorry about...well, you know."

"I know."

"Take care of yourself, and may your next boyfriend be all you've ever wanted."

I blinked back a tear. The Perry who stood before me was a much more sensitive version than the one I was used to.

"Of course, good luck finding one as sexy and talented as me."

Or maybe not.

Anne Marie gaped at me from her side of the sofa. "Yowza. Makes my Christmas of attending midnight Mass, eating obscene amounts of food, and exchanging presents seem very *bourgeoise*."

Chuckling, I said, "It was actually a pretty typical holiday. Well, aside from pretending Will was my boyfriend and coming home to find out the guy I was *really* dating had a sizzling suck-face session with the girl he was pretending to be in a relationship with."

Anne Marie leaned forward to top off my glass of wine. "Yeah, aside from all of that."

I let my head drop back toward the ceiling. "Who am I kidding? It was a disaster."

"How could Sidney do that to you? To me? I'm her secretary, and I'd never have introduced you to her if I'd known she'd stab her claws into your man."

"I should be mad. But I don't care enough." I frowned. "Isn't that sad?"

"What's sad is that you slept in the same bed with your lifelong crush for three nights and nothing happened, while my slutty boss was throwing herself at your boyfriend." She cocked her head at me. "By the way, I can't believe you didn't tell me you had feelings for Will."

"He's your boss's boyfriend. I didn't want to put you in the middle. And besides, I didn't think I'd still like him after nine years."

"But you did."

I gulped my wine. "I did."

"Does he like you?"

I brought my glass to my mouth and let my lips linger on the edge for a moment before taking a sip. "James thought so. Will had nothing pleasant to say about Perry, and James said it was because he was jealous that Perry was my guy. I wanted it to be true, and that's when I knew I had to end things with Perry no matter what." I thought back to dancing with Will and how right it felt to be in his arms. He'd called me sexy. But I didn't miss the regret in his eyes immediately after he said it or the way he hoofed it to the porch to get away from me later. He was holding his phone when I followed him outside. He probably missed Sidney and wanted to hear her voice. "I think Will might have gotten caught up in the moment and the performance of it all, but he has no intention of breaking up with Sidney."

Anne Marie harrumphed. "Wait until he finds out what she did."

"I'm not going to tell him."

"You're a much better person than me."

Shrugging, I said, "It's not my place or my business." My phone rang and I picked it up, gasping when I saw who was calling.

Will.

Chapter 16

Sidney

After Will left my apartment, I stretched across the length of my couch and remained there for an hour. With effort, I lifted myself to a seated position, feeling as if my body was weighted down with concrete cinder blocks. I removed my wine glass from the table and stared into the bottom, tempted to swallow the backwash. Instead, I returned it to the silver Hammertone coaster with a loud sigh. Despite putting my best effort into my expression of remorse, I was prepared for it to not be good enough. But I hadn't expected Will to end things between us for any other reason than my infidelity. It had never even occurred to me that simply asking Will to play along with the swap was akin to treating him like shit and making it clear his feelings didn't count nearly as much as my own. Once I decided the boyfriend swap was more than just a drunken suggestion by Anne Marie, but the perfect antidote for mine and Robyn's holiday dilemma, no one else mattered. When had I become so focused on winning that I'd do anything to get my way? Success at all costs was the name of the game, at least the one I'd been playing for most of my life.

I might have been oblivious to how my dysfunctional personality affected my romantic life all these years—or just too busy winning to notice—but based on their outburst at Christmas dinner, my family knew something I didn't. I wondered who else was in the know. Lisa? She'd never said as much to me, but considering how open I was to unsolicited advice—not at all—it didn't mean anything. There was only one way to find out. I removed my phone from where it had been charging in my kitchen, headed to my bedroom, and called her.

After telling Lisa about my indiscretion with Perry and my subsequent breakup with Will, I said, "And that's what's happening with me. What's shaking in your neck of the woods?" The resulting silence on the other end of the phone unnerved me. "You there, Li?"

After another beat, Lisa said, "Yeah, I'm here. I'm trying to come up with an appropriate response."

"You're my best friend. Just say the first thing that comes to mind—appropriate or not."

Lisa clucked her tongue. "Here goes nothing then. The boyfriend swap was not one of your wisest schemes—something I would have told you if you'd asked my opinion *before* going through with it—but it's not as if you would have listened to me anyway. When Sidney Bellows devises what *she* considers a brilliant plan, God help any naysayers. In short, nice going, friend. Hashtag fail."

I whistled through my teeth. "Wow. Don't sugarcoat your feelings or anything."

Lisa snorted. "You told me to say the first thing that came to mind." In a softer voice, she asked, "How are you doing with the breakup? Are you going to call Will?"

I squeezed the smiley face stress ball I kept by my bed. "There's no point. I really messed things up, and losing him is the price I have to pay. Maybe I'll feel differently when it all sinks in, but I don't think Will was the one anyway. If such a concept even exists outside of Hallmark movies. Speaking of which, how was Meat Guy?" After receiving Lisa's virtual spanking, I needed a break from my own drama.

"Meat Guy, also known as Evan, was actually kind of cool."

My eyes opened wide. "You mean Frank got it right for once?"

"It's too soon to say we'll be starring in our own Hallmark

movie, but a one-on-one date is not out of the question."

"He didn't smell like roast beef?" I put the phone on speaker so I could simultaneously unpack my suitcase.

Lisa laughed. "If he did, it was in a good way."

"Cute?"

"Very." I could hear her smiling as she said this.

"Go Frank. Keep me posted."

"Will do."

"Is Jake married?" I held my breath. Will definitely wasn't the one if instead of sobbing into a gallon of Häagen-Dazs over his dumping me, I was sweating another ex-boyfriend's marital status.

"Jake who?" Lisa asked before answering her own question a second later. "Jake Harrington?"

"Yes, Jake *Harrington*. What other Jake is there?" The simple question took more effort to ask than I'd ever admit. My heart was beating as quickly as if I'd just sprinted to the finish line in a 5K run. "I saw a picture of him with kids and was wondering if they were his." *No big deal.*

"Yes. He got married a couple of years ago."

My stomach dropped. "So those boys in the picture...are his?" I kicked the suitcase against the wall and sat on the edge of my bed. I'd do it tomorrow.

"They had twins." Lisa was quiet for a moment. "You're not upset about it, are you? I never told you because I didn't think you'd care."

I closed my eyes and contemplated my answer. What would be the big deal in admitting I might have made a mistake? Lisa, of all people, wouldn't judge me. Before I could change my mind, I blurted out, "I've been thinking about him a lot lately and wondering if I blew it."

"How do you think you blew it?"

"My ambition. In the battle between my grades and love life, my grades won every time. Maybe I was misguided." I pinched my lips together.

"For one thing, there's nothing wrong with wanting to make

the most of a very expensive Ivy League education. Your dad had some high expectations of you joining the family practice. And let's not forget Jake was your *college* boyfriend. College relationships rarely make it to the altar."

It would have been so easy to accept Lisa's answer and let go of any responsibility I held for the failure of my relationship with Jake, but something was nagging at me. The floodgates had opened and I couldn't let it go. "How do you explain the rest of my relationships not going anywhere?"

"I can't."

"My family thinks my drive to succeed impedes my ability to fall in love. Do you agree?" I held my breath. Maybe she'd say no. My relationship with Will ended prematurely, but at least it hadn't been contentious while it lasted.

"Honest answer?"

Her need to ask my permission to voice her true opinion wasn't a good sign. "Obviously."

"I don't think you blew it with Jake, but—"

"But?"

"But until now, I had no idea you even cared about finding someone special. Whenever you talk about a guy you're dating, you'll tell me how cute he is or how great he is in bed, but nothing else. You even kept Will at arm's length by refusing to introduce him to your parents. Kind of extreme. I just assumed you weren't looking for anything deep. Are you?"

"Yes. No? I think so." I scratched my head in frustration. "I don't know."

Lisa laughed. "How decisive of you."

I sighed. "I have no idea what I want, Li. But I really need to figure it out."

"What's your plan?"

"I don't have one. Any suggestions?" Not having a plan of attack was foreign territory for me, and I didn't like it.

"Maybe it's time you made some changes."

"Brilliant idea, Captain Obvious. But how?" My left leg

bounced uncontrollably.

"I don't know, but if anyone can figure it out, it's you. You have everything you need at your disposal—you're wickedly intelligent and your parents have more money than many small countries."

"I'm not sure cash will solve this problem." I leaned back against my headboard and closed my eyes. "I wish I had time to sort it all out, but beginning Monday, it's back to the grind. Billable hours trump self-reflection at Bellows and..." I stopped speaking and opened my eyes.

"You still there, Sid?"

"I'm here. More importantly, I'm a genius." I vaulted out of bed and hoofed it to where I'd left my laptop on my coffee table.

Lisa snorted. "And she's back."

"I have to go, but I promise to share this plan with you *before* I implement it, okay?"

"I'll believe it when I see it, but fine. Call me tomorrow."

"Will do. Keep me posted on Evan the cute Meat Guy. And Lisa?"

"Yeah?"

"Thank you."

Robyn

"Hello?" I recoiled as the word came out like a question instead of a greeting, but I wasn't expecting to hear from Will again so soon, if ever.

"Hey, Snow. It's Will."

As if someone else would call me Snow. "Miss me already?" I asked before gnawing on a fingernail.

Will chuckled. "The absence of a choir performing twenty-four-seven in my apartment is disconcerting."

I smiled. "It wasn't twenty-four-seven. We did sleep, remember?" I glanced at Anne Marie, who didn't try to hide her desire to listen in.

"You've got me there."

I waited for him to get to the reason for his call, but when he didn't say anything, I took the initiative. "What's up?"

"I just left Sidney's place."

"Oh?" Since I didn't know whether Sidney had confessed to getting frisky with Perry, how else was I supposed to respond? I couldn't think of another reason he'd call to tell me he'd been to his girlfriend's apartment, but I had to be careful. I wasn't lying when I told Anne Marie I wouldn't be the one to break the news to Will.

"Have you seen Perry yet?"

I stood up from the couch and twirled a strand of hair around my finger. "Yes. He left a little while ago."

"Are you all right?"

"I'm fine. Why wouldn't I be?" Now I was pretty sure he knew and wondered if, like me, he was afraid to be the bearer of bad news. "Did Sidney tell you something?" One of us had to say something or we'd be here all night.

"You mean about her and your boyfriend?"

"My *ex*-boyfriend."

"You did it. Good for you."

I rolled my eyes. "Yes, you've made your feelings about my relationship with Perry quite clear, Will." With an apologetic glance at Anne Marie, who was still paying keen attention to my side of the conversation, I took the phone to my bedroom and closed the door.

"Like I said, he's not good enough for you, and I think he proved it this week."

"Sidney isn't exactly innocent either." I wasn't trying to defend Perry, but I resented Will placing all the responsibility on Perry.

In a quiet voice, Will said, "I know she's not. I broke up with her too."

"I'm sorry." And I was. I never wanted things to go down this way.

"Don't be. I'm not."

Sitting on the edge of my bed, I said, "Well, that's good then." An awkward silence ensued until I said, "Was there another reason for your call?" I took a sip of my wine.

"I was thinking we should go out for karaoke."

Like a Pavlovian response, my heart instantly beat in double time. "Just the two of us?"

"Yes. We could have a country theme—cheating exes." Will laughed.

As much as I wanted to see Will again, my stomach dropped in dread of spending all night talking about Sidney. "Sorry, but I have zero desire to commiserate over the sordid behavior of our former partners."

"You're right. Who needs them? Forget I mentioned it. We have plenty of other things to talk about."

"You really want to go out?" The room suddenly got very hot. I cracked open a window, but when the sounds from the street twenty-seven floors below felt like they were coming from right outside my door, I closed it again.

"Why not? Let's go on a real date and show them how it's done."

I'd often fantasized about Will asking me out and how I'd respond. In my daydreams, I always played it cool on the outside even as I sweated thunderstorms on the inside. Sometimes I imagined him coming backstage after a concert to tell me how amazing I was or even running up to the stage with flowers. Other times, he followed me into the bathroom after our first kiss, shut the door behind us, and ripped my clothes off. And in other versions of my daydream, he climbed into my bedroom window and we fooled around under my parents' roof. There were more scenarios than a choose-your-own-adventure book, but they had one thing in common. I *never* dreamed he'd call me on the phone an hour after breaking things off with someone else because she cheated on him. He really had no clue. "Is this a joke to you?" I looked out my window, remembering when I had a view of the Bradys' house a few doors down.

Will paused before responding. "Of course not. I'm completely serious."

In all my fantasies, I was the happiest girl in the world. I never would have guessed I'd be angry when it really happened. "Perry and Sidney messed around. Let's show them by doing it too?"

"That's not what this is, Snow," Will said in quiet voice.

"Are you sure, Will? Because it feels more like tit for tat than a genuine desire to go out with me."

"I like you, Robyn. It has nothing to do with Sidney."

"If that's true, then how come you never mentioned dating me before now? You had plenty of opportunities this week."

Will sighed. "You were taken, and I don't go after other guys' girlfriends."

"I told you I was breaking up with Perry. You never once mentioned ending things with Sidney."

"I was conflicted, Snow. I was attracted to you, but I still had feelings for her."

I let his words sink in. I was pretty sure Will believed what he was saying, and I wanted to believe him too. There were moments we spent together when I felt something between us and knew in my gut it wasn't one-sided. But the timing of his confession was questionable—mere hours after learning of Sidney's deceit. Less than twenty-four hours earlier, Will was ready to resume things with Sidney and never see me again. How could I trust what he was saying? I didn't want to be his consolation prize.

"You still there?"

I nodded as if he could see me and removed my finger from my mouth. "You need to know my mom wasn't exaggerating about the extent of my crush on you when we were younger. If she didn't believe our farce, she never would have purposely embarrassed me by announcing it at the dinner table. But I knew we weren't really together, and let me tell you, I was mortified." Unveiling the magnitude of my feelings was the opposite of playing it cool, but I didn't care. He needed to know.

"Like I said, you have nothing to be embarrassed of. It was a high school crush."

My eyes welled up. "It was bad, Will. I barely knew you, but I wanted you so much. I thought about you almost constantly. Going to school was fun, not only because I was Snow White and naturally cheery, but because there was a chance I'd see you. On weekends, no matter where I went, I kept my eye out for you, hoping you'd show up. Even if you were with Adrienne, I was happy because I got to look at you. My feelings were silly and based on nothing but teenage hormones, but it didn't matter because they consumed me. My ability to keep it together the night we kissed was nothing short of miraculous because I was dying inside. *Dying*. And when you left for college, I cried like my dog died. But I got over it. With you out of the way, I was able to give other boys a chance. I moved on. And then I met Hurricane Sidney and she came up with the asinine plan to trade boyfriends for the holiday. She mentioned her boyfriend's name was Will, but it never occurred to me it was you. But it was."

"Snow—"

"Wait. Let me finish. I promise I'll get to my point soon."

"Go on," he whispered.

"By the time I found out it was you, it was too late. I couldn't suddenly renege on my agreement to go through with it, and besides, high school was a long time ago. I'm not the same innocent girl I was then. I'm an experienced woman. I've had many boyfriends and plenty of sex." I cleared my throat as my cheeks turned pink. "I figured I could handle a few days with Will Brady. Maybe I'd find I wasn't the slightest bit attracted to him and laugh about my silly high school infatuation. Right?"

"Um—"

"Wrong. For one thing, you're still sexy as all get out. And funny. And, well, you really are an appallingly bad singer, but you're a good sport. And a fabulous dancer. And I like being with you, and my family adores you. We exchanged more words in four days then we did in four years and I like you, Will. I really like you. Not the idea of you as the older popular boy in the neighborhood, but the real grown-up tone deaf Will Brady."

"I like you too—"

"Which is why I can't go on a date with you."

"You can't...I don't understand. If you like me so much, why wouldn't you want to go on a date with me? I'd think you'd be happy I finally shared your feelings. Better late than never, right?"

I was sick to my stomach and certain it had nothing to do with drinking wine only an hour after eating almost an entire bag of mini marshmallows. The knowledge that Will Brady professed to like me in real life instead of my imagination and I was turning him down was mind boggling even to me. I was the one making it happen. It felt wrong, but not as wrong as saying yes. "That's the thing. I don't believe you like me, Will. I want to believe it. I really do. But I think it's a knee-jerk reaction to breaking up with Sidney on the heels of our four days together. It would be convenient, wouldn't it? If we hit it off. But it's not something you've thought through. It can't be, considering you just broke up with Sidney a hot minute ago. If you were anyone else, I'd say, 'Sure, let's go on a date. If we hit it off, great. If not, no biggie.' But I can't do that with you, Will. Dating you was my teenage fantasy, but if I'm going to take my fantasy into the real world, it has to be for the right reasons or else it's better off remaining in my dreams." I waited for Will to respond, but there was silence on the other end of the phone.

Finally, he spoke. "I understand, Robyn."

"You do?" My lips quivered, and I fought not to tell him I changed my mind even though part of me really wanted to.

"Yes. It makes perfect sense you would think that."

"Good." I gulped.

"You're pretty amazing, Robyn. I'll talk to you soon." He hung up before I could respond, and I remained frozen to the spot, staring at my phone.

My hands were still shaking ten minutes later.

Chapter 17

Sidney

The first day back after a vacation, I liked to get to work early to go through emails and get myself in work mode before everyone else arrived. The office was usually a ghost town the week between Christmas and New Year's, but even when our clients were sipping exotic drinks with tiny umbrellas while basking in the sun in St. Barts, they still managed to have legal issues they needed us to handle at a moment's notice. I finished the Venti coffee I'd picked up at Starbucks, and desperately in need of more caffeine, I resorted to the firm's free stash. When I entered the pantry, I was surprised to see Anne Marie. She was stirring a container of Quaker instant oatmeal.

"Miss this place, did you?" I asked.

Appearing startled, Anne Marie looked up. "Did you say something?"

I waved a hand at her and smiled. "I was teasing you for being here so early. How was your holiday?"

Anne Marie's face flushed and she pursed her lips. "It was nice," she said before turning back to her breakfast without another word.

I opened my mouth to press for more details but shut it as it hit me why she was being so cold. She knew. I made my coffee in silence and she was gone by the time I finished. I walked past her cubicle on the way back to my office, tempted to apologize or at least explain my side of the story. But no matter who told the tale, I was still the backstabbing bitch who climbed on her roommate's boyfriend. Rather than express my regrets or offer an explanation, I stepped into my office and closed the door behind me. I was more determined than ever to put my plan into action.

Not a minute later, there was a knock on my door. "Come in." I grimaced when Michael Goldberg entered, wearing a tacky flamingo-printed tie and a smug look on his face. "Merry Christmas, JB."

"*Feliz Navidad*, Mike. What can I do for you?" I flipped through my desk calendar for my appointments for the week. Anne Marie added all my meetings to the Outlook calendar, but I still liked to use my old-school printed calendar for backup.

Michael sat in my guest chair uninvited and reclined with his arms clasped behind his head. "No time to chat?"

I rolled my eyes. "When have you ever come in here to chat?"

"Maybe it's a New Year's resolution."

"It's only December twenty-eighth. Seriously, Mike, cut the bullshit."

Mike laughed. "I'm sure Stan will send a firm-wide email soon, but I wanted you to be among the first to know. I managed to solidify the Sparks account last week. B&B will be the lead firm for all film deals moving forward."

My eyes opened wide for half a second in surprise. The Sparks account was huge. Stan had been trying to segue occasional licensing work to a more permanent footing with the company for years. "Way to go, Mike." I was genuinely pleased for the firm but wished it had been the result of someone else's effort. Mike was such a douchebag.

"There's more."

"Oh?"

"Stan and Harvey were so impressed, they spoke to the management committee and have decided to promote me to partner."

I leaned forward. "The partners for this year were chosen already."

Mike shrugged nonchalantly. "They made an exception for me."

"Terrific. Congrats. I'm so pleased for you."

"That's kind of you to say. Assuming you genuinely feel that way." He looked me dead in the eye, practically begging me to demonstrate how I really felt.

But I was too good to walk into his trap. "Of course I do. We're colleagues."

He nodded. "It's refreshing to know Bellows & Burke bases its decisions on performance as well as...other things." He looked pointedly at the gold nameplate on my desk when he said the last bit, clearly alluding to my family connection to the firm, and stood up. He walked to my door and turned around to face me. "And Sid?"

"Yes?"

"Technically, we're no longer colleagues. I'm one of your bosses now."

After he left, I tried to go through the rest of my emails and sort high priority from low, but it was useless. I'd planned to wait until after lunch, but I wasn't going to be able to focus on work until I spoke to my father.

I knocked on his office door, and when he looked up from his computer, said, "You have a minute?"

"Sit." He motioned to my designated visitors' chair. He had two, but I always sat on the one to the left when facing him.

I sat down with my back straight.

"You doing all right with the whole Perry situation?"

Confused, I echoed, "The whole Perry situation?" And then I remembered my family was under the misconception I was recovering from a broken heart. I had just ended a relationship, but it was with Will, and my heart was more bruised than broken. "I'll live," I said, waving my hand. "I was hoping to talk to you about something else. Is Mom around? This concerns her too."

My dad's lips pressed together and he furrowed his brow. "What's this about?"

"Just call Mom."

My dad removed the phone from the receiver, put it on speaker, and dialed my mom's number. When she answered, he said, "Barb, I've got Sid with me. She has something to tell us both."

My mom squealed. "You've reconciled with Perry and you're engaged."

While I rolled my eyes at my dad, we could hear my mom clapping through the phone. "I knew the breakup wouldn't last. He's the perfect match for you."

"Mom."

"Please don't tell me you want a destination wedding. You're our only offspring and we deserve to plan a proper celebration."

"Mom." I said it louder his time. "I'm not marrying Perry. We're not back together." I contemplated telling them the truth then and there, but I wanted to get to the point of my call.

"Oh," my mom said, the disappointment evident in her voice. "What did you want to tell us?"

I told them.

"Absolutely not," my father insisted. "You're not taking a gap year. You're not eighteen years old, or even twenty-two, for crying out loud."

I sighed. "I just need a break, Dad. Maybe it will be a few weeks, maybe a month, maybe a year, but I need it and I'm doing it."

"What is this about, Sidney?" my mom asked in a much calmer voice than my dad.

"I'm tired of going, going, going. Something's gotta give."

"*You're* tired? Try being in your late fifties and running your own law firm and then we can talk." Under his breath, my dad muttered, "She's tired."

"You all said it yourselves at Christmas. I'm so focused on the bottom line and winning that the rest of my life is suffering. I need to find balance, but I can't without giving myself time and space to decide what really makes me happy. I think law and beating our adversaries bring me pleasure, but it's all I know."

"Is this about Goldberg? Because—"

The next words out of my father's mouth didn't matter. "It's not. I made this decision over the weekend, before I knew about Michael."

"What will you do?" my mom asked.

"Barb. Don't humor her." My dad glared at the phone as if my mother could see him.

Ignoring him, I said, "I want to go to Barbados for an extended vacation. It could be a few weeks or it could be three months, but I'll purchase a return ticket to keep immigration off my back. I'm not even asking you to pay."

"Good. Because the answer would be a resounding no," my dad barked. "As if I'd pay for my daughter to abandon her responsibilities."

I groaned. "Dad. I won't leave for another two weeks or so. I'll make sure all my cases are in order first. I've always done the right thing in the past and think I've built up a lot of goodwill to demonstrate I'm not a screw-up and would never put the firm in jeopardy. I'm not planning to start now. I genuinely need to go and find myself, as corny as it sounds."

"It sounds very corny," my dad mumbled.

"Is this about losing Perry?" my mom asked.

"No! This has nothing to do with Perry." I pulled on my hair. "He wasn't even my boyfriend. We made it up. You happy now?" I sat up sharply, my fingers curled tightly around the rim of the chair.

My parents gasped in harmony before going silent.

I'd done the impossible—I'd rendered Harvey and Barbara Bellows speechless. Dropping my shoulders, I said, "I'm sorry. I didn't mean to yell. It's not about Perry. It's about me. But, yes, I was so desperate for something of my own that I chose to bring home a flaky actor as my boyfriend thinking he wouldn't register on the Bellows & Burke radar scale. In the process, I hurt my real boyfriend, and he decided he didn't want to be with me anymore. I was wrong about everything, and I'm sorry I lied to you." I was remorseful about so many things and desperately needed this recess.

"I thought Perry really liked us," my mom said, her tone heavyhearted. "But it was all an act."

In hindsight, the surprising shine my mom took to Perry was endearing. "His fondness for you guys wasn't for show, just his affection for me. But that's not the point."

"I'm still waiting for you to get to it," my dad said. At least he didn't seem too shook up over my trickery.

"I've spent all my adult life chasing one goal after another. First it was the LSAT so I could follow in Dad's footsteps by getting accepted to Columbia Law. Then it was Law Review, followed by the Bar exam, working more hours than any summer associate ever." I gawked at my dad. "What summer associate bills three hundred hours a month? They're usually drinking or feasting on caviar, but not JB here. And now it's a constant battle to prove I earned this job. I'm only as good as my last month's billables. Just five minutes ago, your newest partner rubbed it in my face that the firm rewards hard work and performance over nepotism. As if I'm so entitled to think you'd make me partner because you're my dad." I let out a deep, frustrated exhale. "I'm so used to battling it out in here that I don't know how to live out there without having my guard up or being uber aggressive. I must win all the time, from arguments, to silly competitions, even to hailing taxis. If you make me stay, I'm going to resent you and my job, and guess who will suffer the most besides me?"

My dad blinked at me. "Who?"

"The firm and its clients. On the flip side, if I take this time, I might just come back a new person."

"What if you're so new you don't want to be a lawyer anymore?" my dad asked.

Seeing the fear and vulnerability in his eyes—something he didn't display very often—threatened to bruise my heart more than any breakup ever had. He deserved my honesty. "If that happens, you won't have to pay my salary anymore." My dad opened his mouth to respond, but I cut him off. "But I'll always be your daughter, and I'll always make you proud. It's in my blood."

My dad stared at me for a moment. Finally, he gave a reluctant smile and nodded. "What do you say, Barb?"

"When Cherry Bomb's mind is set, there's no stopping her," my mom said. "I think she gets it from her father."

Robyn

"It says here Fender Music Foundation donates instruments to school music programs by selecting in-need, ongoing, and sustainable schools," Lance said, pointing to his computer screen. We'd met at a local coffee shop to commiserate and brainstorm possible solutions in the event the rumors were less back-fence talk and more fact.

"Except we don't know if we even need new instruments. If we don't, this grant would be meaningless. Maybe it's our salaries the school won't be able to afford. If so, no amount of free instruments will make a difference," I said.

Lance shrugged his broad shoulders. "We have plenty of instruments and they're in decent shape. The string section could be updated, but that's about it. Horns and woodwind are new." Lance took a sip of his coffee. "What should we do?"

I frowned. "I'm not sure it makes sense to do anything until we confirm the rumor. Our school might not even qualify as a school in need." It was a public school with kids from mostly middle-income families.

Lance scratched his goatee of black hair. "I asked around, and apparently affected teachers aren't given much notice in circumstances like this. We might not find out until the end of the school year when we're supposed to be given our assignments for fall semester."

I knew where he was going with this. "We might not even be told until after the summer is over."

"When it's too late," we muttered at the same time.

"Without enough notice, we'll never have enough time to apply for grants," Lance said, his brown eyes wide with fear. With two children under the age of five and a stay-at-home wife, I knew Lance couldn't afford to lose his job or even a pay cut from reduced classes.

"What should do we do?" Lance asked again, this time with a pleading look.

I was more worried about the kids than myself only because I didn't have anyone depending on me, and I knew my folks would help me out with money until I got a new job. I felt it my responsibility to play cheerleader and calm Lance down as best I could. "Until we know what we're dealing with, we can't do anything. I'll talk to Principal Hogan."

"You will?"

I nodded. I didn't want to, but there was no other option.

Lance let out a sigh of relief and beamed at me. "You're so great, Robyn. Like a Disney princess."

Or like Snow White. Lance was beaming at me, but all I saw was Will's face.

My phone rang as I stood before my closet deciding what to wear on the first day back at school. The second semester always felt like a new beginning, and even though I wasn't a student anymore, I got the jitters. My outfit needed to be uplifting. It was James on the phone. I'd been both dying to talk to him and dreading it. I knew the topic of Will would come up immediately, and it was a subject I'd been unsuccessfully trying to distract myself from for the last week. Even dancing the year away with Anne Marie and some of our other friends on New Year's Eve wasn't a good enough distraction, because each time a guy tried to dance with me, I wished it was Will. I picked up the phone. "What should I wear the first day back at school: a red ombre long-sleeved mini dress over black tights, or black and white gingham pants with a hot pink cable knit sweater?"

Without hesitation, James said, "The dress."

I smiled. I hoped he would choose the dress since I'd been wearing pants for the last two weeks and needed a change. We were always in sync. "Thank you for confirming my instincts."

"How did you end things with Will?"

"You don't waste time, do you?" I said in an attempt to waste time.

"I fully expected you to call me the second you got back to the city. It's been almost a week."

"Ah, Will. He was so last year," I joked.

With a snort, James said, "Terrible attempt at humor, but if you want to go there, Will Brady was last year as well as most of the first ten years of the twenty-first century."

I sat on the edge of the bed and placed a hand over my tummy. I was nauseous.

"Rob?"

"He asked me on a date," I whispered.

James gasped. "Wow. This is just...wow. More exciting than when Nathan fell for Hailey in *One Tree Hill*."

"I said no."

"This is momentous news. I can't believe you held out on me. Wait. You said no? Why? It's Will Brady. Your dream man. It's like Rachel and Ross in reverse."

"Aren't you going to even ask what happened to Perry and Sidney? You know—my boyfriend and Will's girlfriend?"

"Who cares? They're supporting players whose main purpose is to add conflict and drama to the main love story—you and Will."

I chuckled despite myself. "Sounds like something Perry would say."

"Okay. I need to know. What happened with Perry and Sidney?"

"They messed around in a pantry closet. No sex, but Schuester rose to the occasion." I'd told James about the nickname Perry gave to his penis because...well, because it was too funny to keep to myself.

James whistled through his teeth. "Geez. I couldn't have written this better if I were the producer of the aforementioned *One Tree Hill*."

"I was planning to break up with Perry anyway. What you said at Billy Murphy's was right. We weren't going anywhere. It was time. But then he told me what happened."

"I'm actually impressed with Perry's honesty. Unless he was planning to dump you for Sidney."

"Don't be impressed. He fessed up only after he thought I knew. But, no, he isn't dating her. It was a one-time thing. He said it never should have happened. The pathetic part was I didn't care. My heart barely registered the news."

"I'm glad you're not heartbroken, sweetheart. His hotness factor notwithstanding, he's not good enough for my Robyn."

"Will said the same thing. Of course, he didn't call me 'his Robyn.'"

"Which brings us back to Will. When did he ask you out?"

I told James how Will called me the same night Sidney confessed her indiscretion and suggested we go out and show them how it was done, and that it felt more like a need to get back at our cheating exes than a genuine desire to date me. "I don't trust he really wants me."

"There's something between you for sure. I saw it at the bar."

"I felt it too, but even after I told him I was breaking things off with Perry, he didn't say anything about liking me."

"I'm guessing the only reason he didn't make a move in your childhood bed was because he already had a girlfriend. He's too decent to cheat or make a move on someone else's girl. Unlike Perry."

"What if he just can't handle being single? Even when he wasn't dating Adrienne in high school, there was always a girl waiting in the wings." Faces of all the girls who got to kiss Will for more than five seconds during a game of Spin the Bottle flashed before my eyes. "There was Jill, Debbie, and Kaurie." I slid up my bed, leaned against my headboard, and closed my eyes. "I don't want to be his second-choice rebound girl because he needs a warm body."

"It's a possibility."

"You really think so?" It was easier for my heart to believe Will didn't really like me than accept I might have made the biggest mistake of my life.

James sighed. "I can't believe after all these years Will Brady asked you out and instead of being the happiest girl in the world, you have all these doubts. It's not fair. You deserve to live happily ever after with your own Troy Bolton."

James's reference to *High School Musical* reminded me of something, and I sat up straight in my bed. "Did I tell you how horrid his voice is?"

"Will's?"

"Yes. Oh, James. If Will's singing was a food, it would taste like a rotten egg."

James laughed. "Oh, man. Bad singing doesn't bode well for a Lane Christmas. What did your parents do?"

"They ate it up." My mind flashed back to my mom hugging Will and whispering "I love this guy" to me. "They loved him."

"What about their daughter? Does she love him too?"

I swallowed hard as the ache in my stomach got sharper. The answer to James's question was yes. The man I loved asked me out, and I'd turned him away. Still, Will didn't seem too upset when we hung up. Maybe I was right all along. Had I made the biggest mistake of my life by rejecting him, or saved myself from getting my heart broken? I wasn't sure it mattered, since my heart already felt shattered.

Chapter 18

Sidney

I swallowed the last of my beer and swiveled my barstool to order another one just as Izaiah, my favorite bartender, placed one before me. "You're the best," I said. Since I'd arrived in Barbados three days earlier, I'd kept mostly to myself aside from the resort's daily happy hour by the pool, when I made chitchat with the friendly bartenders and whoever else happened to be around.

"I got you, girl," Izaiah said, pointing a finger at me.

"Thank you." I shook out my air-dried hair and turned to face my new friends—Robert and Douglas. "As I was saying, I'd never cheated on a boyfriend before, and it brought up so many questions. Why did I really do it? Would I still be with Will if I hadn't, or would he have dumped me anyway? And I question whether I was truly falling for him or just passing time like I've done with every other guy since Jake."

I didn't know if it was the beer (I was on my third) or the hot sun that provoked me to confide in two strange men. I was a skilled liar and could have easily concocted a fake story as to why I was in Barbados. For instance, I'd been left at the altar and celebrating my honeymoon solo. Or I was writing a novel set in the Caribbean and was there for "research." But the truth felt good. It was liberating, and it might help me come to terms with what had gone down at Christmas three weeks earlier. I explained what happened when Perry outed our break-up at the Christmas table and how the members of my family chimed in about my relationship issues.

"Once I got over the hurt and humiliation of being psychoanalyzed so harshly and publicly, I accepted the truth in their words. I'm so used to being the boss of me and everyone else, I never learned how to let someone else take care of me. I think maybe I want romance?" I spoke the words like a question because until that moment, I didn't know how to articulate what was missing from all my romantic interludes. Romance. Jake had been a romantic, and I stomped all over it. And I never gave Will a fighting chance. Maybe if I'd confided why I didn't want him to meet my folks, he would have understood and we could have figured it out together. Instead, I kept him in the dark.

Douglas, a stocky guy in his late thirties with thinning brown hair and tattoos on both his arms, raised an eyebrow. "I can't comment about Will, but there must have been some crazy chemistry between you and Perry."

I shook my head vehemently before taking a sip of beer. I wasn't much of a beer drinker in the States, but this Banks stuff was more than decent. "No. He drove me bat-shit cray cray." I shrugged guiltily.

Robert, the older of the two, with a shaved head and a fit body, motioned to Izaiah. "Two more beers," he said, pointing to himself and Douglas. "And put Sid's next one on our tab too." The guys had met in a bowling league and won the trip for themselves and their significant others in a tourney. The women had gone on an excursion to see the turtles and weren't back yet.

I was in my happy place. A nice buzz was the perfect distraction from guilt and contemplation. "Thank you so much, Robert."

"My pleasure. Call me Bobby. How did Perry get you so wound up?"

I didn't even know where to start. His first offense was changing the story of how we met to make me look like a pathetic stalker. It got worse from there when, no matter what nonsense he spewed and how dumb he made me look, my family members were charmed as if he'd put a spell on them. Then he repeatedly dissed me at my own party, embarrassing me in front of my relatives. I finally forgave him, just in time for his grand announcement of our breakup, resulting in my public shaming at the dinner table. And what was with the stupid nickname he gave me—Cherry Bomb? But my new friends didn't need to know the details. "Basically, the swap was a genius of my creation, yet Perry refused to follow my rules. He insisted his way was more interesting. He couldn't follow my lead—he had to be contrary every time. When I'd confront him about it, he'd play dumb and laugh at me. I couldn't shake him and it drove me batty." He was such a piece of work, I had to laugh. "It sounds silly now, but at the time, it really set me off."

"It seems like Perry was trying to have fun and loosen you up. When you didn't take the bait, he went out of his way to provoke you and push you out of your comfort zone," Bobby said.

Bobby had a point. Even when Perry tried to be nice to me and free me from my father's claws, I held it against him. It was like I was more comfortable working against him than with him.

"Maybe if you hadn't insisted on taking charge of every moment, he wouldn't have been so contrary," Douglas said. "Sometimes, you need to be the woman in the relationship."

My inner feminist didn't like this and I scowled at him. "The *woman* in the relationship?"

Bobby laughed. Patting Douglas on the shoulder, he said, "I don't think Doug means any disrespect."

Doug shook his head. "I don't. Men like to show off to their women sometimes. Be the tough guys. The one who opens the tightly screwed pickle containers, mows the lawn, carries the heavy packages. If you can do it all yourself, what do you need us for?"

I raised an eyebrow. "I can think of one or two things."

They laughed, and Bobby continued where Doug left off. "All we're saying is there's nothing wrong with kicking butt at work, but every once and a while, sit back and let your man take the lead at home. Even if you're rolling your eyes on the inside, it will make him happy with little effort on your part. All you need to do is relinquish control and let go. Not all the time, but sometimes. You might even enjoy it."

"We're not excusing Perry's actions, but they support our arguments that strong men don't like to be controlled. And you," Bobby said, nudging me lightly in the arm, "need a strong man."

My head was spinning from the beers and the complimentary head-shrinking by my mini therapists. I needed a nap. I asked Izaiah to close out my bill and climbed off my barstool. I regarded my new friends with a weak smile. "Thank you for your interesting perspectives. You've given me a lot of food for thought." With a final wave goodbye, I headed back to my room.

Robyn

"In a pot," I sang.

"In a pot," my kindergarten class repeated.

We sang together, "We stir the letters up and then, you boil it 'til it's good and done."

"Who's got the K?" I sang.

Five-year-old Tommy Capshaw called out, "I've got the K!" When his classmates snickered, he threw his freckled hand against his mouth before repeating himself, this time in song and to the tune of "Hot Cross Buns." Then he sprinted to the front of the classroom, affixed his magnetic letter K to the board next to the letter J, and rushed back to his fellow students.

When he sat back down, his breathing ragged and his normally fair cheeks flushed from exertion, I grinned at him and sang, "Alphabet soup."

The kids repeated, "Alphabet soup."

"In a pot," I sang as my classroom phone rang. "One minute, guys." My phone didn't ring often during class, and it usually meant one of the children was needed somewhere else. I picked up the phone. "Hi. This is Miss Lane," I said while keeping an eye on my students. If one restless five-year-old got bored sitting still, the rest would copy like monkeys at the zoo.

"Hi, Robyn. It's Principal Hogan. Sorry to disturb your class."

"No problem," I said as my hands shook. Despite my promise to Lance, I hadn't garnered the courage to confront Principal Hogan about the rumors since I'd returned to school a week earlier and, instead, was avoiding him. What I didn't know couldn't hurt me. "What can I do for you?"

"Could you stop by my office after this class? I think you have a free period, right?"

I gulped. "Of course. I'll see you soon." This was it. He was going to deliver my fate.

After we hung up, I finished the last round of Alphabet Soup and turned the classroom into the Lane Discotheque. I let the kids choose a popular earworm from the radio, played it on my iTunes, dimmed the lights, and let them dance freestyle. The Lane Discotheque was a student favorite. I usually reserved it for special occasions, like holidays, student birthdays, and the last day of school, but I feared I might not see the precious faces of these twenty-three kindergarteners when they advanced to first grade next year. I wanted to remember them happy in case my remaining lessons were tainted with the knowledge I wouldn't be returning to the school. I knew I was getting ahead of myself, but between the rumors heard by Lynn and the strange conversation Lance heard in the teachers' lounge, it was challenging to remain calm and optimistic.

I turned off the music two minutes before class was officially over to give the kids time to calm down in advance of being picked up by the kindergarten teacher.

A little while later, I knocked on Principal Hogan's open office door.

He looked up and smiled at me. "Come in, Robyn." He gestured to the guest chair on the opposite side of his cluttered desk.

I sat down, careful not to knock over any of the photos of his picture-perfect four-person family that lined the outer surface of his desk. Besides his multiple diplomas, the walls of his office were almost entirely hidden by pictures students had drawn for him over his years as a teacher, vice principal, and now principal. The students loved him, and he seemed to genuinely like children and his job. I felt very fortunate to work with him after all the horror stories I'd heard about school administrators while I was still getting my degree. The cynics, of which there were many, argued that only in his early forties, Hogan was still too young to be jaded.

"Did you have a nice holiday, Robyn?"

It was a loaded question, and I bit back a giggle picturing his reaction if I answered him honestly. What would he say if I told him I'd brought someone else's boyfriend home and pretended he was mine? The temptation to laugh disappeared as soon as I remembered how much I missed Will, and I answered with a simple, "It was nice. How about you? Your daughter's a Christmas baby, right?"

Hogan's light blue eyes widened in surprise. "Yes. My son was born on Valentine's Day and my daughter on Christmas Eve. You think we should try for Thanksgiving with our next?"

"If you can make that happen, you might end up with your own reality show."

He scratched his wavy brown hair. "On second thought, I think we'll try for June. No holidays in June."

"Smart," I said with a laugh.

"I heard you had a little disruption during your holiday."

I blinked in confusion. How could he possibly know what happened?

"I'm referring to Aimee Clay's unauthorized phone call." He leaned forward.

"Oh, yes. She was so upset about her polyps. It broke my heart."

Hogan nodded. "Mine as well. But her parents said she felt much better after speaking to you. I wanted to personally commend you on how you handled the situation."

I smiled timidly. "Thank you. I didn't know what else to do."

"It was a brilliant idea suggesting she work as your assistant.

A plan both her parents and I support wholeheartedly. I also appreciate you telling her you'd need to check with me first."

"Of course." I planted my feet securely to the ground to stop my legs from shaking in anticipation of Hogan's next words.

"Keep up the good work."

I stared at him. "That's it?"

He smiled. "Was there something else you wanted to discuss?"

I licked my lips. This was it. I could either face my fear by asking him straight out, or I could leave his office and continue to toss and turn at night waiting for the delivery of my pink slip. "Can I be blunt?"

He looked at me strangely, presumably because it was a strange question. "Shoot."

I let out a long exhale. "Is my job in jeopardy?"

Hogan jerked his head back. "I certainly hope not. You're one of the favorite teachers here."

I was too nervous for the compliment to register. "I'm not so much worried about me as I am about the music program in general. There's been talk about budget cuts." My heart raced just saying the words.

Understanding washed across his face. "You've heard the rumors, huh?"

I nodded, resisting the urge to chew on a fingernail.

"Between us, there *was* a danger due to an increased interest in foreign language curriculum at the elementary level. We were discussing possible work-arounds to avoid a complete shut-down, but it won't be necessary. At least not in the immediate future."

My eyes widened. "What? How? Why?" I realized I probably sounded like a high school journalist and blushed.

Hogan chuckled. "I don't have all the details because it went through the superintendent, but the funds came from a law firm's private charitable fund and were specifically allocated to the music program at this school for the next five years."

My mouth fell open, but the only word I could form was, "Wow."

"It looks like you're stuck with us for a little bit longer, Ms. Lane. Are you okay with that?"

Faking calmness, I answered, "Yes. Yes, I am," and presented Principal Hogan with a smile. But as my legs resumed shaking like tree branches during a hurricane, I feared they'd give out before I made it back to my classroom.

The funds came from a law firm's private charitable fund.

After work, I (easily) persuaded Anne Marie to meet me at one of our favorite neighborhood bars, Dive 75, for happy hour.

"Cheers to you not being out of a job and me not needing a new roommate after you're forced to move back in with your parents in Philly." Anne Marie raised her five-dollar pint of Bud Light and clinked it against mine. We were sitting at the bar so Anne Marie could flirt with her crush, Steve the bartender, but the place was at capacity and he had little time to chat.

I took a gulp of my beer. "And cheers to the students not missing out on a music education because they're too busy learning to converse with German tourists."

"On behalf of my German ancestors, I must defend the ability to speak fluently in German. *Prost*," she said before lifting her glass again and smiling at Steve, who grinned back and slid a bowl of Reese's Peanut Butter Cups in front of us. Besides the cheap happy hour specials and friendly bartender, another reason we loved Dive 75 was the free candy. The place didn't serve food, but patrons were allowed to bring it in from other places. Most of the millennials who frequented Dive 75 were more about liquid sustenance than solid eats anyway.

I pulled a piece of chocolate from the bowl. "The only word you know, I presume?"

Anne Marie shook her head. "*Nein.* I also know *bier*, *lederhose*, and *Oktoberfest*."

"All of the essentials." I chuckled. "I'm not adverse to foreign language curriculum, but I'm happy my school doesn't have to choose."

Despite being thrilled my school's music program had been rescued, I couldn't get over Principal Hogan's comments that the hero was a law firm. "Do you think it was Sidney's way of apologizing for kissing Perry?" I asked Anne Marie, who had pulled her blonde hair out of the ponytail holding it captive and replenished her lipstick, presumably because Steve was now talking to two cute girls sitting at the other side of the bar.

She smirked at me. "Not likely. How would she know about your school? It's not like she asked me. And besides, she's on a leave of absence from work."

I didn't truly think it was Sidney, but I felt the need to rule her out as a possibility before letting my mind wander to who else it could be. "Why is she on leave?" I asked, before taking a bite of my peanut butter cup and snarling because beer and chocolate were as bad a combination as toothpaste and orange juice.

"Harvey cited personal reasons." In response to my blank expression, she clarified. "Mr. Bellows. Her dad. Big man on campus."

I smiled. "Gotcha."

"I'd like whatever personal issues she's having. She's in Barbados."

My stomach dropped. "You think she's with Will?" Maybe they'd gotten back together. They'd only been broken up a matter of hours before he called me. For all I knew, they'd made up. Maybe he realized I was right about his interest in me being directly related to losing her. What if she begged him to take her back with reminders of her advanced sexual talents and he caved? This possibility should have made me feel justified in my decision to turn him down and it did—a little. But it mostly made me mad with envy.

Anne Marie looked at me like I'd sprouted horns. "You're joking, right? You know it was Will, and all you need to confirm it is the name of the law firm." She narrowed her eyes at me. "Or you can just ask him yourself." She chugged the rest of her beer and called out for Steve. When he glanced our way, she said, "Can we get another round and two Redheaded Slut shots?" before typing something on her phone.

I narrowly escaped choking on my beer.

Anne Marie looked up from her phone. "According to food.com, it's Jägermeister, peach schnapps, and cranberry juice."

"I know how to make them, Marianne," Steve said, using his nickname for Anne Marie. His nickname for me was Lainie. This worked well when we were hit on by undesirables, although up until recently, Perry was usually with us.

"Make one for yourself too," Anne Marie said.

Steve wordlessly placed another clean shot glass onto the bar, finished mixing the ingredients, and placed one in front of each of us. "What are we toasting?"

Anne Marie lifted her shot glass. "To banishing all ginger-haired sluts to Barbados."

Steve and I raised our shot glasses to our mouths, but Anne Marie held up her hand. "I'm not finished yet." She stared me down. "And to childhood crushes and sexy attorneys slash saviors of music education." She slid the shot down her throat.

Steve looked at her curiously and held his glass up to mine. "To what Marianne just said."

I clinked my glass against his and whispered, "To Will," before slamming the shot.

Chapter 19

Sidney

I was bored. The life of leisure wasn't all it was cracked up to be. On the plus side, lack of activity and plenty of sleep provided much opportunity during my waking hours to consider the advice bestowed upon me by Bobby and Doug. Once my buzz faded, I wished I hadn't confided in them. Their suggestions to let my man take charge in the relationship, or least think he was, bothered the feminist, stubborn, and competitive side of me. But the part that craved the romance, or even someone to nurse me sometimes, wondered if they were right. I was tired of always taking care of myself.

Interrupting my rumination, a woman at the table to my left in the hotel's outdoor café said, "I hope the next twenty-four hours go by very slowly. I never want to leave."

Her male companion said, "I know. Even during the hour it rains, stormy Barbados is paradise compared to the brutal winter in Mount Kisco."

This caught my attention since Mount Kisco wasn't far from my folks' estate in Scarsdale. I glanced over at the thirty-something couple just as the woman scrunched her sunburned face in irritation. "It's not even the weather. It's those awful Millers. God knows what our lawn will look like when we get back."

The waitress came by with my lunch, and after ordering another glass of iced tea, I cocked my head at a better angle to eavesdrop on their conversation. I craved drama, and fighting neighbors would do nicely.

"I know. The nerve of them cutting our hedges without our permission. How would they feel if we painted their mailbox in neon green or drew a hopscotch board on their driveway?" the man said.

The woman frowned. "I know we promised to fix things, but did they really expect us to cut hedges in the middle of winter?"

Smirking, the man said, "I guess so, considering they couldn't wait until the spring before doing it themselves."

A lawyer on sabbatical was still a lawyer, and it occurred to me what their neighbors did was not only unneighborly and ballsy, but it might be illegal. Perhaps it wasn't my business, although it never stopped me before, but I believed my fellow beachcombers might want to hear what I had to say. "Excuse me," I said.

When the couple failed to answer me, I cleared my throat. "Pardon me," I said in a louder voice until both heads turned my way. "I couldn't help but overhear your predicament. I'm an attorney." When both sets of brown eyes opened wide in what I took as horror, I waved my hand. "You have nothing to worry about. In fact, I think you might like what I have to say."

The two exchanged a glance before looking back at me. With a timid smile, the woman said, "By all means then."

"You said your neighbors trimmed your hedges without your permission?" I asked.

The man nodded. "They complained our hedges had grown so long, they blocked their light."

"They asked us to trim them and we were planning to, but the request came on a Thursday night and we were going away for a long weekend. We said we'd handle it when we got back, but Mother Nature had other plans," the woman added. "I went to take out the garbage on Saturday morning the week before Christmas and there was Mr. Miller bundled up in his winter jacket, hat, and scarf. He was humming Broadway show tunes like it wasn't at all unusual he was trimming our hedges."

An image of Perry in a quilted parka and knit hat singing songs from *Sweeney Todd* flashed before my eyes, and I jutted my head back. Where did that come from? I shook off the hallucination and resumed my lawyer role. "If your hedges fall squarely on your own property, your neighbors aren't allowed to trim them. It's against the law."

My new friends gaped at me in silence until the Mrs. asked, "Really?"

Nodding, I said, "I suggest you hire a surveyor to determine exactly where the property line is. If anything they did damaged the trees, they can be liable." I motioned for the waitress to bring over my check so I wouldn't be stuck at the table until dinnertime. Since I'd arrived almost two weeks earlier, I'd learned Barbados time was very different from New York time.

The woman focused on her partner. "What do you think?"

He put down his coffee cup and turned to me. "This is really helpful. Thank you so much...What's your name?"

"Sidney," I said, my lips curling up.

"I'm Jack, and this is Diane. And yes, we've heard it before."

Chuckling I said, "Cute."

Diane beamed at me. "I feel so much better now. Lucky for us you were sitting here."

I felt myself flush as a bolt of adrenaline rushed through me. Next time someone accused me of being nosy, I'd tell them how my meddling once helped an anxious couple to relax on their vacation. "I'm so happy I could offer my assistance. And it's free of charge," I said as the waitress placed my bill in front of me in record time.

Jack smirked at Diane. "Betcha we never hear that phrase again from a lawyer." He turned to me and shrugged. "No offense."

I snickered. "None taken. The bottom line is your neighbors were probably not within their rights. Your only obligation is to abide by a reasonable expectation to keep your property safe and not cause injury to your neighbors' property. If you confirm the hedges are on your side of the property, you'll have grounds to sue. I wouldn't suggest being litigious because you still have to live next door to these people. But it's something you can throw in their face to prevent them from taking liberties in the future. They should have waited for you to cut your own hedges in the spring." I signed my bill and stood up. "I'm staying in the hotel, so if you have any questions, I'll be around."

"Thanks again," Jack and Diane said in unison.

With a final wave, I left the restaurant and headed over to the lap pool. I threw my bag and towel over an empty beach chair and climbed the steps into the water. I was ultra-awake and figured laps was a productive way to work off my excess energy. As I pushed my arms and legs through the water with the breaststroke, I felt high on life. I had never practiced residential real estate, but evidently some of what I learned in law school and through studying for the Bar stuck. I had skills. When I reached the other side of the pool, I pushed against the edge and turned around.

Not only was I a talented attorney, but I liked what I did. I enjoyed counseling clients and making their lives easier. My heart was racing, and I knew it wasn't only because of the calories I was burning. It was because I knew without a doubt I still wanted to be a lawyer. Not because my last name was Bellows, but because it made me happy. This time, when I reached the other side of the pool, instead of turning around, I pushed myself over the edge, stood up, and returned to my chair. I was on the cusp of an epiphany and needed a minute to capture my thoughts.

I lay back in my chair with my eyes closed and let the hot sun dry my body. A few moments later, I opened my eyes and sat up. I observed the couples holding hands poolside, the small children splashing around in the water, and the groups of girlfriends working on their afternoon buzz. Then I took a sweeping gaze of my surroundings—the bright blue sky, glistening pool water, and rise and fall of the ocean waves in the distance. It was a sight to behold. But it was time to go home.

Robyn

"Hi, Mom." The ache festering in the back of my throat left me short of breath as I answered the phone. Since coming home after the holidays, I'd managed to bullshit my way through our telephone conversations for almost a month. When she asked how Will was doing, I said, "fine." As far as I knew, it was the truth. My confidence with respect to maintaining the lie was wearing thin in light of the newest development. I also craved her advice, which she wouldn't be able to give until I was honest with her.

"Hi, honey. How are you?" My mom's voice was calm, as if she wasn't expecting this phone call to be any different than the ones we usually exchanged, during which we confirmed our mental and physical wellbeing, shared any newsworthy events, traded "I love yous," and hung up. She could be in for a big surprise.

I sat on my bed with my feet dangling over the edge. "Back to school. Back to reality," I sang it to the tune of the song "Back2Life" from the late eighties. My parents played the tape in the background pretty often during my toddler years.

Predictably, my mom said, "I wonder whatever happened to Soul II Soul," before releasing a wistful sigh.

"There's this thing where you can look stuff like that up, you know? It's called the internet." I chuckled.

"I'm way ahead of you, kid." I heard her tapping the keys of a computer. "How's school?"

"They want me to direct a mid-winter concert this year the second week of February, right before mid-winter recess. I only have about three weeks to prepare." Thankfully, the concert would be limited to the fourth and fifth graders. They were easier to train than the younger kids. I was too thrilled the music program was intact to complain about the extra last-minute work on my plate.

"Holding another concert is a good sign for the fate of your position at the school though, right?"

"I'm pleased to report my job is safe, and more importantly, so is the music program." My lips curled up at my expression of happy news.

My mom squealed. "That's wonderful. By the way, according to Wikipedia, Soul II Soul disappeared in 1997 but have been back in action since 2007. I have to tell your dad. Maybe we'll catch a gig. Back to you. Tell me more about the school."

I breathed deeply in and out of my nose. I could lie and say Will saved the day because I was his girlfriend, but it wouldn't be right. And it wouldn't be true. As the knots twisted in my belly, I braced myself for what I was about to say. "A law firm used its charitable foundation to gift the funds. It will be enough to keep the program going for the next five years."

My mom whistled. "Wow. What firm? A rich parent?"

I chewed a nail. My first instinct had been whoever was responsible did it on my behalf. I hadn't even thought about it being an unrelated third party. But it could have been anyone. I wasn't the only concerned individual in the story. Lance might have talked to someone. Even Lynn. Or perhaps an active parent in the PTA got wind of the budget troubles and pulled some strings. "I don't know exactly. It went through the superintendent, but I intend to find out." Despite the broader array of possibilities from which to choose, my gut stuck to my original conclusion. In a much lower voice, I said, "I think Will might be responsible."

"What do you mean, you *think*? Have you asked him?"

"Not exactly."

My mom was silent for a beat. "You two aren't fighting, are you?"

I closed my eyes and blew a stream of air through my lips. "Mom, there's something I need to tell you."

Chapter 20

Sidney

"I knew you'd be back," my father said. He was reclined in his office chair, one foot leaning against his wooden desk and his arms locked behind his head.

My dad's cocky expression could rival Perry's at his most obnoxious. If I weren't the fruit of his loins, I'd be tempted to pop him one in the nose. "You did not." I recalled the fearful look in his eyes when he finally agreed to let me take a break. He was terrified I'd take a bartending gig like Tom Cruise in *Cocktail* and never come back.

He removed his foot from the desk and pushed his chair closer. "I'm your father. I always know. And by the way, you're a chip off the old block. I've never taken more than a two-week break from the office in my entire career, and I knew you wouldn't be able to either." He cackled. "You didn't even make it a full two weeks."

My mouth instinctively opened to make my next argument, but I managed to close my lips before I uttered another combative word. Yes, I had come to realize during my time in Barbados that I loved being an attorney and part of my job was to have the last word, silence the opposition, and win at any cost. But during my brief hiatus from work and life, I'd also discovered I didn't have to bring my career skills with me everywhere I went. It was okay to let someone else win on occasion, and by doing so, I might end up being victorious in other ways. Harvey was my father. What would be so horrible about letting him think he had one over on me? It would make him happy and might reduce my own stress from the energy I exerted fighting. The bottom line was I was back at work, ready to serve my clients and earn my partnership. Nothing else mattered.

"On a serious note, I'm glad this little moratorium confirmed what I've known all along: you're perfect just as you are." My dad's expression oozed affection and tenderness.

Even as my heart warmed at his comment, and despite my resolution to maintain a more agreeable attitude on all things unrelated to my career, I felt the need to correct him this one time. "I love you for saying that, and until a few days ago, I would have agreed with you."

"What happened a few days ago?" my dad asked. He placed an elbow on the desk and rested his chin in his hand.

"I know you think my little getaway was whimsical and a costly waste of time and airline miles, but I got exactly what I needed from it. I knew I would. I just thought it would take longer." I gave him a sly smile. "It's because I'm highly intelligent."

My dad chuckled. "Do you care to share what you learned with me?"

I blew out a breath and leaned back in my chair. These types of conversations were outside of my comfort zone. I rarely admitted weakness to myself, much less other people. But confiding in my father was a perfect way to kick off my commitment to be more in touch with my softer side. "You all did a number on me at Christmas dinner." I got a phantom ache in my neck whenever I recalled looking from one side of the table to the other like it was a game of volleyball as various members of my clan chimed in with their two cents on my relationship foibles.

My father frowned. "It was that damn La Faraona. It turned us into vultures."

"That's right. Blame it on someone, or in this case something, else. You're such a lawyer sometimes," I joked. "I'm glad it happened. Yes, the respite from work made me realize how much I do enjoy being an attorney. I missed it. But it also taught me that not everyone in my life is an adversary, and I don't have to treat them as such. Sometimes I need to relinquish control and let someone else win. Moving forward, you're going to see a gentler Sidney Bellows."

My father studied my face for a few moments as if waiting for me to continue talking or say "just kidding." I braced myself for his response. I was certain he was going to roll his eyes, make a teasing comment about believing it when he saw it, or both. Right at the moment the wait became unbearable, his mouth opened and I curled the fingers of both of my hands around the edge of my chair.

"Knock, knock."

I turned around as Mike Goldberg entered my father's office. He did a double take when he saw me. "JB. We didn't expect you back so soon." His attempt to look happy to see me did nothing to hide his displeasure.

The old Sidney would have thrown back a sarcastic reply faster than he could say "douche," but the new Sidney was suited up and ready for action. "Hi, Mike. My vacation was really nice, but I actually missed this place. I just need a few hours to go through pending cases and return some emails, but I'll be back and ready to assist you and the other partners by lunchtime." I smiled.

Mike blinked at me as if he thought he might be living an alternate reality. "Okay, then. Glad to have you back." Then he turned to my dad. "I'm sorry to barge in here, but when your meeting with Sidney is over, can I get your thoughts on the email I just sent you? I have a meeting with Sparks this afternoon and need input on one issue."

I stood up. "We just finished."

My dad motioned for me to sit back down. "Actually, we need a few more minutes. I'll give you a call in a bit."

Mike nodded. "Great." To me, he said, "Later."

"Bye," I said cheerily. After he walked out, I faced my dad again. He was gaping at me. "Who was that?"

I furrowed my brow. "You mean Mike? Are you having a senior moment, Dad?"

"No, not Mike." He rolled his eyes. "You."

I knew my dad was referring to my companionable exchange with Mike, but it was fun to bust his chops. "Oh, that." I waved him away. "Like I said, Barbados has made me a new woman."

He smirked. "We'll see how long it lasts."

I let my gaze fall to the floor as my stomach dropped in disappointment, but I wasn't going to let my father's cocky cynicism get to me. I knew I could better compartmentalize the different aspects of my life. I'd need to completely retrain myself and react to people and situations at a slower rate to avoid letting old habits take control, but I refused to be discouraged. When I felt my dad's eyes on me, I looked up at him.

He smiled at me with warm eyes. "What I was about to say before Mike came in was that your mother and I would be history ages ago if I didn't let her win sometimes. Of course, I only let her *think* she's winning, but it accomplishes the same thing. It's how it's done, kiddo. Like I said, you're a chip off the old block."

I felt my face brighten. "Yeah?"

"Yeah," he said with a nod. "I would caution against you turning into a doormat, but a turnaround of such magnitude would require a lobotomy." He snickered. "Balance is the key."

I glanced at my watch and blanched. "Geez. It's almost ten." I stood up. With my back to him as I walked toward his door, I said, "Good advice. Thanks, Dad."

"Oh, and Sid?"

I turned around to face him.

"Mike is still your enemy." He chuckled.

"I know. I was merely making a point." I winked at him and stepped out of his office.

Robyn

"What do you need to tell me?" my mom asked.

I stood up and walked to my window. Snow was falling lightly outside but seemed to be melting mid-air because nothing was sticking to the ground below. I felt like I was watching a black and white movie—not a fun one like *It Happened One Night* or *The Philadelphia Story*, but a depressing one like *The Grapes of Wrath* or *To Kill a Mockingbird*. "Will's not my boyfriend, Mom."

"Aw, honey. What happened?" My mom's voice dripped with concern and disappointment.

I stared down at the chipped royal blue polish on my fingernails. "Nothing happened. He's never been my boyfriend. We made up the whole thing." I closed my eyes and braced myself for her response. The silence on the other end of the phone was unsettling. "You there, Mom?" I sat back down on my bed.

After a pause, she said, "I'm here. I'm just trying to comprehend the last words out of your mouth. Did I imagine the whole week? Was I hallucinating? I only tripped on acid once and it was decades ago. Maybe I need a CAT scan."

I laughed nervously. "You don't need your head examined. It wasn't a bad flashback either. I did bring Will home with me to Christmas. And you don't need your hearing checked either, because he *is* that tone deaf. But we lied about being a couple."

My mom gasped. "What? Why?"

I let out a deep exhalation. "Because I couldn't bear more nagging from you guys about dating Perry. Having to defend my taste in men to you, especially when you're artists yourselves and chose each other—fellow singers—is exhausting." Before my mom could weigh in, I continued. "At our wine-tasting party before the holidays, Anne Marie's boss complained about bringing her boyfriend—another attorney—home for Christmas. She was afraid her father, the head partner in her firm, would suffocate them with legal talk and her mother would smother her with questions about their future. She wanted a flaky creative who would be of no interest to her parents, and I wanted a boyfriend with a retirement fund to get you guys off my back. Anne Marie made a joke about trading boyfriends for the holidays and Sidney thought it was a brilliant idea. It took some convincing, but I got on board eventually. I'm so sorry." My belly twitched in guilt.

"We'll talk about your father and me in a bit. Of all people to pretend you were dating though—Will Brady, the sole object of your teenage fantasies. How in the world?"

I thought back to my mom cuddling with me the night of my one and only kiss with Will. I'd described it in agonizing detail to root the experience permanently in my memory. Instead of brushing me off as a silly teenager, she listened intently, braided my long hair, and promised Will enjoyed the kiss as much as I did, even if he didn't admit it. "Sidney referred to him as 'Will,' but it never occurred to me it would be *my* Will." My heart hurt at the sound of his name. "I only found out when she introduced us. I practiced nonchalance like it was an acting exercise, but still managed to spill my wine glass across the table. Since I'd already agreed to the swap, I left it in the hands of Perry and Will, assuming they'd be appalled by the idea and I'd be let off the hook. Only Perry was cool with it once Sidney heaped on the incentives for him in the way of networking opportunities and unlimited access to the family's Steinway & Sons. Will, on the other hand, adamantly refused to participate at first."

My mom snickered. "Why am I not surprised by Perry? I understand why Will would be hesitant though. Pretending to be someone else's boyfriend is not a small favor. How did his reluctance make you feel, given your lifelong crush on him?"

I bit my lip as I recalled my paranoia that Will thought I was a freak in high school. "Relieved and hurt at the same time. I questioned if he said no because he didn't want to go through with the plan in general or because he didn't want to pretend to be my boyfriend specifically. But somehow Sidney got him to change his mind. She knows how to get her way."

"So Will isn't your boyfriend. Is Perry?"

At least I could tell her something I knew she'd want to hear for once. "No. We broke up. So did Sidney and Will." I told her about Sidney and Perry's dalliance.

"I think I need a few minutes to let all this sink in." She sighed.

"Scratch that, can you just fast forward to now? How did you leave things? What does any of this have to do with the music program? Do you have genuine romantic feelings for Will? Because if not, you deserve an Emmy award and so does he. He bought you a gift from Pandora, for the love of Apollo. A fake boyfriend wouldn't go to that extreme."

There was no point in holding anything back at this point. I told her everything. When I finally confided how Will had asked me out after learning of Sidney's betrayal but I turned him down, my voice was breaking. The tears, which had been building up behind my eyelids, could no longer be held back and blurred my vision. Wiping my eyes with a tissue, I said, "And that's it."

"That's all? I think I'll give it three stars. It was kind of one note."

I was too sad to appreciate my mom's attempt at humor. "He asked me out and I said no. Even though it was everything I ever wanted, I refused. I didn't want to win his affections by default or be his consolation prize." Chewing on a fingernail, I said, "But what if I misread him? What if it was his law firm that saved the music program? He wouldn't go to such levels if he didn't care for me, right?" I tossed the used tissue in my garbage can and blew my nose with a fresh one.

"There's a lot to say here, but I'll start with an apology."

"I'm the one who owes you an apology—for lying and making a complete farce of Chrismukkah." I absently grabbed a fistful of raven hair from the back of my head and pulled it over my forehead. It was long enough to touch my breast bone, and I imagined for a second what I'd look like with short hair. Mine had never been cut above mid-back.

"And I'm sorry you felt the need to bring home a fake romantic partner because you think your parents have no tolerance for your real-life creative boyfriends."

"I don't think it. I know it." I closed my eyes, letting my hair tickle my lids.

"Maybe it seems like we have a problem with your boyfriends' chosen career paths, but we don't."

I opened my eyes and brushed my hair away. "Then how do you explain your relentless teasing while I was dating Troy?" I dated Troy, an actor, right before I met Perry. Troy moved to Los Angeles after landing a supporting role on *The Bold and the Beautiful.*

My mom snorted. "Troy's vocation wasn't the problem. Troy was. He was a pompous jerk."

"He just took himself too seriously." Troy studied method acting. He accompanied me to a rehearsal for one of my spring concerts and directed my students to dig deep into the motivations of their characters. One little boy wanted the Christmas tree he was playing to steal all the presents for himself, a little girl wanted her silver bell to be heard by her grandparents in Florida, and a boy playing a snowman wanted to freeze off his older brother's fingers. It was chaos. My mother had a point. I giggled. "Fine. I'll give you Troy."

"Then there was Phil."

"What about him?" I clenched my teeth thinking about the guy I dated my senior year of college. I didn't really need my mother to remind me of his shortcomings.

"Have you forgotten when he came over for Passover and wouldn't break character? He was playing the starring role in the school's performance of *If You Could See What I Hear* and insisted you cut his food, dress him, and lead around him the house for two days as if he were actually blind. I'm sorry, Robyn, but we'd support you dating an artist if he were remotely normal. And even if his quirkiness was more annoying than endearing, we'd learn to love him if you did. Robyn, your dad and I didn't embrace Will because he was a solid attorney. We adored Will because it was obvious you were crazy about him and him about you."

"I always thought you didn't want me to get involved with an actor because you were afraid we'd suffer financially. I've been wrong all this time?" My heart beat triple time in the realization I'd misjudged my parents for so long.

"Not entirely. Let's face it, you're usually drawn to the struggling and them to you. It's not an easy life, especially since creatives are so intense and feel things like rejection and insecurity so deeply. We lived it and want more security for you, but we'd never stand in the way of true love. I admit to harping on the financial side of things, but it's mostly because I'm too nice to attack your boyfriends' less-than-stellar personalities unsolicited."

I bit on a fingernail. "Confession?"

"Another one? I'm not sure I could handle it, but go on."

"The reason I've always dated actors and the like is because I assumed no regular guy would find me attractive." I'd never said it out loud before. The knots in my belly tightened.

There was a beat of silence and I braced myself until my mom finally responded. "On what did you base this assumption?"

I sighed. "The only boys who expressed interest in me in high school were other theater geeks. No one else asked me out." The explanation sounded beyond silly as it slipped off my tongue, and I couldn't believe I'd let it rule my life for so many years.

"The only boys you *spoke* to in high school were theater geeks." My mom grunted. "And the only so-called 'regular' boy who mattered to you was Will. He didn't ask you out, and you attached his disinterest to every other regular man since."

My cheeks burned at my mother's accurate psychoanalysis and I curled myself into the fetal position on my bed. "Uh-huh."

"Will's legal profession certainly qualifies him as a regular person. Can you live with it?"

My heart ached at how much I missed Will. Even running stupid errands with him was fun. "I was a goner from the moment I saw him again. He called me 'Snow,' and it was like I'd time traveled to when I was fifteen years old and lovestruck." I groaned. "More than ten years later and nothing's changed."

My mother yelped. "How can you say nothing has changed? *Everything* has changed. You know each other now. Will told you he likes you. More importantly, he showed you. He went to bat for you and your school. He's the Prince Charming to your Snow

White."

Her words both frightened and thrilled me, and my limbs tingled in a combination of both emotions. "You think it was him? The lawyer who rescued the music program—you think it was Will?"

"I do, but it doesn't matter what I think. Do *you* think it was Will? And if so, what are you going to do about it? The Robyn from yesteryear was too inexperienced and shy to let her affection for Will escape the confines of her daydreams. And it's very possible the Will from high school wasn't ready for someone like you anyway. The adult version has already expressed his interest though, even after spending three days with your crazy family. But is the grown-up Robyn ready to take things with Prince Charming into the real world, or would she rather keep dating Dopey, Grumpy, and Sleepy? I'd include Bashful, but your ghosts of boyfriends past, especially Perry, have been anything but."

"Twenty-something Robyn is definitely ready. Being with Will feels right." I imagined a reality in which Will and I were an actual couple and my heart swelled before pounding in fear. "But what if I'm wrong? What if it wasn't Will who rescued the music program? What if my first reaction—that he only asked me out as an anger-inspired knee-jerk reaction to what happened between Sidney and Perry—is right? I'm not sure I could dust myself off if he told me I was right all along and he isn't interested." I hadn't heard from him since our telephone conversation. If he went through the effort of getting his law firm to sponsor my school's music program, wouldn't he want to tell me?

"I didn't raise my children to live in fear. What do you think about taking chances? How about jumping off the ledge?"

"Thank you, Celine Dion." I chuckled, but I knew my mom was right. I had to take the risk. If Will was the mastermind behind saving my school's music program, I needed to thank him and apologize for doubting his intentions. Considering the way I'd blurted out the intensity of my crush on him over the phone, he shouldn't be too surprised to know my desire to date him for real trumped everything else I wished for in my life, aside from world peace and a cure for cancer. If the offer was no longer on the table, it would hurt, but I'd get on with my life eventually. What I couldn't live with was not knowing. Until I knew for sure, the longing wouldn't go away. It would fester and infect me from the inside out. My decision was made.

Chapter 21

Sidney

I slipped on the cashmere cardigan I kept on my chair at work and rubbed my hands together. The average temperature had dropped at least three degrees a day over the last week, reminding me I wasn't in Barbados anymore. Although such a thought would probably depress most people and make them long for their next vacation getaway, I was still riding the high of my return to work even two weeks later. Time away from the Big Apple and my overflowing responsibilities at work made me appreciate both. I functioned much better in the city that never slept, where my schedule was too full to waste time dillydallying, than I did in the Caribbean, where lazy days stretched as far as the sandy beaches.

There was only one thing keeping me from loving my job. (Two things if you counted Mike Goldberg, with whom I was still playing nice even though it was killing me softly.) I still hadn't resolved my issues with Anne Marie. I couldn't hold her loyalty to Robyn against her—she was her roommate and close friend, and I was the homewrecker who likely caused Robyn and Perry's breakup—but I missed our easy working relationship and the friendship we'd begun to forge until the fateful day of their wine party when the boyfriend swap was born. I took a deep breath and lifted myself to a standing position. With my almost-empty coffee cup in tow, I approached her desk outside my office. "Hey, Anne Marie."

She lifted her blonde head and met my eyes. "What's up,

Sidney?" Her tone wasn't nasty, but it wasn't congenial either—strictly professional.

I pretended I didn't notice the lack of warmth. "I was thinking of heading to Lord & Taylor after work. I can't keep pretending it's not cold enough to wear a hat and scarf. Do you want to join me for some shopping? Maybe get a glass of wine after?"

Anne Marie's mouth fell open. "Um...I..." She pressed her lips together and bit down on her bottom one.

I could tell she was wracking her brain to come up with a believable excuse, but it was late in the day and I'd kept her too busy with work assignments and probably drained all her creative juices. Putting her out of her misery, I said, "I know you're not happy with me these days, and I don't blame you. What happened with Robyn's boyfriend—"

"Ex-boyfriend," Anne Marie uttered in a soft voice, confirming my suspicions that Perry and Robyn had broken up.

I patted down my bangs. "I won't try to make excuses for what we did, because no matter how you slice it, it was wrong. I'm so sorry for hurting your friend and betraying your trust. I can't turn back time, but I'm asking for your forgiveness. I miss you, Anne Marie."

Anne Marie sighed. "Robyn wasn't even hurt. She was going to end things with Perry anyway. I was shocked by how well she took the news. But you didn't know that." She shook her head. "I can't believe you messed around with my friend's boyfriend. I trusted you." Her face turned red. "I never would have supported your stupid boyfriend swap idea if I didn't."

My first instinct was to defend the boyfriend swap idea. It was brilliant—in theory—but I swallowed down my pride in the knowledge this was one of those battles I needed to let someone else win. Even I had to concede the plan had some disastrous consequences. The guilty feelings gnawing at my stomach were another reminder I should keep my mouth shut except to apologize again. "I'm so sorry. I got caught in the moment. Perry...he was..." I closed my eyes and I was back in the pantry with Perry right before

I launched myself at him. I opened my eyes. "Forget it, there's no justification. We were wrong. Period. End of story. Please let me try to make it up to you." I looked at her pleadingly.

Anne Marie studied my face for a moment as if trying to gauge the level of sincerity in my words. Eventually, she let out a long sigh. "Fine. It doesn't make sense for me to hold a grudge on Robyn's behalf."

I felt like a fifty-pound kettle bell had been removed from my back. "I'm so glad. So...Lord & Taylor?" I really did need a new hat.

Twirling a hair around her finger, Anne Marie said, "I actually do have plans tonight, but I'll take a rain check for that drink." She paused. "Your treat," she added with a smirk.

Snickering, I said, "My treat for sure." I glanced at my coffee cup. "I need more caffeine. Can I get you anything?"

"No, thanks."

I took two steps away and hesitated before turning back to Anne Marie. "So Robyn isn't upset about Perry, huh?"

Anne Marie shook her head. "You might have even done her a favor. Now maybe she can be with Will." Her face drained of color and she clamped her mouth shut.

"What?" I grabbed onto Anne Marie's desk. "Robyn and Will?"

Grimacing, Anne Marie said, "Nothing's happened."

I pictured Robyn and Will together, fully prepared for my blood to boil and my nostrils to flare in anger, but it didn't happen. Then I waited for my chest to burn in jealousy and a desire for revenge to bubble out of me. Nothing. I nodded at Anne Marie. "At least something good should come out of this." If Will fell for Robyn, it would explain why he acted so strangely at my apartment even before my confession.

Anne Marie shrugged before returning her attention to her keyboard, and I made my way to the pantry.

"Sidney?"

I pivoted so I was facing Anne Marie again. "Yes?"

"As much as I appreciate your apology, I'm not the one you wronged. Even if Robyn ends up with Will, Perry was Robyn's boyfriend, and you shouldn't have gone there."

She resumed typing before I could comment, but her point had been made and taken. Instead of going to the pantry, I went back to my office and closed the door behind me.

Apologizing to Robyn wasn't only a way to put my new life lessons to the test, it was the right thing to do. I was certain Robyn and Will hadn't given into their attraction while they were still involved with someone else. I was in the wrong no matter what happened now.

I stared at my phone for a few beats before pressing the call button. I tried to predict Robyn's reaction. Anne Marie had said she wasn't too broken up over splitting with Perry and suggested she might be halfway to dating Will. But I had my doubts she'd welcome my call.

"Hi, Sidney." Her usual singsong voice was flat of emotion.

No pretense was necessary. I got straight to my point. "I'm calling to apologize for what happened with Perry. I should have done it sooner, but I was figuring some things out." Robyn didn't respond, and the only evidence she was still on the line was the sound of her breathing. "Robyn?"

"I'm here. I just don't know what you want me to say. Are you expecting me to tell you what you did was okay or offer my forgiveness?" Once again, her tone didn't register as angry as much as matter-of-fact.

"You don't have to say anything. I just wanted you to know I take responsibility for my actions and am sincerely remorseful." I nervously tapped my fingers along the surface of my desk. "For what it's worth, I'm actively making changes in my life and the way I treat others." I winced. I was certain the poor girl had no interest in my self-improvement plans.

"That's good," Robyn said, this time with a tiny bit more heart. "I wish you the best of luck." She sounded sincere.

Prompted to keep going, I said, "I can be a bit bossy and selfish sometimes, and, well, I'm a work in progress."

Robyn let out the smallest of laughs. "None of us have our crap all together. I applaud you for recognizing your issues and working on them. Good luck."

"Thank you, Robyn. By the way, I don't want to pry about what may or may not be happening between you and Will, but if you're together, I do hope you'll be happy." My throat closed up and I thought I might cry. I took a deep breath—apologies were hard. There was a pause before Robyn said, "Um, thanks. Goodbye, Sidney."

"Bye." I hung up the phone, lowered my head to my desk, and wept. When all my tears had been shed, I wiped my eyes, grabbed my coat and purse, and headed out.

At Lord & Taylor, I lifted a crème-colored knitted beret from the shelf, placed it on my head, and gazed at myself in the mirror. I liked how the color contrasted with my red hair and brought out the pink in my cheeks. Most women would probably try on several more hats before making a decision, but I didn't want to waste time when my mind was already made up. My mission accomplished, I paid for the hat and a matching scarf and contemplated my next move. I could either leave the store and take myself for a drink before going home or continue to shop as long as I was already here.

While I was checking out Yelp for wine bars in the area, an announcement sounded over the loudspeaker. I must have heard it wrong because there was no way it said what I thought it said. I put my phone in my purse and waited for them to repeat it.

"Excuse the interruption, but will Cherry Bomb please make her way to the Ray-Ban counter on the first floor? Your party is waiting for you. Cherry Bomb, please head to the Ray-Ban counter on the first floor. Thank you."

I froze in place with my mouth open. Then I closed my eyes for a second and laughed. There was only one person in the world who would call me Cherry Bomb. Actually, my folks found the nickname quite amusing, but not comical enough to draw attention to themselves or their daughter in a crowded department store. Perry, on the other hand, would think nothing of disrupting a store full of shoppers to get my attention. Simply walking up to me and saying "hi" would be too boring. Perry didn't do boring. As I made my way toward the sunglasses section of the store, I wondered if Perry thought I'd be angry. Considering the turbulent nature of our relationship over the holidays, I'd bet he hoped so.

When I arrived at my destination, Perry was leaning against a column to the side of the Ray-Ban counter with one hand tangled in his thick dirty-blond hair, grinning at me like the devil himself—if the devil could also win sexiest, if not most infuriating, man alive. If I didn't know better, I'd think I was witnessing a photoshoot. His black jeans and royal blue sweater fit his skin like the designer created the items with Perry in mind. His brown leather jacket was draped across his arm like a supermodel. "Hey. It's Cherry Bomb. I thought it was you," he said.

I adopted my most put-upon expression to contrast his sly smile, but as soon as I got within two inches of him, I lost it and burst out laughing. "I can't believe you had them call for Cherry Bomb over the loudspeaker." I shook my head. "On second thought, I'm not at all surprised."

He shrugged. "I was buying a pair of gloves when I spotted you French kissing your reflection in the mirror. I was going to say hi but came up with a less conservative approach instead. I figured you probably had a rough day at work and could use the laugh."

"I did, and I could. Thank you."

Perry jerked his head back.

"What?"

"My ears must have deceived me, because I could swear you expressed gratitude. I was positive you'd rip into me for embarrassing you." In a high-pitched voice, he said, "My name's not Cherry Bomb."

I wiggled a finger at him. "I know how much it pains you to be wrong, but let me be the first to say you misjudged me this time." I smiled. My joy at seeing him was disconcerting, but I would take my time and ease into the emotion. "How did you get them to agree to the announcement in the first place? Cherry Bomb is so obviously a fake name."

"The person at security was a woman," Perry said plainly.

"I see." No further clarification was necessary.

He studied me curiously for a moment. "What's going on with you?" He banged his shoulder against mine lightly.

"The usual. Working hard. I actually took a couple of weeks off and went to Barbados."

Waggling his eyebrows at me, Perry said, "And how did that go?"

"It was a learning experience. Enlightening." When Perry regarded me another curious look, I said, "And what about you? I heard you signed with Marshall. Congratulations. I'm genuinely pleased for you." At least one participant in the boyfriend swap accomplished his goal that week.

"I couldn't have done it without the support of your parents. I sent them a thank-you note."

My mouth dropped open. "You did?"

He nodded, looking shy if that were even possible. "I also apologized for embarrassing their daughter at Christmas dinner. I really am sorry, you know."

"I know," I said in a soft voice. "I can't believe you sent them a thank-you note."

"I wanted to send one to you too but wasn't sure how you'd take it, considering how I messed things up with you and Will."

I waved him away. "It wasn't all your fault. There were two of us in that pantry."

He pressed his lips together. "Whatever happened with Will?"

"He broke up with me after I confessed what happened."

"I'm sorry."

"It's okay. We weren't right together."

"Neither were me and Robyn." His eyes locked on mine.

An awkward silence ensued until I said, "Anyway, I look forward to saying, 'I knew you when.' Just remember the Bellows when you accept your Academy Award."

Perry nodded. "I will." He bowed his head down for a second before meeting my eyes again. "It will probably be a while before that happens. Can I buy you a drink now to thank you in the meantime?" He shrugged. "You can say no if you want. I'll understand if you've had enough Perry Smith to last a lifetime. I am a handful." He stuffed his hands in the pockets of his jeans.

"That's for sure." I took him in from head to toe and inhaled sharply. "But I'll still take you up on the drink offer." I wasn't ready to say goodbye.

Perry's gorgeous eyes opened wide. "Really? Great!"

I clasped his elbow and allowed him to lead me to the exit.

"Where should we go?"

"Let me see." With the hand of my free arm, I reached into my bag for my phone. I hadn't reviewed the results from the Yelp search I'd conducted earlier. As I went to pull up the screen, I remembered the advice of my good friends, Doug and Bobby from Barbados, and returned the device to my purse. "How about you choose?" I said.

Perry stopped walking. "Is this a trick?"

I chuckled. "Definitely not. I'll go wherever you want, and I promise not to hate your suggestion."

And it was a promise I intended to keep—even if it killed me.

Chapter 22

Robyn

I peeked through the curtain at the audience. It was a full house. My heart walloped furiously. I was terrified my legs would give out when I led the students to the stage in less than twenty minutes. My fear had nothing to do with the concert, despite having less than four weeks to prepare, and everything to do with one particular showgoer. But as far as my eyes could see, Will wasn't there yet.

I'd left a message on his voicemail telling him the music program had been saved, I couldn't be happier, and I wished I could thank the person responsible face to face. Then I invited him to the mid-winter concert and said I hoped he'd be there. I didn't state positively I knew it was his law firm who donated the funds in case I was wrong. And it also gave him an easy out if his employer had nothing to do with it or if he simply had no desire to see me again. He'd never returned my call. Each time my phone rang or pinged the arrival of a text message, I thought I might go into cardiac arrest wondering if it was him. And then my stomach dropped in disappointment when it wasn't. Tonight was the big night, and I held out hope he'd show up. But I made a promise not to beat myself up if he didn't. It would only mean he didn't share my romantic feelings after all, which was something I couldn't control. And besides, I was used to it—been there, done that.

"Robyn."

At the sound of Lynn's voice behind me, I let the red velvet curtain close. I turned to her with a smile and opened my arms.

Pulling her into a hug, I inhaled the vanilla and jasmine scent of her perfume. "I'm so glad you could make it. I didn't give you much notice."

We separated and Lynn smirked. "My dance card is usually pretty empty mid-week in the middle of the winter. Most of my ancient friends are hibernating in Florida." She beamed at me. "You look radiant."

"Thank you so much." I chose a simple purple fit and flare dress for the occasion, opting not to add "uncomfortable outfit" or "clothing malfunction" to my list of things to worry about. I still hoped Will would think I looked pretty, but considering he'd seen me when I woke up in the morning, I doubted his attraction to me hinged on what I wore.

"You're always gorgeous, but can I assume some of the brightness in your cheeks is due to the music program not being in jeopardy after all?" Lynn's eyes lit up.

"You heard?"

She nodded. "Some law firm saved the day. Kensworth and Associates. Maybe one of the student's parents works there."

I took a sharp intake of breath. I'd chickened out on investigating the name of the law firm. Part of me was afraid to find out. What if it wasn't Will? What if it was? I decided to allow the mystery to be solved naturally. But I'd heard him mention the name of his employer a few times over the holidays and was pretty sure it was Kensworth and Associates. He really did it. He was Prince Charming to my Snow White. I glanced down at the Pandora bracelet on my wrist and at the newest charm, courtesy of Will.

Lynn studied me with concern. "Are you all right, Robyn?"

Before I could respond, I saw Aimee Clay approaching me and my worries were temporarily forgotten. Wearing her red hair in an updo with a few curly pieces left out for the "messy" effect, she looked adorable and every part the junior production assistant. Since she'd helped me pick out the songs for the concert and even assisted in stage direction, her role was not in name only. She was trying so hard to make the best of the situation, but I'd caught her gazing longingly at the students during rehearsal a few times. I knew she missed being front and center and still held out hope she'd be able to sing again after her polyps completely healed.

She looked timidly from Lynn to me. "Are we almost ready, Ms. Lane?" Pointing to the rowdy students behind her, she said, "They're getting restless and won't listen to me when I tell them to keep their voices down and line up."

I put a hand on her shoulder. "We'll see about that." It occurred to me I'd completely abandoned my duties in favor of scoping out the auditorium for Will and then talking to Lynn. Regardless of whether Will was here and if his appearance meant I could finally kiss him again after ten years, this time without spinning a bottle in his direction, there were more than a hundred people waiting to hear their nine- and ten-year-old daughters, sons, sisters, brothers, granddaughters, and grandsons sing their little hearts out. It was my job to make that happen. I turned to Lynn. "I need to tame the lions. You know how it goes."

She winked. "I sure do."

I hugged her again. "I'm sorry we couldn't talk more, but I'm so glad you're here."

"Wouldn't miss it. Break a leg."

My pulse raced in a mixture of usual pre-show jitters and renewed anxiety over seeing Will again. "I will." I only prayed my leg wouldn't take my heart along for the ride.

The students' performance of "Rhythm of Life" was flawless, and I was still riding the high when I turned around to face the audience, who were on their feet. My cheeks ached from the smile I couldn't remove while I waited for the applause to die down so I could announce the intermission. Aimee had already led the students backstage with the help of Lance and the fourth- and fifth-grade teachers. "Thank you," I said into the microphone over the clapping. "Thank you so much."

After a few moments, everyone took their seats. "I'm so glad you're enjoying the concert so far." Since I faced the students while conducting the songs, I hadn't had an opportunity to look for Will. At first, I was very conscious of the possibility he was there and watching me, but I quickly got lost in the music. But now, I allowed my eyes to sweep the crowd while I spoke. "The students worked diligently to learn all the songs in a very short amount of time and I'm so proud of them. Although this is the only school I've worked at, I can't imagine another one with more talented, hardworking, enthusiastic children than the ones here, and their passion for music warms my..." My pulse raced as my eyes locked on Will sitting third row center. *He came.* He smiled at me and my quivering lips curled up in response. My next words escaped me and I struggled to remember where I'd left off. Oh, yeah. "Their passion for music warms my heart." I paused. "Which brings me to another subject. We are so very lucky to have music education as part of our curriculum. And I'm not just saying that because I'm the music teacher." The audience chuckled, and I giggled with them before continuing. "Music education is not a given in many schools across the country, and I'm so very grateful to be able to help provide it to your children." I focused my attention on Will. "Thank you from the bottom of my heart."

As the audience clapped, my eyes remained fixed on Will. He winked at me and my knees wobbled. I cleared my throat. "We'll be back for another few songs in fifteen minutes. Take the time to snack on one of the delicious desserts available from the bake sale going on next door. All proceeds go toward the athletic program." I placed the microphone back on the stand. "Thank you," I said one more time before heading backstage.

The other teachers always covered for me during the majority of the intermission to give me a short break, but I would catch up with them as soon as I caught my breath. I kneeled behind a chair, put my head between my legs, and breathed in and out. I smelled him, rich lavender combined with cocoa—masculine but clean— before I heard his voice.

"You all right, Snow?"

I brushed my long hair out of my eyes and looked up at him. He was standing over me with his brows furrowed in concern. "Um, yeah. Just taking a breather." I swallowed hard and slowly raised myself to a standing position. "Hi, Will." I cursed my voice for shaking like someone was pounding on my back while I spoke. Even though I'd pictured his face every night as I settled into bed (and nearly all day), I'd forgotten the small details, like the sprinkling of light brown freckles around the bridge of his nose. I wondered how many there were, but figured it wasn't a good time to count.

His eyes danced merrily. "Hi back at you. Security is pretty weak here. I managed to sneak backstage. I hope you don't mind."

"Not at all. I'm glad you made it." I smoothed out my dress.

"So am I. The concert is great so far."

"Thank you." I bit down on my lip. "Was it you?" I couldn't bear going back onstage without hearing it from his lips.

Will studied my face. "Was what me?"

I swallowed hard. "Did you ask your law firm to rescue the music program?"

He nodded his answer.

Even though I only had the tiniest of doubts by now, I was overwhelmed by the admission. "I can't believe you did that for me. It was..." I gulped. "I don't even know what to say or where to start thanking you."

Will waved me away. "It was nothing, Snow. The firm has a charitable foundation and needs to donate a certain amount of money each year. I merely proposed they consider helping a local public school out and they agreed. Turns out, the managing partner has a soft spot for education. His wife is a retired schoolteacher from a lower-income district."

Shaking my head, I said, "It wasn't nothing."

He gave me a wry grin. "There's something in it for them too. It's a tax break and they'll get free advertising in exchange, so—"

I grasped his arm. "Stop downplaying it. It might not be a huge deal for your firm, but it's the nicest thing anyone's ever done for me. Why?"

His eyes probed mine. "Why do you think?"

My hands shook and I wished I could amputate them for the length of this conversation. "You care about me?"

Still gazing at me, Will nodded again. "Very much. And while I understand and respect your doubts and can't deny my execution could have been better, I didn't only ask you out because Sidney cheated on me, and I didn't only break up with her because of that either."

"I believe you," I said, my voice croaking. Sidney's apology had come as a pleasant, albeit awkward, surprise—although it took a few minutes for my anger to simmer. Sidney didn't know I'd been planning to break up with Perry when she launched herself at him, and it was a blatant breach of the girl code. But her honesty and vulnerability won me over by the end of the call. I also had to wonder if it could have been her on the receiving end of the apology. If Will had owned up to his feelings while I was still with Perry, would I have waited until I was truly single to satisfy my urges or would I have given in to my lust like she had? I liked to think I would have exercised self-control out of respect for Sidney and Perry, but as my eyes locked onto Will's lips like a magnet on metal, I wouldn't swear my music collection on it.

Will lessened the distance between us. "And I didn't only want you to dump Perry because he's a tool who's not good enough for you. There was another reason."

I blinked back the tears desperate to explode from the back of my lids and looked up at him. "What other reason?"

He shook his head and let out a laugh. "I thought I knew what being jealous felt like before, but I didn't have a clue until I spent almost a week with the most adorable, sexy, and sweet girl in the world knowing she was dating..." He rolled his eyes. "A blond god. I wasn't jealous because Perry was with Sidney; I was jealous because Perry was really dating *you*, and I was falling for you big time."

I was tempted to halt the conversation to pinch myself and confirm this was really happening. "You had me at 'Snow,' Will." In case he missed the *Jerry McGuire* reference, I said, "You're the one I want, not Perry." I shrugged. "I didn't think I could compare to someone like Sidney."

Will took both of my hands in his. "I don't want someone like Sidney. I want you. And I have a feeling I always will." He chuckled. "Even when you're seventy-one."

I pressed my lips together in confusion, and then I remembered the song we danced to at Billy Murphy's. I stroked his jaw with my hand and reveled at the sensation. It felt better than I ever imagined. "And what happens when I turn seventy-two? I might not be sexy anymore, and I might be adorable in an old-lady way, but I'll still be sweet. Will you still want me?" I held my breath.

Will drew me closer to him. "I'm willing to bet my firm's entire charitable foundation you'll still be sexy, adorable, and sweet when you're *ninety*-two. And, yes, I'll still want you."

I chuckled. "That's a mighty risky wager. And considering my school's music program needs those funds, I'm not sure I'm comfortable with it."

He took a few locks of my hair and rubbed them between his fingers. "We'll wait and see then. But my money's on you, Snow White. It's on us. If you're looking for a date for your family's Passover or Easter celebration, I'd like to confirm my availability."

"You mean Eastover?"

Will's eyes opened wide. "Is that a thing?"

I smiled. "I have no idea. I totally made it up."

He shook his head at me. "Clever. So what do you say? Can I be your date for Eastover?"

"Yes. On one condition." I gave him a meaningful look. "No pretending this time."

"Considering I was only pretending to pretend during most of Chrismukkah, you drive an easy bargain."

I was afraid if my heart swelled any more, it would be visible from the outside. "Which means you have to kiss me. And I'm not talking about little pecks. I mean full-on making out." I waggled my eyebrows. "I might even put out."

Will ran a finger along my bottom lip. "I'm in, Snow. But do we have to wait until Eastover to get started?"

I shook my head. "No." I slowly moved in to seal the deal with a kiss. I was still in a state of disbelief this was really happening, but in case I was dreaming, I was desperate to kiss him before I woke up. His lips were less than an inch away from mine when Principal Hogan called out, "Three-minute warning."

Will pulled away from me and grunted. "Talk about bad timing."

I bit back a groan of frustration. "I need to go to my students. I'm sorry."

"I should get back to my seat." Will stroked my cheek and smiled at me. "To be continued?"

I nodded. "Definitely." My skin tingled from his touch.

"I'll wait for you after the show."

"You'd better," I said with a smile. As I watched him walk away, I knew I couldn't do it. I couldn't wait another minute. I ran after him and put a hand on both of his hips to stop him.

He turned around and frowned in concern. "What's up, Snow?"

I didn't know what came over me. And I had no answer for him. There was nothing to say. There was only something to do. I grabbed his head with both of my hands and kissed him. And, oh my God, it was even better than it was at Oliver's party in high school, even though, just like back then, he kissed me back. And just like then, he held my face in his hands. But although that was our first kiss ever and one I'd never forget, this kiss was the first kiss of the rest of our lives. This kiss was...I heard someone call my name, but it would have to wait. I wasn't quite finished yet. As Will tapped me on the back, I pulled on his hair. It was so soft.

Wait...how could Will have one hand on each of my cheeks and another one on my back? I pulled away and looked at him. He stared back at me with a glazed expression on his face. And then there was giggling.

"Ms. Lane. The curtain's up." Aimee had a hand clamped to

her mouth, but it wasn't enough to suppress her chuckles. I followed her finger as she pointed it at the audience, who were gawking at us. I felt my face drain of color as I realized Will's firm might have saved the music program, but I was probably out of a job. I glanced at them helplessly. "I'm so sorry." Then I heard clapping from behind me—Principal Hogan. I turned to face him.

To the audience, he said, "I'm happy to report there will be no extra charge for the romance portion of the evening. It's almost Valentine's Day, after all." He flashed me a genuine smile and resumed clapping while the rest of the audience joined in. I faced Will and laughed as he took a bow.

"Looks like I ended up with an entertainer after all," I joked.

"At least I didn't have to sing," he said with a snicker before pulling me close to him again.

I whispered, "We still have their rapt attention." I gestured to the audience, who were still riveted to the stage.

Will raised an eyebrow. "Are you thinking what I'm thinking?"

My answer was another kiss.

Meredith Schorr

A born-and-bred New Yorker, Meredith Schorr discovered her passion for writing when she began to enjoy drafting work-related emails way more than she was probably supposed to. After trying her hand penning children's stories and blogging her personal experiences, Meredith found her calling writing chick lit and humorous women's fiction. She secures much inspiration from her day job as a hardworking trademark paralegal and her still-single (but looking) status. Meredith is a loyal New York Yankees fan, an avid runner, and an unashamed television addict. To learn more, visit her at www.meredithschorr.com.

Books by Meredith Schorr

JUST FRIENDS WITH BENEFITS
A STATE OF JANE
HOW DO YOU KNOW?
THE BOYFRIEND SWAP

The Blogger Girl Series

BLOGGER GIRL (#1)
NOVELISTA GIRL (#2)

Henery Press Books

And finally, before you go...
Here are a few other books
you might enjoy:

JUST FRIENDS WITH BENEFITS

Meredith Schorr

(from the Henery Press Chick Lit Collection)

When a friend urges Stephanie Cohen not to put all her eggs in one bastard, the advice falls on deaf ears. Stephanie's college crush on Craig Hille has been awakened thirteen years later as if soaked in a can of Red Bull, and she is determined not to let the guy who got away once, get away twice.

Stephanie, a thirty-two-year-old paralegal from Washington, D.C., is a seventies and eighties television trivia buff who can recite the starting lineup of the New York Yankees and go beer for beer with the guys. And despite her failure to get married and pro-create prior to entering her thirties, she has so far managed to keep her overbearing mother from sticking her head in the oven.

Just Friends with Benefits is the humorous story of Stephanie's pursuit of love, her adventures in friendship, and her journey to discover what really matters.

Available at booksellers nationwide and online

Visit www.henerypress.com for details

THE BREAKUP DOCTOR
Phoebe Fox

The Breakup Doctor Series (#1)

(From the Henery Press Chick Lit Collection)

Call Brook Ogden a matchmaker-in-reverse. Others bring people together; Brook, licensed mental health counselor, picks up the pieces after things come apart. When her own therapy practice collapses, she maintains perfect control: landing on her feet with a weekly advice-to-the-lovelorn column and a consulting service as the Breakup Doctor: on call to help you shape up after you breakup.

Then her relationship suddenly crumbles and Brook finds herself engaging in almost every bad-breakup behavior she preaches against. And worse, she starts a rebound relationship with the most inappropriate of men: a dangerously sexy bartender with anger-management issues—who also happens to be a former patient.

As her increasingly out-of-control behavior lands her at rock-bottom, Brook realizes you can't always handle a messy breakup neatly—and that sometimes you can't pull yourself together until you let yourself fall apart.

Available at booksellers nationwide and online

Visit www.henerypress.com for details

BLOGGER GIRL

Meredith Schorr

The Blogger Girl Series (#1)

(From the Henery Press Chick Lit Collection)

What happens when your high school nemesis becomes the shining star in a universe you pretty much saved? Book blogger Kimberly Long is about to find out.

With her blog, she works tirelessly by night to keep the chick lit genre alive, helping squash the claim that it's dead" once and for all. Not bad for a woman who by day ekes out a meager living as a pretty-much-nameless, legal secretary in a Manhattan law firm. While Kim's day job holds no passion for her, the handsome (and shaving challenged) associate down the hall is another story. Yet another story: Hannah Marshak, one of her most hated high school classmates, has popped onto the chick lit scene with a hot new book that's turning heads—and pages—across the land.

With their ten-year reunion drawing near, Kim's coming close to combustion over the hype about Hannah's book. And as everyone around her seems to be moving on and up, she begins to question whether being a "blogger girl" makes the grade in her offline life.

Available at booksellers nationwide and online

Visit www.henerypress.com for details

GIRL MEETS CLASS
Karin Gillespie

(from the Henery Press Chick Lit Collection)

The unspooling of Toni Lee Wells' Tiffany and Wild Turkey lifestyle begins with a trip to the Luckett County Jail drunk tank. Her wealthy family finally gets fed up with her shenanigans. They cut off her monthly allowance but also make her a sweetheart deal: Get a job, keep it for a year, and you'll receive an early inheritance. Act the fool or get fired, and you'll lose it for good.

Toni Lee signs up for a fast-track Teacher Corps program. She hopes for an easy teaching gig, but ends up assigned to a high school that churns out more thugs than scholars.

What's a spoiled Southern belle to do when confronted with a bunch of street-smart students determined to make her life difficult? Luckily a handsome colleague is willing to help her negotiate the rough waters and keep her bed warm at night. But when she gets involved with dark dealings in the school system, she fears she might lose her new beau as well as her inheritance.

Available at booksellers nationwide and online

Visit www.henerypress.com for details

CPSIA information can be obtained
at www.ICGtesting.com
Printed in the USA
LVOW13s1744011117

554607LV00013B/1551/P